THE SONS OF PHILO GAINES

THE SONS OF
PHILO GAINES

MICHAEL R. RITT

THORNDIKE PRESS
A part of Gale, a Cengage Company

GALE
A Cengage Company

LIBRARY OF CONGRESS CIP DATA ON FILE.
CATALOGUING IN PUBLICATION FOR THIS BOOK
IS AVAILABLE FROM THE LIBRARY OF CONGRESS.

ISBN-13: 978-1-4328-7104-8 (hardcover alk. paper)

Published in 2021 by arrangement with Cherry Weiner Literary Agency

Printed in Mexico
Print Number: 01   Print Year: 2021

This book is dedicated to my wife and redheaded sweetheart, Tami, who understands the necessity of giving me my alone time in which to pursue my passion for writing. To her is aptly applied this description found in the book of Proverbs.

"Many women have done excellently, But you surpass them all."

It is also dedicated to my sons, who are on their own journey to discover their place in this world. They make me as proud as a father can be.
Soli Deo Gloria

PROLOGUE

April 2, 1865, Eastern Tennessee
Major Morgan Burnett dismounted from his grulla mare inside the clearing hidden well back within the grove of hickory trees. He chose this location for his meeting because it was secluded and offered a measure of protection from any Yankee patrols that might be in the area. But, truth be known, Major Burnett was more worried about discovery by his own side than by any Yankees. If his men went along with his plans, it would make them all outlaws . . . on both sides of the Mason-Dixon Line.

He leaned back against the shaggy trunk of one of the old trees and lit a cigar. The smoke drifted upward and dissipated in the leaves of the branches above.

Within moments, they appeared: six riders, all in Confederate uniforms and mounted on splendid looking horses that they had managed to steal somewhere along the way. One by one, they dismounted and stood by their horses waiting for further orders.

A red-bearded man with sergeant's stripes approached the major and spoke in hushed tones. "All of the men you requested are here, Major, but ummm . . ."

"What is it, Sergeant? Speak up."

Sergeant Decker fidgeted and looked uncomfortable. "Begging the major's pardon, but are you sure about Private Walker?" The sergeant gave a sideways glance toward one of the men who had arrived with him. The private in question was pouring some water from his canteen into his hat for his horse to drink.

Major Burnett followed the sergeant's eyes until they rested on Private Walker. "What are your concerns, Sergeant?"

The sergeant took a half step closer and lowered his voice even more. "Well, sir, for one thing, the rest of the men are single and unattached. Walker here has a family — a wife and a young daughter." He waited for the major to respond, but Burnett remained silent, puffing on his cigar as he waited for Decker to finish. "Walker is also a religious man, Major; he is forever reading that Bible of his. I'm afraid he has too many moral scruples to go along with your plan."

The major took another puff and blew a smoke ring over the sergeant's head. "That's what I'm counting on, Sergeant." He took several steps past the sergeant and addressed his men. "All right, men, gather 'round."

The men walked forward, made a half circle in front of the major, and waited for him to speak.

"Each one of you," he said in his slow Alabama drawl, looking each man in the eyes as he spoke, "has been 'specially chosen. You have each proven yourselves to be brave and excellent horsemen. But above all, you each possess the singular quality I prize above all others in a man . . . your loyalty. I trust each of you with my life." He gauged the impact of his words on each man present and was encouraged to continue.

He removed his hat and hung his head for a moment. "Over the past several months it has become painfully clear to me, and to most of my superiors, that the end of this great conflict is upon us. I am afraid the south has lost this war, gentlemen."

The men all commenced speaking at once.

"There's still plenty of fight in us, Major. Just point the way!" shouted one private.

"We ain't ready to give up yet, Major!" shouted another.

"General Lee will show them blue-bellies what's what!" shouted yet another.

The major held up his hands to quiet his men. "Please, men . . . please let me continue."

After a few more exclamations enumerating the glories of the Confederacy, the men quieted to hear what else the major had to say.

"I received a dispatch this morning. Pickett has abandoned Petersburg."

There were groans and shocked exclamations from the men. Most of them understood the significance of the news, but Major Burnett spelled it out for them so there would be no misunderstanding.

"With the defenses at Petersburg gone, the Yankees have an unobstructed march to Richmond, where Lee is outnumbered four to one."

His men looked on in silence, some of them hanging their heads. A few had tears running down their dirty, bearded faces.

Burnett continued. "The Yankees are well armed and supplied. On the other hand, our boys haven't even enough weapons to go around and are reduced to eating grass and shoe leather. It might be a week, it might be two, but Lee will have to sur-render, and that will be that."

The men were devastated by the major's remarks and several wept openly, shame-lessly mourning the loss of their beloved Confederacy. This continued for several minutes. At last, one young private, who couldn't have been more than seventeen years old, looked up. He had locks of curly, blond hair protruding from under his cav-alry cap that had earned him the nickname "Curly" from his companions. Eyes wide with uncertainty, he asked, "What do we do now, Major?"

The men gathered together in the hickory grove looked up as if one man. Trained to take orders, they wanted to be told what their next move should be.

This is the moment Burnett had been waiting for. If he handled this correctly, he was sure the men would go along with his plans. They might even think it was their idea. Men were more likely to take an ac-tion if they could also take credit for the idea that spawned it.

"Men, I can no longer, in good con-science, stand before you and give you orders. For all practical purposes, the war is over. I am no longer your commanding offi-cer." He placed his hand on his collar and, with one swift motion, ripped away the single gold star that designated his rank as that of major. The men looked at each other but remained silent.

Burnett continued, "I can't tell you, men, what to do, but I can tell you this . . . you can go back to your homes if you like, but the South we knew and loved . . . the South we fought for . . . the South so many of our friends have died for, no longer exists. Our cities have been shelled by the Yankees. Our farms and plantations have been burned and looted, our livestock stolen, our slaves set free. And don't think that it will stop with the last shot fired. In the months to come, you will see the boot of Northern oppression stomping through the South, bringing Yankee government and Yankee laws to further subjugate our people. Is that the kind of place you want to go back to? Is that the kind of place you want to call home?" He waited for their response.

"No, sir!" one man shouted.

"I can't live like that, Major," exclaimed another. Most of the men nodded their heads in agreement. "But what'll we do? Where do we go?"

"I've given this a lot of thought, men, and this is what I propose." He looked at the face of each man in turn. With the exception of Private Walker, they were eagerly straining forward to hear what he had to say. Walker looked like he wanted to speak up, but he held his tongue.

Burnett continued. "There's nothing for us in the south and we certainly can't go east or north. That leaves us one option."

Curly smiled. His face looked as though he had recognized an old friend in a crowd. "We go west!" he shouted.

"Exactly, Curly, we go west."

Just as quickly as it came, the smile left Curly's face, and lines of uncertainty furrowed his brow. "But what'll we do out west, Major?"

"Curly, out west there won't be anyone to tell us what to do. We can do whatever the hell we want. We can start over again — make whatever we want to out of our lives — and there won't be any man to stand in our way. I believe there will be a huge demand for beef. We could leave the war behind and set up a ranching operation . . . be our own bosses."

The men talked excitedly among themselves. "What the major says makes a lot of sense," said one man. "Hell, there ain't nothing to go home to," said another. "Why not go west with the major and start over again?"

A tall, lanky corporal named Jed spoke up. "How we gonna get us a ranch, Major? Don't that cost a lot of money?"

Burnett took a final draw off of his cigar. Dropping the stub, he ground it into the dirt with the toe of his boot. He took a few steps forward and motioned to his men to move in closer. They formed a circle around him while he bent down and arranged some twigs on the ground before him.

He pointed with his finger while he talked. "This here is us in Tennessee," he said, pointing to one side of the line of twigs. "North of us is Kentucky." The men paid rapt attention to Burnett's words. A few of them nodded in recognition of the crude map he had laid out before them.

Burnett looked up to make eye contact with his men while he continued. "For years now, the Yanks have been marching throughout the South looting our cities and homes and taking whatever it is they wanted."

The men nodded in agreement.

"I say we give them a taste of their own medicine."

"How so, Major?" It was Private Walker who spoke up. He had been looking more and more uncomfortable as the major had laid out his plans.

Burnett picked up a stick to draw on his

map in the dirt. "I propose that we cross the border into western Kentucky here." He traced a route on his map. "A short ride north from here we cross the Ohio into Indiana and Illinois." He pointed out their respective locations on his map.

He looked up again to ensure he had everyone's attention. The men were fully engaged in listening. Several of them had squatted down on their haunches for a closer look at his map. Only Private Walker held back.

"The banks up north are full of Yankee dollars. I say we visit a few of them and make a withdrawal." Burnett looked at his men. Some smiled and laughed, others patted each other on their backs.

Curly danced a jig, his feet stomping a beat to an imaginary tune that played in his child-like imagination. He gave a whoop and said, "Then we can start our ranch, right, Major?"

"That's the plan, men. What do you think? Are you with me?"

One by one, each of the men, with the exception of Walker, came forward to shake Burnett's hand and give their hearty consent to his plan.

Private Walker made his way back to his horse and adjusted the cinch. He untied the reins and slipped his boot into the stirrup. Throwing his leg over the back of his horse, he sat in the saddle and waited. Silence fell on the group as, one by one, the men turned to look at Walker.

"I can't go along with you, Major. I've got a wife and daughter back home. It may not be much of a home when I get there, but we're young enough to start over. Besides, what you are planning isn't right. It's not what soldiers do. It's what outlaws do. The war is over, Major. Let it be."

"If that's the way you want it, Walker, then go in peace. I won't force any man to follow me who doesn't want to."

"Thank you, Major."

Walker turned his horse and had taken about two steps when Burnett drew his sidearm and fired. The bullet hit Walker square in the back. He toppled from his horse and lay motionless in the grass.

Burnett holstered his weapon and turned to speak to Sergeant Decker. "Now, when they find his body, they'll think he was killed by a Yankee patrol. They'll figure the rest of us were either killed or captured. That will give us a good head start before anyone thinks to look for us. After a few months, they'll forget all about us. By then, we'll have left the Mississippi far behind and be

16

well on our way to a new life somewhere out west."

Decker grinned. "You think of everything, don't you?"

The men mounted up and followed single file as former Confederate Major Morgan Burnett led them out of the secluded clearing in the hickory grove and north toward the Kentucky border.

■ ■ ■ ■

PART ONE
THE SCHOLAR

■ ■ ■ ■

"When I first met the new school teacher, he looked like a doe-eyed calf, brand new to the world and innocent as a newborn babe. But something told me there was a lot more thunder and lightnin' in him than what most people saw."

— Casey Hicks,
owner of Hicks Livery,
Mustang Flats, Texas

CHAPTER ONE

September 1873, Mustang Flats, Texas
Matt Gaines stepped down from the train onto the platform at the depot in Mustang Flats and looked around at his new home. A tumbleweed blew across the dusty main road that cut the small west Texas town in half. A shift in the wind caused it to veer toward a buckskin gelding tied to the hitching rail. The horse jumped in the air and kicked out its hind legs as the tumbleweed rolled underneath it and bounced off of the edge of the boardwalk. The pens at the other end of the train depot filled the air with the pungent, dusty smell of cattle. It was a far cry from the ivy-covered walls of the College of New Jersey.

A Negro porter followed him onto the platform a second later and handed him his leather grip. "Here you is, suh."

Matt took his bag, pressing a coin into the porter's hand. "Thank you, George. I appreciate all your help."

A man and woman, who had been standing off to the side watching passengers disembark, approached Matt as the last of the passengers stepped onto the platform. The man was the first to speak. "Are you Mister Gaines?"

Matt held out his hand. "I'm Matthew Gaines. And you are . . . ?"

The man shook Matt's hand. He was a handsome man in his late twenties or early thirties. His weathered complexion made him look older than his actual years. He stood six feet tall, a couple of inches taller than Matt. His firm grip and callused hands marked him as a man familiar with hard work. Matt's handshake was equally as firm, but he had the soft hands of an academician. College professors didn't worry about calluses, only the occasional paper cut.

"I'm Tom McCutchen. This is my sister, Katie."

Katie McCutchen was as lovely a young lady as Matt had ever seen. She had a pile of red hair tucked up under a straw bonnet that had sage-green and beige fringe with handmade flowers on the side. She wore a light-green cotton dress with a dark-green bolero.

"I'm pleased to meet you, Mr. Gaines. I

hope you had a pleasant trip." She smiled and offered her hand.

Matt held her fingertips and bowed slightly. He was socially awkward, especially around women. He had a habit of weighing his words carefully before replying, so much so that it often seemed to people as though he wasn't attentive. "The pleasure is all mine, Miss McCutchen."

"Katie here is head of the school committee," Tom offered. "The town board asked us to meet you and escort you to the school. Our wagon is this way." Tom indicated the direction with a nod of his head. "Can I help you with the rest of your baggage?"

Matt lifted his single bag. "This is all there is." He saw their quizzical looks. "I like to keep my life simple. My needs are few."

"All right then, shall we go?" Tom led the way as the three of them walked to the one-horse Studebaker wagon that waited nearby.

Matt walked with a slight limp that he was still self-conscious about. He was sure Tom and Katie had noticed. Like most people, they were too polite or too embarrassed to mention it.

Matt helped Katie aboard while Tom climbed into the driver's seat. There didn't seem to be much room on the seat of the wagon, so Matt went to hop into the back.

Katie scooted over closer to her brother. "There's plenty of room here for you, Mr. Gaines." She smiled and patted the empty space on the seat next to her. Matt climbed aboard, and, with a flick of the reins, the horse pulled the wagon down the center of town.

Mustang Flats was much like any other western town, struggling to make a place for itself in the commercial life of the nation. The war had taken its toll on the town, as it had in every other town in the former Confederacy. A shortage of able-bodied men and material had left many things neglected and in need of repair. But the war had ended eight years ago, and Mustang Flats was slowly working its way out of the depressive state caused by the war. There was an influx of new settlers in the area, people displaced by the war. Some looking toward the future. Others running from their past. Some, like Matthew Gaines, were doing both.

Tom talked about the town as the wagon bounced along the dusty main street, pointing out businesses and giving Matt the lowdown on some of the locals.

"Mustang Flats has about eight hundred residents, but it's been growing steadily since the end of the war."

"A lot of the children don't attend school," Katie added. "They're needed to help their families on the farms and ranches in the area. But you should have about thirty students for the beginning of school. They will be of all ages, of course, and at varying levels in their education, but you indicated in your correspondence with the school committee that you wouldn't have a problem teaching the different grades."

"That won't be a problem at all, Miss McCutchen. I look forward to the opportunity."

Tom continued his tour of Mustang Flats as they drove east from the train station. Matt took note of the various businesses. There were four saloons, a general store, a hardware store, and a bank that was building on a second story. That seemed to be a good sign, thought Matt. He also took note of a blacksmith and livery, a hotel, and three restaurants.

"I was surprised to discover I could take the train all the way to town," Matt remarked. "Towns generally need to be larger than this to justify a rail depot."

Tom nodded. "You're right about that. The fact the railroad is here at all is a happy accident for the town. During the war, when the Union was blockading southern ports, the Confederacy had a plan to smuggle supplies over the Rio Grande from Juarez. They were going to haul the supplies in wagons down out of the hills right here to Mustang Flats. The railroad built this spur line to haul the supplies the rest of the way to Fort Worth."

"That sounds like an ambitious plan," Matt remarked.

Tom clicked his tongue and gave the reins a shake. The horse picked up his pace. "The plan was abandoned before it got underway, but, as a result, the town wound up with a rail depot. The tracks end here in town, and the train only comes twice a week, but that can change, and we're in hopes it does. There are a lot of cattle ranchers around here, including me, that would like to be able to ship our cattle without having to drive them north to Kansas."

"How big is your ranch, Tom?"

"We run about three thousand head. We're not the biggest ranch around, by any means, but we're comfortable."

The pride in his eyes and the smile on his face were evidence that Tom loved the life he had. It wasn't always about the biggest or the best or the most. All some men needed was an honest way to make a living and a way to provide for the needs of their families. In his experience, Matt had found that the happiest men were the ones that worked hard to put food on the table and a roof over the heads of their loved ones and got to enjoy the fruits of their labors.

"Who owns the largest ranch in these parts?"

The smile left Tom's face. Matt noticed Tom and Katie glance at each other. Katie was the one to answer. "That would be the A-bar-T ranch. It lies north of town and borders our ranch on the west. It's owned by a man named Amos Tolliver. You'll get to meet him soon enough. He also owns the bank, the general store, and the largest saloon in town."

Matt grabbed hold of the edge of his seat as the wagon's right front wheel dipped in and out of a pothole. "I take it from your reaction, Tom, that this Mr. Tolliver is not the best of neighbors."

Tom turned the wagon south as it approached the outer edge of town. "He came in a few years back and bought up several of the smaller ranches and consolidated them into the A-bar-T. Then he started buying up businesses in town. He's been trying to get his hands on our place, but I won't sell. Our parents founded the ranch. They had to fight the Comanche and the Apache to do it. Then they had to fight the Mexicans

27

to keep it, and I'll be damned if . . ."

"Now, Tom . . ." Katie broke in. This was obviously a touchy subject for the young rancher. "You'll have to excuse my brother, Mr. Gaines. He and Amos aren't of the same mind."

Matt noticed that Katie said "Amos," and not "Mr. Tolliver" and sensed more than a casual familiarity between the two. "What about you and Amos?" It never occurred to Matt that his question might be inappropriate.

He saw the blush on her cheeks and thought her all the more lovely for it.

"Amos is a charming, handsome, and educated man. The fact that he is ambitious should be considered as a mark of the quality of his character, not a detriment to it."

Tom shook his head and sighed. "What you consider ambition others call greed."

He pulled the wagon up in front of a newly constructed wooden frame building and brought it to a stop, set the brake, and tied the reins to the handle. "Here we are," he said, hopping down from the wagon seat.

Matt climbed down, carefully gripping the side of the wagon as his bad leg met the ground. He then offered his hand to Katie as she stepped down to stand in front of the school building with the two men.

It was approximately twenty feet wide and sixty feet long. It had three windows on each side and a door on either end. There was a porch built onto the rear part of the structure, and set off to the side were his and her outhouses. The building sat on the edge of a field of about five acres, on the far side of which was a small creek lined with old cottonwoods and massive, twisted live oaks.

Katie led them through the front door as she explained the layout of the building. "This first room takes up about two-thirds of the structure and is the school portion."

The schoolroom was spacious, with rows of desks for the students — plenty for the number expected. The town was obviously planning for growth. The teacher's desk was on the far side of the room. There was also a blackboard and a small bookshelf full of math, English, and history books of various proficiencies.

Katie continued. "On the wall behind your desk, and to the right, is a doorway into your living quarters." Katie led Tom and Matt into the twenty-by-twenty room, which contained a bed, a stove, a table and two chairs. There were shelves on one of the walls for dishes and cooking utensils, and a small closet for his clothes and linens. Matt was happy to see a small wash basin in the corner with an indoor pump handle. At least he wouldn't have to haul water from the creek.

"This isn't much," Katie said. "I hope you'll be comfortable here."

"This is more than adequate," Matt assured her. "I have no doubt I'll be quite comfortable."

The three of them walked outside together. Tom helped his sister into the wagon and then climbed up onto the seat next to her.

Katie turned to Matt. "If there's anything more we can do for you, or if there is anything more you require for the school, please let me know. The school committee feels very fortunate to have been able to retain you to teach our children, and we want you to feel at home here."

"I'm the one that feels fortunate to be here, Miss McCutchen."

"Let's not stand on formalities, Mr. Gaines. I will call you Matt if you promise to call me Katie."

"That's an easy promise to keep, Katie. I hope you'll give me more of a challenge sometime."

Katie smiled down at him from her seat in the wagon. The sunlight glistened like fire off a lock of red hair that had escaped the confines of her bonnet. "In that case, Matt, you can promise me you'll come out to the ranch Saturday evening for dinner. Some of the town's most prominent citizens will be there. You'll have a chance to meet them and become acquainted with some of the parents of the children you'll be teaching."

"It would be my pleasure. How do I find your ranch?"

"Take the road north out of town about three miles. You can't miss it. You can hire a horse from the livery if you wish. We'll eat about six o'clock, but feel free to come early."

"That sounds good. I'll see you then." Matt shook hands with Tom and watched as the wagon made its way down the dusty road back towards town.

He walked back into the school and took his seat behind the desk at the front of the class. He looked out over the empty benches and imagined them full of students paging through textbooks and writing on their slates. This was all new to him. Not the teaching, but the surroundings that were so different. He had never been to Texas before. He had never been west of the Mississippi.

Born in Monroe County, Tennessee, on the banks of the Sweetwater Creek, Matt was the eldest son of Philo Gaines, who had become somewhat of a legend throughout the West. Philo had been a mountain man, Indian fighter, Texas Ranger, and army scout, prior to his appointment by the Tennessee legislature to the U.S. Senate. Matt was not like his father, or even his younger brothers, who felt at home sleeping under the stars or astraddle the back of a horse for days on end. He was more comfortable with a book in his hands than a hunting rifle, and it was his mother who saw to it that he received a good education.

He enrolled in the College of New Jersey in Princeton when he was seventeen and continued his studies there throughout his postgraduate years, majoring in philosophy and theology. He had spent the last eight years as a teacher at the college. He was used to academia, to city life . . . to restaurants and shops and theatres. Now here he was, living in the back of a shack on the western plains of Texas, with coyotes and jackrabbits for neighbors.

As Matt thought about his past and wondered about his future, he realized that he was rubbing his bad leg. The scarred flesh from his burns often tightened up during periods of inactivity, and Matt would have to rub the pain and the stiffness away.

That night as he lay asleep in bed, he awoke with a jolt and sat up, perspiration ringing his brow. It took him a few seconds to realize where he was. The cries still echoed in his head from the dream that had awakened him. It was a dream he had had many nights previous. It was a dream of burning flames and searing pain and of a woman's screams.

CHAPTER TWO

"I'll need a horse."

The old hostler pushed his hat back on his head and rubbed his grey whiskers while he gave the new school teacher the once over. Matt wore fawn colored pants with a dark sack coat and lowcut vest. Around his neck, he wore a light-brown cotton cravat over a white cotton wingtip shirt. His hair was cut short and slicked back in the style of the day, and he was topped off with a black, felt derby hat. The wire-rimmed spectacles perched on top of his nose helped to give him the appearance of a bookish person. He looked better suited for San Francisco or New York than for Mustang Flats.

"You're the new school teacher, ain't ya?"

"Yes, I am. My name is Matthew Gaines." Matt removed his hat and stepped forward, extending his hand.

The hostler hesitated like he was unsure

of what to make of him. He paused long enough to make it awkward, then stepped forward and shook hands with Matt. "My name is Casey Hicks. I own this here livery. Are you looking to buy a horse or rent one?" Casey maneuvered the wad of tobacco in his mouth from one cheek to the other. With the precision of a marksman, he let fly a stream of juice that knocked a grasshopper off of a stem of grass not far from Matt's brown, leather brogans.

Matt sidestepped to avoid any splash back. "If the price is right and the horse is in good shape, I might be interested in buying. I'd like to ride around a bit and become familiar with the countryside. I'll be riding out to the McCutchen ranch later this week. Miss McCutchen has invited me to dine with her and her brother." Matt was generally quiet and not much of a talker. But when he did start to talk, he often said more than what was necessary. It was his way of dealing with his social awkwardness.

"Miss McCutchen, huh?" There was a twinkle in the old hostler's eyes and a hint of a smile on his leathery face. "That there is one fine looking filly."

"She is a fine looking woman," Matt replied, more to himself than to the hostler.

Casey turned on bowed legs and moseyed

to the corral on the other side of the barn. "Follow me, young fella. We'll pick you out a nice, gentle horse for the day."

Matt returned his derby to his head and followed behind Casey as he led him through the barn to a corral with about a dozen horses inside. They both stood with their arms resting on the top rail of the corral, looking over the stock inside. After a few minutes, Matt pointed out a chestnut mare about sixteen hands tall. She had bright eyes and a sleek, shiny coat. She pranced around the corral like she had someplace to be and was in a hurry to get there. "I'll take that one if she's available."

Casey stepped back and looked Matt over from head to foot. "That's a lot of horse, young fella. Can you ride?"

"I'm quite a proficient equestrian," Matt replied, matter-of-factly.

"You're a what?" The hostler looked dumbfounded.

"I can ride."

The old man shrugged his shoulders. "If you say so." He let loose with another stream of tobacco. The victim this time was a fly on a nearby fencepost. "You know, you talk real fancy, even for a school teacher. Where're you from?"

"Actually, I was born in Tennessee. But,

more recently, I've lived in Princeton, New Jersey. I attended the College of New Jersey and have been a professor there for the past eight years."

"A professor, huh? What did you profess?"

"Most of the time I taught philosophy."

"Well, there ain't much use for 'philosophy' around here."

The old man retreated to the tack room while Matt waited by the corral. He emerged a moment later with a bridle. Opening the gate to the corral, he walked right up to the chestnut and proceeded to fit the bridle in place. To Matt's surprise, she took the bit without a fuss. Matt watched as Casey led her out of the corral, tossed a blanket and saddle on her, and cinched it in place.

He led her over to Matt. "That'll be a dollar a day if you want to rent her. If you're lookin' to buy, it's one hundred dollars for the horse. I'll toss in the saddle and bridle for another thirty dollars. How's that sound to you?"

Casey watched as Matt put his foot in the stirrup and mounted up. The horse pranced around the yard but responded nicely when he pulled the reins, first to the left, then to the right. Then he trotted her in a circle

37

around the yard and stopped her in front of the hostler.

"She will do nicely," Matt said, reaching forward to rub the horse on the neck. He took five dollars out of his pocket and paid the hostler. "I'll try her out today, and, if I like her, I'll give you the purchase price tomorrow, if that meets with your approval."

Casey reached up to shake hands with Matt. "It's a pleasure doing business with you."

"The pleasure is all mine." Matt shook hands and turned the horse to exit the livery yard.

Before the mare took more than a few steps, Casey yelled after him. "You seem like a nice fella. I hope you aren't thinking about tossing a loop over her."

Matt turned the horse again to face the old man. "I'm afraid I don't understand."

"I'm not talking about the horse," he replied. "I'm talking about Katie Mc-Cutchen. She's already roped and branded by Amos Tolliver, and he doesn't take it kindly when someone rustles his stock."

Matt turned the horse to leave again. "I'm here to teach school. That's all."

He dug his heels into the horse's sides and leaned low over her neck as she raced out of the yard towards the edge of town.

Mustang Flats sat among the sage and mesquite, between the Llano Estacado to the north and the Pecos River to the south. To the west was an expanse of sandy hills overgrown with prickly pear. Further west were the Sierra Guadalupe Mountains, which stretched north from the Rio Grande into New Mexico. Any other settlements worthy of notice were to the east, but, even so, it would take several days' worth of saddle sores to reach one of them. If it wasn't for the railroad, Mustang Flats would be cut off completely from the rest of the country.

CHAPTER THREE

The next morning, Matt paid a visit to the mercantile store to pick up a few items. He stopped the chestnut in front of the general store and tied her to the hitching rail, where she could drink from the trough. Looking up, he read the sign above the store, stenciled in red and gold letters: TOLLIVER'S MERCANTILE.

The bell above the door rang as he pushed it open and stepped inside. There was an elderly woman behind a counter, folding bolts of cloth. She smiled as Matt walked over and removed his hat.

"Good afternoon," he said. "I'm Matt Gaines, the new school teacher."

"Oh, my," the woman exclaimed, stepping around the counter to extend her hand, "the new school teacher." She shook Matt's hand and then called out, "John, come meet the new teacher."

John had been on the other side of the

store stocking canned goods onto the shelves. He stopped and came over to shake Matt's hand.

"John," the woman continued, "this is Matt Gaines. Mr. Gaines, this is my husband, John Lathrop, and my name is Violet. We both serve on the school committee, and we're excited to have you here in our humble community."

"I'm happy to meet both of you," Matt replied. "I hope I can do justice to the confidence the school committee has shown in retaining me for the position of teacher."

"Well, you have an impressive resume, Mr. Gaines." Violet continued her conversation with Matt as John went back to his work. "I hope we can all live up to your expectations."

"So far, everyone has been very kind. I am sure I'll enjoy living here."

Matt glanced around the store. "There are a few items I'm in need of."

"Of course, Mr. Gaines. What can I help you with?" Violet returned to her place behind the counter and assumed her role as clerk.

Matt handed her a list. "Here are some grocery items I need. I would also like to purchase some additional items for my wardrobe."

She pointed him in the direction of some shelves containing shirts and pants of various styles and sizes. Matt picked out several sets of clothes and returned to the counter. Placing them on the countertop, he inquired, "Is there a tailor in town where I can have some suits made?"

"There's no tailor, per se, but just about any woman in town who can sew would be happy to make your suits for you. I've sewn dozens of them for our own customers. I would be happy to make them for you if you want."

After taking his measurements, they agreed on a style and price, which Matt thought quite reasonable. A professor of philosophy doesn't make a great deal of money, but Matt had been frugal with his finances and had made some good investments. He had sold most of his belongings before the move to Texas, in the belief that it would be easier and less expensive to buy new things than it would be to haul his old belongings across the country. He had left behind, in the care of some friends in Princeton, several boxes of books and papers.

He bid Violet and John good day, picked up his grocery order, and walked outside. After stowing his packages into his saddlebags, he mounted up and set out for the train station. There was a telegraph office there, and he wanted to wire his friends to send his books the first chance that they got.

Back in his room behind the school, Matt got ready for dinner at the McCutchen ranch. He shaved and splashed some water on his face from the wash basin, then put on one of his new shirts. He had carried an extra pair of suit pants in his grip, but he had to brush his suit coat the best he could to make it presentable.

As he finished up his preparations, he found himself thinking about Katie Mc-Cutchen. His mind fought against the notion that he was primping for her benefit. He wanted to make a good impression on everyone, he told himself. Besides, there seemed to be some kind of relationship between her and Amos Tolliver. It's like he told the hostler: he was only here to teach school, nothing else. He did have to admit, however, that he couldn't remember what Tom McCutchen was wearing the other day. But Katie? He remembered every detail about her. She was a vision worth holding onto.

CHAPTER FOUR

Later that afternoon, Matt followed the road north out of town as Katie had instructed. It was still early, and he had plenty of time, so he was content to keep the chestnut at an easy walk while he took in the surrounding countryside. Although the land to the west and south of town was hilly, the land to the north was flat prairie land. The McCutchen ranch bordered the southern end of the Llano Estacado.

After almost an hour, the road forked, with the right-hand fork leading through a gate with a sign hanging over it. The sign had a capital *M* with a horizontal line through the middle signifying the Bar-M, the brand for the McCutchen ranch. Matt pointed the chestnut through the gate and down the dust-covered, rutted road. Off in the distance, about half a mile, he could make out some buildings which he figured must be the ranch house and outbuildings.

To his left, about a hundred yards from the road, was a rather good-sized stream with cottonwood thickets lining both banks. As he continued down the road to the ranch, he saw three riders emerge from the trees. They stopped their horses when they saw him, then spurred them forward at a gallop to intercept him.

Matt pulled back on the reins as they approached and halted the chestnut. She pranced uneasily in the road as the three riders positioned themselves between Matt and the ranch house in the distance.

The man in the middle was the first to speak. He was a stocky man in his mid- to late forties. He had red hair protruding from under his hat, and a bushy, red beard covered his face. "This is private property, mister. What are you doing on Tolliver range?"

Matt looked confused. "I understood this was the McCutchen ranch."

The youngest of the three, a man in his mid-twenties with curly, blond hair, laughed. He looked at the red-haired man and said, "Not for long, huh, Red?"

The red-headed man looked at the younger man and snapped, "Be quiet, Curly." He turned back to look at Matt. "That doesn't answer my question, mister.

Who are you and what are you doing here?"

Matt sat facing the three men, who were all wearing sidearms and carrying rifles. Matt, on the other hand, was not armed. He didn't care for guns and avoided them whenever he could. Back in Princeton, people handled their problems in a civilized manner without resorting to violence. He couldn't believe that these men would want to start trouble with a complete stranger. Was west Texas that barbaric of a place?

"My name is Matt Gaines. I have an invitation to dine at the McCutchen ranch this evening. If I've made a wrong turn, perhaps you can point me in the right direction."

"Are you a friend of theirs?" Red continued with his questioning.

Matt looked at the three men in front of him. Of the three, it was the third man that bothered Matt the most. He was the one who had thus far remained silent. He was a Mexican who looked to be in his thirties. He wore a black gaucho hat with silver conchos in the hatband.

"I must say," replied Matt, "that I find your chronic disposition toward inquiry rather invasive. Do you make a point of interrogating all travelers in such a manner?"

46

Curly leaned forward in the saddle and squinted at Matt. "You sure talk pretty, mister. What causes you to talk that way?"

Matt was becoming annoyed. These men had no right to stop him and question him. "If by 'pretty' you are referring to my proper use of grammar and enunciation, and if you are inquiring as to the cause for such use, I would ask you to be more specific. Are you inquiring as to the material cause, the formal cause, the efficient cause, or the final cause?"

Curly's mouth hung open, and he stared with blank eyes. Turning to Red, he said, "What language is he talking?"

Red shook his head. "I have no idea."

"What about you, Pony?" Curly asked. "Any idea what he's saying?" Pony was the name of the Mexican. He shook his head and remained silent.

Curly drew his gun and pointed it at Matt. Pony also drew his weapon, but he waited to see what Curly would do.

Curly sat easy-like in his saddle in a relaxed fashion. He waved his gun in a carefree manner but kept it aimed in the general direction of Matt. "Are you making fun of us with your fancy talk, mister? Where's your gun?"

"I don't have a gun. I'm a teacher, not a

shootist," Matt replied calmly, and with a touch of disdain.

Red spoke up next. "I heard we had a new school teacher in town. I was hoping for a pretty, young gal."

"Sorry if I disappoint you," replied Matt.

At the revelation that Matt was the new school teacher, Curly holstered his gun. Pony did likewise.

Curly walked his horse around behind Matt's chestnut until he was on the opposite side, next to Pony. He beamed with the new information. "Looky here, Pony. We got us a new schoolmarm. He should have a pretty dress to go with his pretty words, don't you think?"

At last, Pony broke his silence. With a heavy accent, he said, "I think you're *pendejo.*"

Curly ignored the insult if he even knew that it was one. "Red, how come the major didn't tell me we were getting a new school-marm?"

"Shut up, Curly," ordered Red. "You talk too much." He walked his horse to the side of the road, opening up the way for Matt to pass. "I wouldn't worry none about getting to know the McCutchens very well. It'd only be a waste of your time."

With that said, the three men galloped off

in the direction of town. Curly laughed as he turned and shouted, "See you later, schoolmarm."

Matt watched as the three men disappeared down the road. Their horses kicked up a cloud of dust that was still visible long after they had merged into the horizon.

He nudged the chestnut down the road toward the McCutchen ranch, wondering what he was getting himself into.

CHAPTER FIVE

The McCutchen ranch was set on top of a slight swell in the land that overlooked a tree-lined creek to the north. The main house was a sturdy, two-story adobe building with red clay tiles on the roof. The house was shaded by several huge live oaks that surrounded it. Smaller persimmon and crabapple trees dotted the property. Blooms from oleander and hibiscus lined a veranda running the length of two sides of the building. Several of the smaller outbuildings were adobe or stucco, but the barn was wooden. All the buildings were painted white and were clean and in good repair.

Matt rode his horse into the yard and dismounted in front of the house as Tom McCutchen walked up to greet him. Tom and Matt shook hands.

"Glad you made it, Matt. Did you have any difficulty finding the ranch?"

"Not at all," Matt replied. "It was right

where Katie said it would be." He let his eyes take in the surrounding yard and buildings. The sweet smell of pavonia and the citrus scent of lemonweed filled his nostrils. "You have a beautiful place here."

Tom smiled. "Thank you. Katie and I have worked hard to make this place comfortable and productive."

He took the reins from Matt. "Why don't you go on up and see Katie. She wants to introduce you to some of our guests. I'll put your horse in the barn."

Matt could see Katie and others mingling on the veranda, so he followed a short, flower-lined path that led up to the front of the house. Katie walked over, smiling. "I'm so glad to see you, Matt."

Matt smiled back at her. She was lovely in a blue, satin skirt with a high bustle. She wore a matching short-waist, basque bodice that fastened up the front, trimmed in black lace. "I would have been foolish to ignore your gracious invitation," he replied.

"I would be the one looking like a fool if you hadn't come," she replied, leaning in closer to whisper. "I have a confession. You're kind of the guest of honor tonight. Everyone wants to meet you."

Matt felt a familiar uneasiness. He had suspected that there would be a lot of

51

people here tonight, but he was uncomfortable as the center of attention. So much for retreating to a quiet corner to spend the evening.

She looped her arm through his and led him onto the veranda, where she introduced him to many of the couples who would have children in the school when it opened.

They worked their way through the crowd of people and found themselves approaching a man who sat on one end of a small wicker loveseat. The man stood up when they drew near.

"Matt, I would like you to meet Amos Tolliver," Katie said.

Matt held out his hand. "I am pleased to meet you, Mr. Tolliver."

Tolliver hesitated a moment and then extended his hand. Tolliver exerted more pressure into his grip than was necessary, so Matt firmed up his own grip to match. He thought he could detect a look of surprise in Tolliver's eyes before he let go.

By this time, Tom had joined them on the veranda. Tolliver maneuvered himself so close to Katie that their arms brushed together. Tom and Matt stood opposite them.

There was a pitcher of lemonade on a silver tray on the table next to Katie, so she poured them all a glass.

Tolliver was a distinguished looking man in his late forties or early fifties. He wore fawn-colored trousers with a tailored, black frock coat. He wore a low-cut black vest over a white shirt and narrow black cravat. He had a neatly trimmed full beard and mustache. He didn't have the weathered look of a rancher, like Tom; he had a more polished, sophisticated look like that of a banker or businessman.

"I understand you own the largest ranch in the area, Mr. Tolliver, as well as several of the businesses in town," said Matt.

"That's correct," replied Tolliver. "I make no apologies for being ambitious. I have big plans for this town." Tolliver slipped his arm around Katie as he spoke. Matt noticed how she leaned in toward him and smiled.

It was plain to Matt that Katie was attracted to Tolliver, and it was easy to see why. He was attractive, wealthy, and ambitious, and that made him powerful as well. Power could be intoxicating to a lot of people. But there must have been more to it than that, thought Matt. Katie didn't seem to him to be the kind of woman who would concern herself with a man's money and his ambition. But what does it matter? He really didn't know Katie. Besides, he was there to teach school.

"I heard you were a professor back in Princeton," said Tolliver. "What subject did you teach?"

"My primary discipline was philosophy," replied Matt.

Tolliver grinned and shook his head, not bothering to hide his disdain. "I think you'll find that the people of Mustang Flats are practical, Mr. Gaines. They take life one day at a time and deal with things head on. There isn't much use for 'philosophy' out here." Full of his self-importance, Tolliver dismissed the subject with a wave of his hand.

Not to be put off, Matt replied, "Living practically *is* a philosophy, Mr. Tolliver. It's a rather ancient school of philosophy called Stoicism, founded by the Greek philosopher Zeno." Matt tilted his glass and took a sip of his lemonade. It was cold and on the tart side, but he liked the conflicting sweet-sour battle that engaged his taste buds. It made his mouth water, even after he swallowed the lemonade.

"Is that the kind of stuff you'll be teaching the children in school?" Tolliver made the question sound like an indictment.

"Oh, please do," said Katie, wide-eyed, her hands grasped together in a manner of supplication. "It would be wonderful if you did."

"But even the Bible says something about this, doesn't it, dear?" Even though he had addressed his question to Katie, he didn't wait for her to answer. "Wasn't it the Apostle Peter who said something about '. . . beware of vain philosophies.' "

"Tell me, Mr. Tolliver. How can you *beware* of something that you are not first *aware* of?" asked Matt.

"Ha-ha." Tom laughed and slapped Matt on the back. "He's got you there, Amos."

"And, actually, that reference comes from the Apostle Paul in his epistle to the Colossians," said Matt to Tolliver. "I taught theology at Princeton also."

The conversation continued for the next ten minutes between Matt, Tom, and Katie. Tolliver said barely a word during this time.

Matt knew that he had somehow offended the rancher. He often said something that rubbed people the wrong way, and people often viewed him as an intellectual snob. But he didn't mean to give that impression. So, he became silent in social situations and only offered conversation when someone asked him a question or addressed him directly.

Tolliver seemed to be an ambitious man

who had plans — plans that included Katie McCutchen. Matt reminded himself that he was only there to teach school. He didn't need to make an enemy out of Amos Tolliver, and he didn't need to be entertaining romantic thoughts about Katie McCutchen.

After a while, Tolliver spoke up. "Gaines . . . Gaines . . . that name sounds familiar. Are you any relation to Colonel Philo Gaines of Tennessee?"

Matt had wondered how long it would be before someone made the connection. He mentally sorted through half a dozen different answers that he kept on hand. "There're no heroes in my family; we're mostly teachers and ministers."

Matt and his two younger brothers had learned early in their lives that being sons of the legendary Philo Gaines was not an easy thing. People's expectations rose exponentially when they found out who their father was. Growing up, there was always someone who wanted to make a name for himself by challenging him or his brothers. All three of them had had more than their share of bloodied noses and blackened eyes as boys, and they had given out as good as they had received. But, as they got older, the challenges became more deadly. They found out that it was easier to deny who they were; or, rather, it was easier for them to be who they were than who people wanted them to be.

"Were you in the war, Mr. Tolliver?" asked Matt.

"Oh no, no . . . not me," Tolliver was quick to deny. "I spent the war in Europe as a cotton broker. I traded cotton for munitions to aid the Confederacy in the war effort."

Matt looked puzzled. "I thought that the Confederate cotton embargo, along with the Union blockade of southern ports, prevented any cotton exports."

"For the most part, that's true. But we were still able to smuggle a good amount of cotton into Mexico, and from there to France."

"I see." Matt took another sip of his lemonade. He licked his lips before setting the glass on the table. "I thought you had served during the war and that's why you're called 'major.' "

Tolliver looked as though he had been slapped.

Tom spoke up. "I don't think I have ever heard Amos referred to as 'major.' Where did you hear that?"

"From the three men I met as I rode through the gate to your ranch."

"What men?"

"Three cowhands, I suppose. They called each other Red, Curly, and Pony."

Tom's eyes narrowed, and the muscles in his jaw drew tight. "What did they say to you?"

Matt noticed that Tolliver was beginning to fidget, tugging on his lapels and smoothing out the crease in his trousers. Katie looked pale and kept her eyes fixed on Tom.

"I didn't mean to upset anyone," said Matt, as he glanced from one to the other.

"What did they say to you?" Tom asked a second time, louder than before.

"It was just a misunderstanding, that's all. They accused me of trespassing on Mr. Tolliver's range. But once they learned who I was, they let me pass."

Tom took a step toward Tolliver. His fists clenched so that his white knuckles stood out in sharp contrast to the bronze skin on the back of his hands. "Amos . . ."

Tolliver stood his ground but held his hands out in front of him to keep Tom at bay. "Just simmer down, Tom. I had nothing to do with this."

"Please, Tom, calm down. I'm sure Amos is not responsible for this," Katie pleaded.

Tom looked at his sister and seemed to relax. He lowered his voice and unclenched his fists but remained standing only inches from Tolliver. "Why were your men on my ranch, Amos? I told you to keep them away from here. And why did they tell Matt that this is your range?" Although he wasn't shouting, Tom's voice was loud enough that some of the other guests on the veranda were looking at the four of them.

Tolliver shrugged his shoulders. "I'm sure my men were just confused . . . Curly especially. He's a good man, but he's simple-minded."

Matt decided to keep to himself that it was the man called Red who had accused him of trespassing, not Curly.

Tolliver held out his hands in a concilia-tory gesture and said, "I'll have a talk with my men, Tom. This won't happen again, I assure you."

Tom spoke through clenched teeth, ac-centing each word with a thrust of his finger. "I'm warning you for the last time, Amos. Keep your men off of my ranch. If I catch any of your hired guns anywhere on my property, I'll put a bullet in him."

Tom turned on his heels and stormed away.

CHAPTER SIX

Amos Tolliver arrived back at his own ranch house sometime after ten o'clock that evening. He had left the McCutchen ranch seething inside at his men. He had made careful plans and wouldn't abide his men ruining his chances to get his hands on the McCutchen ranch. It angered him that they couldn't keep their big mouths shut, Curly especially. Tolliver had warned him many times over the years to stop referring to him as "major." They had left that life behind, and if it ever caught up with them, it could be disastrous.

He reined his horse up in front of the barn and dismounted. One of his men came out and grabbed the bridle to lead it into the barn.

"Where's Red?" Tolliver snapped.

The cowhand flinched at the unexpected greeting from his employer. "I think he's in the tack room oiling his saddle," the man replied. "Do you want me to tell him you're looking for him?"

"Have him come up to the house right away."

Tolliver strode off toward the main ranch house. Once inside, he went straight into his office. Walking over to a mahogany liquor cabinet, he pulled out a bottle of bourbon and poured himself a double. He paced back and forth with his drink in his hand until Red walked in.

"You wanted to see me, Mr. Tolliver?"

Tolliver said nothing. He pointed to an empty chair.

Red took the seat offered.

Tolliver walked over and stood several feet in front of where Red sat. He looked down at his foreman, raised his glass, and drained the contents, then threw the glass past Red, narrowly missing his head. The foremen shied and brought his arms up to shield his head as the glass shattered against the wall behind him.

Tolliver turned and walked over to his desk. He sat on the edge of it, leaning slightly forward.

Red sunk down in the overstuffed chair while Tolliver loomed over him.

"You have a nice thing here, don't you, Red?" Tolliver didn't wait for him to answer.

"You're the foreman of this ranch, and you get paid a hefty sum for the work that you do."

Tolliver was silent now. Red fidgeted in his chair, his eyes on the floor.

After several long seconds, Tolliver said, "How long have you been with me, Red?"

"Hell, Mr. Tolliver. I've been with you since Vicksburg . . . over ten years now."

"That's right, Vicksburg." For a moment, Tolliver stared straight ahead, recalling names and faces and trying to put them together in a way that would jog his memory.

Red waited for him to speak again.

"We ran circles around Grant's men back then, destroyed railroads, burned bridges, disrupted his supply lines. Remember those days, Sergeant?"

"I remember, Major." In the privacy of his study, Tolliver would sometimes grow nostalgic. It was the only time that he allowed anyone to refer to him by his old rank.

"You were a good sergeant back then, Red. Do you know what made you a good sergeant?"

Red wasn't sure if the question was rhetorical or not but felt compelled to say something. "Because I followed orders?"

"Sergeant, every soldier in the army, from

the greenest private to the most seasoned general, had to follow orders." Tolliver stood up straight and started to pace the room again as he continued. "What made you a good sergeant — and someone who was useful to me — was the fact that your men listened to you; you had control of them."

Tolliver stopped his pacing in front of Red's chair. He turned and looked down at the man cowering before him. "Tell me, Sergeant, have you lost control of your men? Are you no longer of any use to me?"

"If this is about Curly running his mouth off to that new school teacher . . ."

"What else would it be about?" Tolliver snapped. "How many times have we had this conversation? That simple-minded fool is going to get us all hung one of these days. Do you understand what's at stake here?"

"Yes, Major, I do."

Tolliver wasn't sure if Red really did understand. They had robbed a lot of banks, stolen a lot of money, and killed a lot of people to get where they were today. At first, they told themselves they were still fighting the war, that the Yankees were getting what they deserved. But they all knew what they had become.

He had been a brilliant strategist during the war, and his skills carried over naturally into their post-war activities. He had planned every job with minute attention to the smallest detail. As a result, they had seen great success, and not a man had been lost. Every man there owed him his life. They owed him their loyalty.

Red stood to his feet, penitently twisting his hat brim in his hands. With his head bowed and his eyes on the floor, he said, "Major, I'm sorry for the actions of my men, and I take full responsibility."

Tolliver reached out his arm and put his hand on Red's shoulder. "Red, I depend on you a great deal. You have proven yourself invaluable to me on more than one occasion. I have come to expect a certain level of performance from you. I guess that's why I am so disappointed in you now."

Red looked hopefully at his boss, eager for the chance to make amends. "You tell me how I can make it up to you, and, I give you my word, it'll get done."

Tolliver directed Red to take his seat again while he walked over to his desk. He opened a cigar box on the corner of his desk and pulled out two cigars. He handed one to Red, who accepted it eagerly. Both men lit their cigars, but neither man spoke. Tolliver walked around behind his desk and took a seat, deep in thought.

After a moment, Tolliver placed both hands palms down on the top of his desk. "Sergeant, I'm afraid Curly has become too much of a liability to all of us. We can't take any more chances with him." Tolliver looked at Red and waited to continue until they had made eye contact. "Do you understand what I am saying?"

Red's mouth drew tight, and he nodded his head.

Tolliver sighed and leaned back in his chair. "If you rather I took care of it myself . . ."

"No!" Red practically jumped to his feet. "I mean that won't be necessary, Major. I'll take care of it."

Tolliver smiled. "Good man." He leaned forward and folded his hands on the desk in front of him. "This may actually work out to our advantage."

"How's that, Major?"

Tolliver smiled and even chuckled as though he were privy to some private joke. "Our good neighbor, Tom McCutchen, has offered up a solution to our problem with Curly. He may have even gift wrapped his ranch for us in the process."

Red looked confused and asked, "What does McCutchen have to do with it?"

Tolliver ignored the question. "This is

what I want you to do. Early tomorrow I want you and Curly to ride over to the Mc-Cutchen ranch. Make sure that you are well onto his range, but south of the house, toward town." He leaned back in his chair again and took a long draw off of his cigar. "And make damn sure no one sees you," he added.

Whether he realized it or not, Red was standing at attention while Tolliver gave him his orders. "All right, Major. Then what would you like me to do?"

"Then I want you to kill Curly."

CHAPTER SEVEN

On the third day after the dinner at the Mc-Cutchen ranch, Amos Tolliver took his foreman, Red, and rode into town to see the marshal. He paid Guthrie good money to look the other way when it was necessary. This was one of those rare occasions when he actually wanted the old lawman to do his job — with a bit of guidance from him.

Tolliver dismounted and gave the reins a couple turns around the hitching rail. He stepped up on the boardwalk in front of the jail and nearly tripped over a dog sunning itself in the middle of the walkway. The short-haired golden retriever gave his tail a series of solid thumps on the wooden planks.

Tolliver squatted down to pet the dog. "How are you doing, boy?" The dog got to his feet, sat in front of Tolliver, and licked his face.

"Who's your friend, boss?" asked Red.

Tolliver got to his feet while the dog remained looking up at him, as though he were waiting for instructions. "I don't know. I've never seen him before. Maybe he belongs to Guthrie."

Red pushed his hat back on his head and grinned. "Well, he sure seems to have taken a shine to you."

"Why shouldn't he," Tolliver replied. "You know what they say about children and dogs: they're good judges of character."

Tolliver bent down again to give the dog a scratch behind the ears and then walked over and pushed open the door to the marshal's office, followed by Red.

Guthrie looked up when he heard the door open. He was seated behind his desk with his foot propped up on a chair. He was sixty-five years old and almost that many pounds overweight. He suffered from arthritis in his hands and gout in the big toe of his right foot. It was almost impossible for him to pull on his boot whenever the gout was flaring up.

"Did you get yourself a dog, Marshal?" Tolliver said as he took the only other chair in the office while Red remained standing.

"You mean that yellow mutt outside? Naw, he's been hanging around for a few days now. I don't know where he comes from." The marshal looked out of the window and raised his voice as though for the dog's benefit. "I'm gonna put a bullet in that mangy cur." Looking back at Tolliver and Red, he explained, "The damn dog growls at me every time I go outside."

Tolliver looked at Red and smiled. "See what I mean? He's a good judge of character."

Red laughed.

"What's that?" asked the marshal.

Tolliver ignored his question. "How's your gout today, Marshal?"

"Oh, it pains me something terrible, Amos." He started to reach for a bottle of Daffy's Elixir that was sitting on his desk, but, before his hand could grasp it, Red stepped over and snatched it off of the desk and out of the marshal's reach.

"What are you doing, Red?" Marshal Guthrie complained. "Stop fooling around and hand me my medicine."

"I need you to be alert, and I need you to pay attention to me," replied Tolliver.

"That's medicine, not whiskey," whined the marshal. "Now give it here."

Red sniffed the neck of the bottle, and then he tilted it back and took a swig. "I'd say that's about a ninety-proof medicine you've got here, Marshal."

Guthrie made a sudden grab for the bottle in Red's hands, but the cowboy was too quick, and the marshal missed as Red nimbly pulled the bottle out of his reach. Red laughed and taunted him with it, holding it out to him and then pulling it back whenever the marshal grabbed for it.

"Now, listen up." Tolliver raised his voice to get their attention. "I have a job for you."

"Oh, Amos," Guthrie protested. "I'm in no shape to go anywhere today."

Tolliver sighed with disgust. Although he paid the marshal to do his bidding, he loathed any man who abandoned his principles for money. He could understand a person who had no principles or ethics to speak of. Someone who was simply motivated by money and sold their services to the highest bidder had a kind of honesty to them. But men like Guthrie, who feigned respectability, who pretended to care about justice and the law, who were willing to part with their principles for a few extra dollars . . . these men were hypocrites.

"I'm serious, Marshal. I need you to do your job," Tolliver snapped.

The marshal squinted his eyes and looked first at Red, and then at Tolliver. "What's going on?" he asked.

"One of my men is missing," Tolliver replied.

"Who's missing?" said Guthrie.

Red spoke up this time. "It's Curly. We haven't seen him for a few days."

Marshal Guthrie waved his hand through the air, ready to dismiss the entire conversation. "Pshhhh, good riddance if you ask me. That crazy nitwit is one scary bastard."

"Well," said Tolliver, "I'm not asking you. Curly has his faults, but he's been with me a long time. He's a good man, and it's not like him to run off."

"Well, all right," said Guthrie. "When did anyone see him last?"

"I saw him three nights ago," replied Red. "He said he was headed into town to see Lori, that gal that waits tables over at Brown's. I talked to her, and she said he never came into town. Plus, Curly's horse wandered into the ranch this morning without him."

"So, he disappeared three nights ago somewhere between your ranch and town. I assume the two of you checked along the road when you came into town today."

"We checked," replied Tolliver, "but that doesn't mean anything. He could have gone off the road to take a shortcut."

The marshal lowered his foot gently to

the floor and eased it under his desk. His head popped up, and he stared wide-eyed at Tolliver. "He would've had to cut across the McCutchen place to do that, wouldn't he?"

Tolliver tried not to smile. The marshal had gone right where he had led him, as easy as if he had had a bit in his mouth. "I suppose that's true. What of it?"

"Why, don't you see it?"

Tolliver could see that the marshal was getting excited and more animated. He had presented him with a rare opportunity to actually do the work of a lawman, and Guthrie had solved the mystery without leaving his desk.

"I was at McCutchen's the other night," the marshal exclaimed. "I and about a dozen other people heard Tom McCutchen threaten to kill any of your men he found on his range. Hell, Amos, you were there. You heard him yourself!"

Tolliver shook his head in feigned disbelief. "No. I can't believe Tom would do such a thing."

"I'm telling you, Amos" — Guthrie brought his fist down like a hammer on the top of his desk — "I heard him my own self. He was mad enough to do it."

Tolliver acted like he still couldn't believe

what the marshal was proposing. "I know Tom was seething with rage, but do you think he would take out his anger on a young man who just wanted to get into town to see his girl?!"

"I'll tell you what I'm gonna do, yes, sir. I'm gonna ride out there right now and have a look around. That's just what I'm gonna do."

"All right, Marshal. If you think that's best. I'll leave the matter in your capable hands."

Tolliver rose to leave, and Red fell in behind him. "Let me know if you find out anything," Tolliver added.

In his eagerness, Marshal Guthrie picked up his boot lying on the floor next to his chair and started to tug it onto his foot, over his sore toe. The effort caused him to wince. Sucking air in through clenched teeth, he moaned, "Oh, good lord that hurts."

Then he remembered his medicine. "Red, toss me that bottle, will you?" he pleaded.

"Sure thing, Marshal." Lifting the bottle to his mouth, Red drained the last of the contents and tossed the empty bottle onto the floor in front of the marshal. He smiled and followed Tolliver out of the marshal's office, not even bothering to close the door behind him.

Once outside, the two men untied their horses and saddled up. They turned their mounts east toward the bank at a slow walk.

The yellow dog jumped off of the boardwalk and fell in behind Tolliver's horse, following him down Main Street.

CHAPTER EIGHT

Marshal Guthrie sat on his horse and looked up at the sky, blue and bright with the afternoon sun. Something was moving in the sky above him, so he shaded his eyes from the glare and tried to focus. It was actually two "somethings" that he saw. No, there were three . . . three vultures circling a mile to the northeast. He lowered his head and closed his eyes for a few seconds while the dark spots continued to circle under his eyelids. He opened his eyes and blinked a few times until the blurriness was gone.

It was hot for this time of year, over ninety degrees. The marshal removed the cork from his canteen and took a long drink of water. When he finished, he aimed his horse toward the circling buzzards and kicked him into a trot.

Fifteen minutes later he stopped at the edge of a small arroyo that broke across the grasslands from east to west. The three buzzards were still circling overhead, and four more were on the floor of the arroyo.

Guthrie got off of his horse, careful not to put too much weight on his bad foot. He walked over to the edge of the arroyo. Bending down, he picked up a good-sized rock and hurled it at the birds as they jostled for position at the dinner table. "Go on. Get out of there!" he shouted. It took another couple of rocks and some more shouts before the birds flew off, only to land a few yards away.

Marshal Guthrie eased himself over the side of the wash and walked over to examine whatever had excited the vultures so. It wasn't difficult to recognize the body of Curly, even though the buzzards had made a fine mess of the carcass. They had pecked out the eyes and ripped open the softer areas of the stomach, groin, and thighs. Sections of the intestines were trailed out of Curly's abdomen where the vultures had pulled on them and fought over them.

Guthrie pulled his bandana out of his vest pocket and held it to his nose. The stench was overwhelming. He thought he might retch, so he walked upwind a ways.

After his stomach had stopped its somersaults, he walked back to have another look at the body. Stooping down, he noticed two bullet holes in the chest.

He stood up and looked around. He wasn't much of a tracker, but he could see there were no tracks inside the arroyo besides his own, not even Curly's tracks.

He walked down the arroyo for about twenty yards until he found a low spot where he could climb up the opposite bank to look around. He walked back to the spot above where Curly's body was laying. There were a few horse tracks visible, but he couldn't tell from how many horses.

He stood there a while, his eyes scanning the country to the north, and tried to piece together the events that led up to Curly's murder, for it was most definitely murder.

From what he could see from the evidence around him, Curly had ridden out this way on his way to town. Instead of taking the road south to Mustang Flats, he had cut across this section of the McCutchen ranch to shorten his journey. It looked as though Tom McCutchen had made good on his threat and had shot Curly as he cut across this part of his range. It looked like Curly fell from his horse into the arroyo; that's why there were no tracks down below. Guthrie saw where a section of the bank had been caved in on top of Curly's body in an effort to cover it up, but the killer must have been in a hurry, because he did a poor job of it.

Guthrie worked his way back to the low spot on the north bank of the wash and climbed down, then up the opposite bank and over to where his horse waited. Mounting up, he turned south and headed back to town.

When he arrived in Mustang Flats, he went straight to the bank, where he expected Tolliver to be. He walked through the front door and veered to his right. Nodding to the teller, he asked, "Is Amos in his office?"

The teller looked up from a ledger he had been writing in. He looked disdainfully at the marshal and nodded his head towards Amos's office.

Guthrie saw the look the teller gave him but ignored it. Officially, he was the town's marshal, but unofficially, and more importantly, he worked for Tolliver. Most folks in town knew how it worked, and, if the arrangement bothered anyone, they kept it to themselves. Some of them, however, like the teller and the McCutchens, looked down their noses at him.

The door was open, so Guthrie walked in. Tolliver sat behind an immense oak desk and reclined in a cowhide-covered chair. He relaxed with a glass of brandy in one hand

and a cigar in the other. Red sat in a chair on the other side of the desk, nursing his own drink, but not looking as relaxed as Tolliver. Red never seemed to relax when he was around Tolliver, thought Guthrie, as he took in the two men. Maybe it was an employer-employee thing, but to Guthrie, it looked more like Red was plain scared of Tolliver.

Guthrie took a few steps into the office but froze in his tracks when he heard a low growl that came from around the corner of Tolliver's desk. He peeked over the top of the desk and saw the yellow dog lying on the floor at Tolliver's feet.

"What in the hell is he doing in here?"

The yellow dog bared its teeth and growled again.

Tolliver bent down and gave the dog a pat on the head. "That's okay, boy. The marshal works for me just like you do." Looking at Guthrie, he added, "Meet my newest employee, Marshal."

"Employee? What does he do for you?"

"I haven't figured that out yet," said Tolliver, adding, "He's unusually loyal. Maybe I'll appoint him town marshal instead of you."

Guthrie stared at Tolliver and the dog. He thought Amos was joking, but he never could tell with him.

"Take a seat, Marshal," Tolliver said, pointing to an empty chair. "What did you find?"

The marshal took a seat next to Red, exhaling a long drawn-out breath as he slumped in his chair. He paused, for dramatic effect, before answering. Tolliver and Red were both waiting for him.

"I found your man, Curly. His body's in a wash about an hour north of town. He has two bullet holes in his chest."

"Well," said Tolliver, "I never thought Tom McCutchen would commit murder. I mean, we all heard him threaten to shoot my men if he found them on his ranch, but I thought he was just excited. I didn't think he would actually go through with it."

Red relaxed and said, "What are you going to do now, Marshal?"

"Well, I'll send some men with a wagon to pick up his body. Do you know if he has any family that I need to notify?" He aimed the question at Tolliver.

"No, Marshal, we were the only family the boy had. I'll see to his funeral arrangements. I'll make sure he has the best."

Red was fidgeting in his chair. "What I mean is, what are you going to do now about Tom McCutchen?"

Tolliver might have been paying him to look the other way, but he was no fool. "I don't know, Red," said the marshal. "I don't have any hard evidence that Tom killed Curly. As a matter of fact, from the powder burns I found on Curly's shirt, it looks to me that whoever shot him was right up in front of him. I doubt Curly would have let Tom get that close. It's more likely the killer was someone Curly knew and trusted — you know, like a friend."

The marshal looked directly at Red, who held his gaze for only a few seconds before lowering his eyes.

Tolliver sat up and leaned forward, resting his elbows on his desk. His eyes narrowed, and he fixed his gaze on Guthrie when he spoke. "Red, shut the door."

Red got up and walked over to the office door and closed it. He gave the deadbolt a turn until it clicked into place.

"Marshal," Tolliver continued, "Curly had become a liability to me. Tom McCutchen is a hindrance to my plans. However it was that Curly met his demise, I can make this work to my advantage, but only if Tom is arrested for the murder."

Guthrie looked at Tolliver. He knew what the man was like. He understood the situation. Tolliver was cold and calculating. For whatever reason, he had wanted Curly dead.

Guthrie turned and looked at Red, who remained standing next to the office door, his eyes still glued to the floor, unable to meet his gaze. He looked as guilty as if he had been caught standing over Curly's body with a smoking gun in his hand.

Guthrie turned back to face Tolliver. After a moment's silence, he said, "Amos, you understand that I don't have jurisdiction to arrest Tom for something that happened outside of town." He had no qualms about arresting Tom or doing just about anything else that Amos told him to do, but Tolliver was someone who believed that any problem could be solved if you threw enough money at it, and the marshal saw an opportunity to insure that some of that money was thrown in his direction.

"No one will say anything, and, if someone does, just tell them that you made the arrest on behalf of the county sheriff." Tolliver reached into his coat pocket and pulled out a leather wallet. "You've done good work. I think it's deserving of a bonus." He counted out a hundred dollars, then thought better and counted out another hundred.

He held the money out for Guthrie, who stood to his feet and reached out for it eagerly. Tolliver pulled his hand back at the last second and asked, "Do we have an understanding, Marshal?"

Guthrie took the money and shoved it into his pocket. "I guess I'll ride out to the Mc-Cutchen place and arrest Tom for murder."

Red unlocked the door to allow Guthrie to leave to make arrangements for picking up Curly's remains.

When the marshal was out of sight, Tolliver clapped his hands together. A smile creased his face. Things were proceeding better than he expected.

Red was still subdued. "Do you think he'll have any trouble arresting McCutchen?"

Tolliver returned to his former position, reclining in his chair. He interlaced his fingers and put his hands behind his head. "That's the beauty of it," he said. "It really doesn't matter."

Red furrowed his brow. "I don't get your meaning."

"Suppose McCutchen puts up a fight. That makes him look guilty. The marshal can deputize as many men as he needs to arrest him, and, if he resists arrest and gets shot, all the better."

"What if he doesn't put up a fight? What if he comes in peaceful?"

"Then he will be swinging from a rope

within a week."

Red shook his head, unconvinced. "I don't know, Major. You heard Guthrie; there's not a lot of evidence for a conviction. Besides, the judge doesn't get here for another two weeks."

Tolliver grinned. "Believe me, Sergeant, a lot can happen before the judge arrives. I don't think the good citizens of Mustang Flats will put up with anyone murdering an innocent boy whose only crime was being sweet on a girl. You've seen what a mob can do. Ordinarily peaceful, law-abiding citizens get together, and, before you know it, they are rioting in the streets. I'm telling you, by the time I get through with McCutchen, he won't have a ranch or a reputation."

"As usual, you've thought of everything."

Tolliver raised his glass. "To preparation."

CHAPTER NINE

The next morning, the news of Curly's murder and of Tom's arrest was all anyone in Mustang Flats could talk about. Matt heard the news from Casey when he stopped at the livery to pick up his horse.

"I know I haven't been acquainted with the McCutchens for very long," said Matt, "but I find it hard to believe Tom would commit murder." He reached under his horse to grab the cinch. Pulling the strap up and looping it through the D-ring, he pulled it tight.

Casey sat on a stack of feed sacks and worked a wad of tobacco around in his mouth. He spat a stream of juice out onto the barn floor before speaking. "Maybe in self defense, but he don't seem the murderin' type to me either." He shrugged his shoulders. "You never know what a man is capable of until he's pushed. I reckon every man has his limits."

"Tom told me Amos Tolliver has been after his ranch for some time."

Casey had stood up and retrieved a curry brush from a nail on the wall. He opened one of the stalls and began to brush a roan gelding. "Amos Tolliver will not be happy until he owns every square foot of range in west Texas and every business in Mustang Flats. I never knew a man to be so dad-burned greedy and power hungry." Casey spat again, not because he had to, but because talking about Tolliver made him want to.

Matt had finished with the saddle and bridle, so he leaned against a stall and asked, "Casey, are you familiar with the story of King Midas?"

"I don't reckon I am. Who's he?"

"The ancient Greeks tell the story of a king by the name of Midas, who was very wealthy. He lived in a beautiful palace and adorned himself with purple robes and gold chains and precious stones. He had everything a man could ever want, including a beautiful young daughter, who was the only thing that he loved more than gold."

"Sounds like he had it made, but I reckon you're working your way around to some kind of a moral."

Matt laughed. "I am. You see, Midas

wasn't satisfied with all his wealth. He was so greedy that he could never have enough gold."

"Sounds like someone I know," Casey said, winking.

"Midas did a favor for one of the gods, Dionysus, the god of wine and revelry. So, as a reward, Dionysus granted Midas a wish, and what Midas wished for was that everything he touched would turn to gold."

Casey slapped his knee and bent over double with laughter.

"What's so funny?" asked Matt.

"Don't tell me, don't tell me . . ." Casey was still laughing. "He went to take a piss, and his pecker turned to gold!"

Now Matt laughed. "No, but you've got the right idea. His daughter came up to him and gave him a hug, and she turned to gold."

Casey chuckled as he wiped the tears from his eyes. "So, because of his greed, he lost the thing he loved the most."

Matt nodded his head. "That's the moral."

"Son, the only problem with your story is that I don't think there's anything Amos Tolliver loves more than gold. I know the good book says that the 'love of money is the root of all evil.' That would make Tolliver about the evilest man I know."

"Things have a way of working out in the end," Matt replied. "The Bible also says, 'Whatsoever a man soweth, that shall he also reap.' Sooner or later, everyone gets what they have coming to them."

Matt climbed up in the saddle and said goodbye to Casey as he trotted out of the livery yard and out into the main road.

As he entered Main Street, a wagon appeared around a corner and nearly collided with him. His horse, as well as the wagon's team, reared, throwing Matt into the dusty street.

Hearing laughter, Matt looked up at the wagon's occupants and saw Red and Pony laughing down at him. Pony had the reins, and Red was sitting next to him on the seat.

"Lo siento, amigo," said Pony. The tall Mexican had a toothpick between his teeth, and he smiled as he looked down at Matt.

From his vantage point in the dust of the road, Matt could see a three-inch scar on the right side of Pony's neck just under the jawline. He hadn't noticed it that afternoon they had first met on his way to the McCutchen ranch.

"No need to apologize to him, Pony," said Red with a grin. "He's just the school teacher, remember? He doesn't carry a gun, so the worst he can do is make you stay after

88

school to clean the slates."

"Ohhhh," Pony's accent was heavy as he exclaimed. "I remember the teacher. I think maybe someone should teach the teacher how to ride a horse."

Matt got to his feet and brushed the dust from his clothes. He picked up his hat and rubbed his hand briskly over it in an attempt to clean it off as well. He gathered up his horse's reins and mounted.

"Where're you off to in such a hurry, schoolmarm?" Red asked. "Are you late for some quilting bee?" The two men in the wagon enjoyed another round of laughter.

Matt looked at them and said, "I find it difficult to ascertain whether it is an education in general that you despise, or whether it is me specifically; and if it's me, why? What have I done to offend you?"

Red looked at Matt and sneered. "You don't belong here, schoolmarm. This is a hard country where men take what they want, and they learn to fight to keep it. Any man that's too scared to carry a gun is a target for those men who aren't. If I were you, I'd take my pretty talk and my fancy eastern clothes and head back where I came from. Texas doesn't want you here."

Pony gave the reins a snap, and the horses

jerked the wagon forward and down the road.

Matt sat for a moment and considered what Red had said. Texas was a hard land, and it would require the best out of hard men to settle it and make something productive and civilized out of it. Maybe he wasn't cut out to be a Texan.

It didn't make any difference. There was nothing for him back in Princeton. Whatever he wanted to make of his life, it would have its start right here in Mustang Flats. Texas may not want him, but Texas had him. And if it took a stronger surge of the blood of Philo Gaines coursing through his veins, then so be it.

CHAPTER TEN

Tom McCutchen sat on the edge of his bunk in one of the three ten-by-eight cells that made up the holding area of the jail. The other two cells were empty, although they would fill up tonight with patrons sleeping off a night's drunk. That was about the extent of the Mustang Flats crime spree, a couple of cowhands who had too much to drink, maybe a brawler or two on occasion. There had never been any excitement like an honest to goodness murder. He had only been locked up for less than twenty-four hours, but already kids outside his cell window threw rocks and horse apples through the bars on his window into his cell shouting, "Murderer, murderer."

Tom jumped to his feet and began to pace his cell, four steps in one direction, turn around, and take four steps back. He kept this up for several minutes before sitting back down on his bunk, only to repeat the process a few minutes later.

He looked up when he heard voices in the outer office. He didn't recognize the voice, but a moment later, the door opened, and Matt Gaines stepped into view.

"How are you, Tom?"

"Aren't you afraid to talk to a cold-blooded killer?"

Matt seized a chair that was kept there in the hall on the opposite side of the bars that separated the visitors and the inmates. He grinned. "I'll take my chances." He moved the chair closer to the bars so he and Tom could talk without being overheard by the marshal in the outer room.

Tom sat with his elbows on his knees, his head hanging with his chin to his chest. He looked up and asked, "How's Katie?"

"Has she been here to see you yet?"

"She was here right after Guthrie threw me in this cell. I could tell how worried she was, not to mention ticked off at me." Tom jumped to his feet and resumed pacing again. "My own sister thinks I'm guilty."

Matt frowned and shook his head. "This has hit her hard, Tom, but I don't think she wants to believe that. However, it doesn't help that you got so angry the other night and threatened Tolliver's men. Everybody in town has heard about it. Tolliver's men are making sure of that."

Tom stepped up to the bars and grabbed them with each hand. His eyes were wide, and worry lines creased his brow. "Matt, I did not kill Curly. I know how bad it looks for me. Yes, I was angry, but I had nothing to do with Curly's death."

Matt sat for a long moment and looked Tom in the eyes. "I believe you, Tom," he said at last.

Tom relaxed after that. He sat down on his bunk and tried to smile. "Well, at least there are two people in this town who think I am innocent . . . and that's counting me!"

"There is at least one other who knows you are innocent, Tom."

"Who would that be?"

"Whoever it was that killed Curly."

"I don't suppose I can count on him coming forward and confessing," Tom joked.

Matt grinned. "Let's call that plan 'B' and see if we can't figure out some other way to get you out of this mess."

"Thank you, Matt. I can't tell you how grateful I am to have your help."

"Well, I'm no lawyer, Tom, but it seems to me that their case against you is all circumstantial. They don't have any hard evidence. All they have is your threat to Amos. I doubt that a judge would even allow this to go to trial without anything more substantial than a threat."

"I agree with you, and I'll take my chances at trial. But what I am worried about is getting my neck stretched before the judge gets here. It will be two weeks before Judge Demars arrives. You've heard how Tolliver and his men have been talking around town. They're telling everyone how Curly was just a boy in love on his way to town to see his girl. He looks like some kind of hymn-singing choirboy. The truth is Curly was crazy and mean, but they've got everybody all worked up and out for blood."

Matt nodded. "I remember my run-in with Curly the night of the dinner party at your ranch, and I'm inclined to agree with your assessment of him."

Tom got quiet and pensive. He shook his head and said, "I know this sounds crazy, but I can't help but think that Amos is behind all this."

"Do you think he would kill one of his own men?"

"Not him personally, although I think he's more than capable of murder. No, he would have one of his men do the butchering for him. He's too smart to get his own hands dirty."

"Who do you think did shoot Curly?"

Tom mulled the question over for a few seconds. "He has a few hard cases working for him, but, if I had to guess, I would say that it was his foreman, Red, or else that Mexican that hired on a while back. I think they call him 'Pony.' Those are two dangerous men. Either one of them could have done it."

"But what is the reason for it? Would he have his own man killed just to set you up?"

"Amos has been after my ranch for years. I have refused to sell, so what does he do? He charms and flatters Katie to the point where she is totally taken with the man. Figures if he gets her to marry him, he can get her half of the ranch and maybe force me out of my half. He saw an opportunity when I threatened his men. He saw a chance to set me up and get rid of me for good. Then he can marry Katie and have the entire ranch to himself."

Matt leaned forward in his chair, rested his elbows on his knees, and interlocked his fingers. "Tell me everything you know about Amos Tolliver. Where did he come from?"

Tom shook his head and answered, "I don't know all that much about his past. He's always been evasive on that subject. He showed up here two or three years after the war ended. He went on a buying spree and grabbed up some of the smaller ranches. He pieced his ranch together from all the smaller ones he acquired. Then, about three years ago, he branched out and bought the bank and foreclosed on a few of the other businesses in town. That's how he got the general store and the saloon."

"What about his men," asked Matt, "particularly Red and Curly? Did they come with him, or did they hire on with him after he got here?"

Tom thought the question over for a minute. "I think he had five or six men with him when he got here, including Red and Curly. The rest he added afterward."

Matt sat motionless for a moment, and then asked, "What happened to the ranchers that Tolliver bought out? Are any of them still around?"

Tom furrowed his brow and inquired, "Why do you ask about that?"

"I'd rather not say right now, but I have a hunch. Are any of them still around?" he repeated.

Tom shrugged and said, "They've all moved on, except for old Casey down at the livery."

"Casey used to be a rancher?"

"Yeah," said Tom. "His was one of the first places that Amos bought."

Tom waited while Matt sat deep in thought. When Matt spoke again, he changed the subject.

"Tom, the law says that in order to convict anyone of a crime, they have to show that three conditions were met; they have to prove that the defendant had means, motive, and opportunity."

"What's all that mean?"

"It means they have to prove that you had the ability to kill Curly, that you had a reason to kill him, and that you had a chance to kill him. Unfortunately, your threat to Amos the other night pretty much establishes your means and motive."

Tom sat back down on his bunk and hung his head. "Katie has warned me often enough that my temper would get me in trouble someday."

"That's not the kind of thing that you want to say in court," Matt cautioned.

Tom looked up and asked, "What about opportunity? How does that work?"

"If we can show you didn't have a chance to kill Curly, then they don't have a case."

"How do we do that?"

"With an alibi," Matt explained. "If we can prove you were somewhere else when Curly was killed, then they have to let you go. Now, it appears Curly was shot crossing your ranch on his way to town the night of the party at your place. You stormed off after your words with Amos. Where did you go?"

Tom scratched his head and thought. "I went riding. That's what I usually do when I need to cool off."

"Where did you go riding, Tom? Did anyone see you?"

Tom shook his head. "No, I doubt anyone saw me, because I didn't see anyone. I rode along the creek, north of the house. About five miles upstream is a deep pool surrounded by cottonwoods and oaks. It's where I go sometimes to be alone. It's quiet and peaceful. It was after dark when I got back home."

"And you didn't see anyone?"

"Not until the next morning when I woke up and went downstairs for breakfast and saw Katie talking to our foreman, Ben, and a few of the hands."

"So, no alibi," said Matt.

The two men sat silently for a few minutes before Matt spoke. "It looks like the only way we can prove you didn't kill Curly is to find out who did."

"How are we gonna do that?"

Matt stood up and pushed the chair back against the wall. "Leave that up to me. I'll check around and see what I can find out."

"How do I keep from being lynched in the meantime? Marshal Guthrie is on Tolliver's payroll. He's liable to turn me over to a mob the first chance he gets."

Matt grinned. "I'll have a talk with the marshal. Don't worry. You'll be safe until the judge gets here."

"Thanks, Matt. I can't tell you how much I appreciate your help."

"Hang tight, Tom. We'll get you out of this."

Matt left the holding area and stepped into the marshal's office.

Marshal Guthrie was sitting behind his desk reading the paper. He looked up when Matt entered the room. "That didn't take you long."

"We said what we needed to say to each other."

"Did he confess to you? I couldn't get him to talk to me. I told him it would go a lot easier on him if he would confess."

"He doesn't have anything to confess to, Marshal. He says he's innocent, and I believe him."

Marshal Guthrie huffed and looked at Matt like he was crazy. "Well, you're the only one left in town who thinks that way. Everyone else knows he killed that boy."

"Why do you and Amos Tolliver keep

referring to Curly as a boy? He was a full-grown man, and not a very pleasant one at that. It wouldn't surprise me at all if there was someone else who wanted him dead, and I'm going to find out who that might be."

"You'll be wasting your time."

"It's my time, Marshal. And let me tell you one other thing: nothing better happen to Tom before the judge gets here."

Marshal Guthrie shrugged his shoulders and replied, "Tom has the whole town worked up over the murder. I can't be responsible if an angry mob storms the jail. I'm only one man."

Matt stepped up until he was standing in front of the marshal's desk. He leaned forward and placed his hands on the edge of the desk, with his face directly in front of Guthrie's. "That wouldn't be justice. That would be cold-blooded murder, and you know it. You are the town marshal. It's your responsibility to keep the peace. If you can't do the job, then let me know. I'll send a telegram to Governor Davis in Austin. He can send someone out here to investigate your office, Marshal. But I don't think that either you or Amos wants that to happen."

Matt straightened up and made for the front door. With his hand on the doorknob, a thought occurred to him. He turned to the marshal and asked, "Tell me something. When you found Curly's body, was he wearing his gun belt?"

"Yeah, he had his guns on. What of it?"

"I remember he wore two guns in a cross-draw rig. Were his guns holstered, or were they on the ground by his body?"

"What difference does it make one way or the other?" replied Marshal Guthrie, clearly annoyed by the questions.

"Humor me. Were his guns holstered or not?"

Guthrie hesitated, rubbing his chin as he considered whether to answer. He couldn't see the harm, but his insides warned him that Amos wouldn't like anyone asking a bunch of questions. He made a mental note to let Amos know that the new school teacher was snooping around.

After a moment he replied, "Curly's guns were both holstered."

"Don't you find that rather strange?" Matt asked. He had turned to face Marshal Guthrie as he spoke.

"What's so unusual about his guns being holstered?"

"Well, it's just that it's inconsistent with the story we are hearing. Curly was shot twice in the chest, correct?"

Marshal Guthrie agreed.

"He was supposedly heading into town to see his girlfriend, so he was riding south. That means that his killer came from the direction of town."

"So, what's your point?"

"The McCutchen ranch is to the north. How did Tom shoot Curly in the chest if he was riding away from him?"

The marshal leaned forward with his elbow on his desk and pointed his finger in Matt's direction. "That don't prove a thing. Tom could have come up from the south and shot him. That don't prove a thing," he repeated.

Matt placed his hands in his pockets as the marshal spoke. Hanging his head, he pursed his lips and listened to the marshal's explanation.

When Guthrie had finished speaking, Matt said, "Except for the arroyo where you found Curly's body, it's as flat as a tabletop between town and the McCutchen ranch. Curly would have seen Tom from way off."

Guthrie smiled triumphantly and exclaimed, "Not if Tom was already hiding in the arroyo waiting for him!"

"How would Tom have possibly known that Curly was going to go into town that night? How would he have known that

Curly would cut across his land, or exactly where to wait in the arroyo for him? I think any jury would be skeptical of that theory, Marshal."

Guthrie looked confused. "Tom could have been coming from town for all we know."

Matt laughed, "You want us to believe that Curly, a hot-headed, well-armed man who knew that he was trespassing, saw Tom, a man who had already threatened to shoot any trespassers on his ranch, and Curly never drew his gun?"

"Well, it might be Curly didn't want any trouble," the marshal added weakly.

"Curly hunted trouble. You know that as well as anyone."

Matt turned toward the door again. "There's more to this killing than meets the eye, and I aim to get to the bottom of it." Matt walked out of the marshal's office and slammed the door behind him.

CHAPTER ELEVEN

"How's that mare working out for you, young feller?" Casey was mucking out stalls when Matt walked into the barn at the livery. "All sales are final, you know."

"Oh, the horse is wonderful," Matt replied. "I'm very pleased with her."

Casey stopped his work and leaned on his pitchfork. "I'm glad to hear it. What else can I do for you?"

Matt upended an empty pail and sat down. "How long have you had the livery, Casey?"

"Oh, let's see now." The old hostler hung his head and tilted it to the side as he did the math in his head. "I bought the place from ol' Ben Tate back in '67. He retired and moved back to Ohio to be with his daughter. So I guess it's been a mite over six years. Why do you ask?"

Matt ignored the question. "I understand you did some ranching before you bought the livery."

"Yep, that's right. I used to have a spread north of town. I didn't care much for ranching, though. I was glad to be rid of it."

"I hear your place was one of the ranches Amos Tolliver bought up."

Casey stopped his work and leaned against his pitchfork. "What's this interest you have in Amos Tolliver?"

Matt shrugged. "I'm interested in one of our most prominent citizens."

Casey removed a plug of tobacco from the pocket of his overalls and bit off a chunk. He looked at Matt with unveiled suspicion. "Young fella, I like you. I think you've got a lot more thunder and lightning in you than you let on. But don't stick your nose into Amos Tolliver's business. He's not the kind of man who's gonna tolerate anyone snooping around in his affairs."

Matt stood to his feet. "Casey, tell me, do you think that Tom McCutchen killed Curly?"

Casey spat out some tobacco juice and wiped his mouth across the back of his grimy hand. "Tom's hot-headed for sure, but that boy ain't no murderer."

"I don't think so either, Casey. I think Amos Tolliver is involved somehow, and I intend to keep Tom from hanging for a murder he didn't commit."

Casey put his hands into his pockets and hung his head, shaking it back and forth. Then he looked up and said, "Looky here, son. Tolliver has some bad men on his payroll . . . some real bad men. Curly was the worst one of the bunch. He wasn't all there." Casey tapped his forefinger against his temple to emphasize his point. "But Tolliver," he continued, "he would make all of them look like a bunch of hymn-singing Bible thumpers. I've been around a long time, and I'm a fair judge of character, and I'm telling you if you ask questions about him, you better watch your back."

"I appreciate the warning, Casey; I really do. But if Tolliver is somehow responsible, then I have to find a way to prove it. I can't let an innocent man hang."

Casey hesitated and then said, "All right, but don't say I didn't warn you. What is it you want to know?"

"When Tolliver purchased your ranch from you, did he pay you with a bank draft?"

Casey shook his head, "Nope. He paid me cash money — two thousand dollars."

Matt stared at Casey wide eyed. "That's a lot of money for a cash transaction."

"Yep, and my place was one of the smaller ones that he bought up. He paid cash for them all."

"Are you sure?" That was a great deal of money for someone to have so near after the end of the war. If he was a cotton broker for the Confederacy, like he claimed, he could have made a fortune. But very few wealthy southerners made it through the war with their fortunes intact.

"I'm sure about it. I knew everyone he bought out, and I know he paid us all cash for our ranches."

"Where do you think Tolliver got his money?"

"Well, he said he sold his ranch up near Denver."

"I suppose that's a possibility," Matt replied, more to himself than anyone else. "Anyway, that's what I needed to know, Casey. Thanks for the information."

As Matt walked away, Casey called after him. "Do you own a gun?"

Matt shook his head. "I don't care for guns."

"Well, if I were you, I would get myself a gun and learn how to use it."

Matt hesitated a moment before he turned and walked out of the barn.

He hopped up on the back of the chestnut. She was a spirited horse, eager to run. Matt liked that about her. But he kept the horse at a slow trot as he headed north out of town. He wanted to get a look at the place where Curly's body had been found. He didn't know if he would learn anything useful, but he thought he should have a look anyway. Besides, he needed to think, and the ride out of town would give him a good chance to do that.

There was something wrong, but he couldn't quite see the whole picture. It was like a jigsaw puzzle. Some of the pieces were upside down, some of them were out of place, and others were missing. Sure, he was upset that Tom had been arrested for the murder of Curly, especially since he was convinced Tom was innocent. Matt was certain Tolliver was behind the murder. He didn't know why he would have had his own man killed, and the evidence he had was only circumstantial. But there was more to it. There was more behind Amos Tolliver than an ambitious rancher and business owner. There was a secret he was hiding. Maybe it was something from his past, and maybe it was really that secret that was responsible for Curly's death. Matt had a feeling that, whatever it was, it would be the piece of the puzzle that would bring the picture into focus.

As Matt rode along the road that took him

north out of town, a theory began to form, one that even Matt found difficult to believe. He would need more proof than he currently had, but, so far, the pieces of the puzzle that he did have started to fall into place. If his theory were right, it would be a miracle that he had stumbled across the truth after all these years, right here in the west Texas town of Mustang Flats.

An hour later, he pulled back on the reins and stopped in the middle of the road. It was easy to make out the tracks from the wagon that Marshal Guthrie had sent from town to pick up Curly's body. The wagon tracks left the road and went east along a depression that grew deeper the further he went. The depression in the prairie turned into an arroyo about ten feet deep and twenty-five feet across.

After about a mile, the wagon had stopped. Matt got down from the chestnut and had a look down inside the wash where Curly had been found.

The marshal had reported that Curly had been killed on the north side of the arroyo and that his body had fallen over the edge and had been found at the bottom of the wash against the north face. Matt could still see where the edge of the wash had been caved in, either from the weight of Curly's body falling over the edge or from a poor attempt to cover his body once it had fallen to the bottom.

As he looked around, he could see that anyone approaching from the south would have been easily seen. Curly would have had ample opportunity to defend himself. Even if Curly had been shot at night — which is what Tolliver and his men claimed — the moon had been bright. A horse and rider would have stood out on the flat prairie.

But, thought Matt, suppose the killer was already on the north side of the arroyo with Curly. He could have been someone that Curly knew. That would explain why Curly never pulled his gun and how the killer managed to get close enough to put two slugs into his chest.

Matt got back on his horse and put her at an easy trot toward the road, but, instead of turning south toward town, he turned the mare to the right. He thought he would visit with Katie. It must be a difficult position for her to be in. Imagine: her own brother accused of killing a man who worked for her . . . her what? Matt had a difficult time coming up with the right word to describe Tolliver's relationship with Katie. He wasn't her fiancé, at least not yet. To say he was her lover seemed crass and may not have been exactly accurate. But he didn't know. Matt settled on "suitor" as the best word to use.

But, no matter what word he used, the idea of the two of them together bothered him more than he wanted to admit.

He rode his horse up to the ranch house and tied her to a hitch rail out front. There was another horse tied up as well, and Matt recognized it as Tolliver's. *He didn't waste any time,* thought Matt.

As he dismounted and walked up onto the veranda, the front door opened, and Tolliver stood in the doorway. He stepped out onto the porch and closed the door behind him.

"Mr. Gaines, what can I do for you?"

"Nothing. I came here to see Katie." Matt took a step towards the door.

Tolliver remained in his path, blocking his way, arms folded across his chest. "I'm afraid Miss McCutchen is not receiving any visitors today."

"I wanted to check in on her and see if there was anything I could do."

Tolliver remained rooted where he was. He smiled without showing any teeth. "Well, that's neighborly of you. However, she is resting right now. She has been through quite an ordeal. The doctor has her sedated so she can get some sleep."

It was clear to Matt that he wasn't getting anywhere near the front door, so he took a step back. "I'm sure Katie could rest a lot easier if you weren't accusing her brother of murder."

"I'm afraid that you're misinformed, Mr. Gaines. I haven't accused Tom of anything. It's the marshal that arrested him, not me."

"Marshal Guthrie works for you and does what you tell him to do." Matt could feel the color rise up in him. Tolliver was an arrogant narcissist who thought that laws were to be manipulated for his own gain rather than to protect society.

Tolliver took a step closer to Matt until they were only inches apart. "You give me too much credit, Mr. Gaines. Everyone heard Tom threaten my men. You heard him yourself. The marshal is perfectly justified in arresting Tom. The judge can decide his guilt or innocence."

"You mean if he even makes it to trial, don't you? Your men are bad mouthing Tom all around Mustang Flats. It's to the point where some of the men in town want to storm the jail and take him by force."

Tolliver shrugged his shoulders. "My men lost a close friend and comrade. They want justice."

"That's not justice. That's murder. And

before I let Tom get lynched by your mob, I will find out what really happened to Curly."

Matt turned and walked back to his horse, untied her, and pulled himself into the saddle. He turned to look at Tolliver, who had stepped up to the edge of the porch. "Tell me, Tolliver," Matt said, looking down at the man, who leaned nonchalantly against a support post, "Do you want this ranch so badly that you'd let an innocent man hang so that you can get it? Why are you doing this?"

Tolliver looked over his shoulder, then to both sides. He and Matt were alone. "Tom brought this on himself. He should have sold out to me when he had the chance. I'm building the largest ranch in Texas. It was never a question with me about 'if' I would get Tom's ranch. The question has always been, 'at what price.' Well, the price just got a lot lower."

"I'm not letting you get away with this." Matt turned his horse up the drive and took off at a gallop, kicking up a cloud of dust in his wake.

After the school teacher rode away, Tolliver turned and went back inside the house. Climbing the stairs to the second floor, he found Katie's room and tapped gently on the door. He didn't wait for a response but turned the knob and walked in.

Katie was propped up in bed with her eyes closed. She looked exhausted and pale. She hadn't slept well since Tom's arrest, so the doctor had given her something to help her sleep. She opened her eyes when he walked into the room. "I thought I heard you talking to someone outside just now. Who was it?"

"It was no one important, just one of the ranch hands." Tolliver walked across the room and sat down on the edge of the bed. "How are you feeling?"

Katie sluggishly threw off the covers and tried to swing her legs over the side of the bed. "I have got to get to Tom. He needs me."

Tolliver stopped her before she got to her feet. He swung her legs back up onto the bed. "What you have to do is get some sleep. You have been through a lot." He reached for the medicine bottle on the nightstand. The doctor had left careful instructions about administering the proper dosage at the proper frequency, instructions that he intentionally interpreted much too liberally. He had needed Katie out of the way these past couple of days so that he could set his plans in motion without arousing her suspicions. He mixed a small amount of the liquid with water and held it out for Katie to take. "Here, take some more of this medicine the doctor left."

Katie weakly pushed it aside. "I don't want any more of that stuff. It makes me too tired."

"Doctor's orders," Tolliver persisted.

"Honestly, Amos, don't treat me like a fragile schoolgirl." The color came back to her cheeks as she swung her arm and knocked the glass out of his hands. "I assure you, I am neither fragile nor am I a girl."

Tolliver stood with his hands on his hips and exhaled a long sigh. "I'm just looking out for your best interests, Katie."

"And I need to look out for Tom's," she shot back.

He sat back down on the edge of the bed and took her by the hand. "All right, I'll tell you what we'll do. If you get a good night's sleep tonight, then tomorrow morning I'll take you into town to see Tom. Is that acceptable to you?"

Katie smiled and took his hand in both of hers. "Thank you, Amos. I know that you are just trying to take good care of me. I promise to go to sleep now."

He leaned forward and kissed her on the

forehead. "That's my girl." He pulled the covers back over Katie as she closed her eyes and settled down to sleep.

A few minutes later, he was back outside on the front porch. Tolliver stood where he was for several minutes, deep in thought. This school teacher was cause for concern. Now that he had Tom out of the way, here was a new thorn in his side.

Tolliver took a seat in a wicker chair there on the porch and reached into his coat pocket, pulling out a long, thin cheroot. He struck a match and lit the end, watching the ash glow dark red as he drew on the other end of the cigar.

The sun began its slow decent in the west. The sky was ablaze with various shades of orange and red and yellow. Tolliver thought about how much he would enjoy sitting on this veranda, watching the sunset, after he married Katie and got possession of the ranch.

He would have to take care of the school teacher, though. It shouldn't be a problem. One school teacher was no match for him and his men. Sitting on the porch watching the brilliant colors of the setting sun gave him an idea.

He stayed on the veranda while he finished his cigar and watched the sun complete its course and disappear below the horizon. When the first of the stars appeared overhead, he tossed his cigar butt out into the yard. He stepped down off of the porch, untied his horse, and mounted. He needed to get back to his own ranch. He had a special job for Red, and he wanted it taken care of tonight.

CHAPTER TWELVE

Matt dropped his horse off at the livery and began the short walk to the schoolhouse. He would have to speak with the school committee about building a small stable for his horse next to the school, but, for now, he enjoyed the walk. It was a pleasant evening with the cicadas singing in the oaks and cottonwoods. As he strolled along, Matt cleared his mind of the events of the day and listened to the sounds of the evening.

When he arrived home, he entered through the door into the school portion of the building, rather than the door on the back that entered into his living quarters. He looked around the room at the empty desks. School would begin on Monday, and Matt looked forward to settling into a routine. He was the kind of person that thrived best when his life was ordered, when there was a structure that lent stability and familiarity to his days.

118

He sat down at his desk in the front of the room and imagined the schoolhouse filled with students, paging through their textbooks and writing on their slates. He had several lesson plans he needed to work on before school started. He knew that his students would range in ages and academic proficiency and that they would be more diverse than the college students he usually taught. He admitted to himself that he was frightened of the responsibility he had undertaken. He wanted his students to like him, but, more importantly than that, he wanted to do a good job and not disappoint the school committee and cause them to regret hiring him.

He got up and walked over to the bookshelf and glanced at some of the titles of the books that were on the shelf. There was a copy of the Bible, so he pulled it off of the shelf and took it over to his desk. He had stopped in town at one of the restaurants and picked up some dinner, so he sat at his desk and ate while reading out of the book of Philippians.

"Brethren, I count not myself to have apprehended: but this one thing I do, forgetting those things which are behind, and reaching forth unto those things which are

before, I press toward the mark for the prize of the high calling of God in Christ Jesus."

Matt had read this verse over and over again on his trip west. To him, it spoke of a new life, of a fresh start and of hope for the future. These were things he desperately wanted, but which, just a year ago, he would not have believed possible . . .

Rebecca Nelson had been the most beautiful woman he had ever met. She was intelligent and graceful, and he felt at ease around her when he had never before been comfortable around any woman.

She was twenty-five when they met in church back in Princeton. He was a thirty-one-year-old college professor who had no difficulty talking to a lecture hall full of students, but who became completely tongue tied when it came to speaking to a young woman.

But she thought the handsome young professor's shyness and innocence were charming, and it didn't take long for her to loosen his tongue. First, it was a few minutes after church on Sunday. Then it was hours, as they took long walks under the chestnuts and elms that lined the streets of Princeton.

Before long, they were seeing each other socially outside of church. Six months later, they were in love and planned to be married.

They had decided to celebrate their engagement with some of their friends by attending the theatre in New York. A New Jersey native named Kate Claxton was a popular actress, and Rebecca had wanted to see her perform for some time. Matt had learned that she was appearing in New York in the adaptation of a French play called *The Two Orphans*.

So one sunny June day, Matt and Rebecca, along with two of their friends, boarded the train for the two-hour trip to New York's Grand Central Depot, where they took a horse trolley south along the East River until they came to a ferry that could carry them across. Once across the East River, they took a coach to the corner of Washington and Johnson streets.

The theatre seated sixteen hundred patrons, and it was filled nearly to capacity that evening. There were three levels of seating, and the only tickets Matt was able to purchase were in the uppermost gallery of seats.

It was after the intermission before the last act of the play was about to begin when the fire started. It began backstage when some canvas from one of the props hung loosely from its frame and came into contact with one of the border lights. Stagehands, in an effort to beat the flames into submission, actually helped to spread the fire to the rigging loft.

The actors had just gone out on the stage to begin the last act when smoke began to billow out from behind the scenery on stage. Despite their best efforts to calm the audience, the theatergoers crowded into the aisles. Within minutes, panic had spread throughout the lower level of the theatre. People packed the aisles in a frantic attempt to reach one of the exit doors.

The people in the two upper galleries had a good vantage point from which to view the chaos below them. They saw the fire engulf the stage and spread through the rigging to other parts of the theatre.

The gallery patrons sprung from their seats and tried to make their way to the ground floor, seeking an exit to the street. Unfortunately, each of the upper galleries had only a single stairway that led to the ground floor, and these stairways could not accommodate the sudden influx of people trying to exit the upper levels. People were screaming and pushing each other in an attempt to escape, but the stairway became packed with people who were trampled to death. After a few minutes, no one could enter the stairway for all of the bodies that were crammed into it.

To make matters worse for the people in the galleries, the head usher opened a special emergency door on the lower level that emptied out into an alley. This certainly helped to save many of the people on the lower level, but the onrush of air added fuel to the flames, which spread more rapidly throughout the theatre.

Matt had stepped outside for some fresh air during the intermission, while Rebecca and their two friends remained in the gallery. He had just reentered the theatre lobby when the doors to the lower level of the seating area burst open, and people rushed out screaming that the theatre was on fire.

Matt hurried to the stairway that led to the uppermost level where Rebecca and their friends were seated. He made it to the second level before he was pushed back and almost trampled by the onrush of patrons shoving past him in the opposite direction.

He fought his way back downstairs, found a corner of the lobby where he could stand, and watched as people descended the stairway. Men and women were being crushed as they attempted to make their way out of the theatre.

Smoke filled the lobby, and Matt hadn't spotted either Rebecca or the other couple that they had come with. He called out her name until he was hoarse from shouting above the cries and screams of the people who were trapped above as well as the ones who managed to find their way out. He studied the faces of the people who had managed to flee down the stairway, hoping to recognize anyone who may have been seated near Rebecca, but none of the frantic faces looked familiar to him.

The lower level of the theatre had been evacuated by this time, and it was only the people in the two upper levels who were still trapped.

Desperate, Matt turned and ran into the main level of the theatre. The smoke choked his lungs and made his eyes water. He could see that the flames had spread throughout the theatre. The stage was completely engulfed, and the orchestra pit was filled with burning debris. Flames crept along the ornately paneled walls at least three-quarters of the way back to the rear exit that Matt had just stepped through. The heat was intense.

He raised his eyes to the uppermost gallery where he had been seated with Rebecca. He could hear screams from both of the galleries above him, but the smoke was too thick for him to see anything.

Although the fire had made its way to the area below the galleries, which were now in danger of being consumed by the flames, several people from the lower gallery were hanging off the side, trying to lower themselves to the main level.

Matt watched in horror as one man slipped as he attempted to climb over the gallery banister. He landed with a crash on a row of chairs beneath. The man cried out in agony but didn't move. Matt could see that his lower right leg was bent at a grotesque angle, with both his tibia and fibula pushing through his skin.

Matt rushed over to where the man had fallen. Placing his arms under the man's shoulders, he dragged him out of the row of chairs and into the aisle, and then along the wall to the nearest door, which led into the lobby. Once in the lobby, Matt handed him off to a policeman who had arrived.

Matt made two more trips to the main level of the theatre for people who had managed to jump from the lower gallery to escape the inferno and pulled them to safety.

His face was black with soot, and his eyes

watered so badly that it was difficult to see. His pants were scorched and ripped, and his jacket had to be hastily pulled off and discarded when his sleeve had caught fire.

On his next trip into the theatre, Matt could no longer hear any cries from the uppermost gallery. The thick, black smoke had risen and filled the upper part of the theatre first. He knew that it would have been impossible for the people trapped up there to take a breath without inhaling the hot, acrid fumes into their lungs.

By this time, the fire had reached the lower gallery, and the people who remained trapped there pushed their way toward the back, away from the encroaching flames. Matt called out to them from below and urged them to take a chance and jump to the main level. But they were all too frightened to hear him or to heed his advice.

Matt took a few steps closer to the balcony so that he could be heard above the screams of the trapped men and women, and above the roar of the fire as the flames curled around the support beams that held up the gallery.

Matt heard the wood creak and then a loud crack as one of the supports gave way. The front edge of the gallery moaned and dropped several feet, causing the gallery to rest at an incline. A number of the people who were trapped lost their footing and slid down and off the edge of the gallery. Some of them landed on top of burning chairs and other rubble, while others landed in a broken heap.

Matt tried to make his way to where several people had fallen in an area that had not yet been reached by the fire, but, before he could reach them, he heard the deafening sound of splintering wood, as the rest of the lower gallery gave way and crashed to the main level.

Matt tried to dive out of the way, but a wooden beam crashed down on his head and knocked him to the floor. He lay there half conscious, dimly aware of the roar of the flames around him and the heat as the fire grew in size and intensity. The last thing he remembered before he lost consciousness was the searing pain in his leg and the smell of burnt flesh.

When he came to, he was lying on a stretcher on Johnson Street, where scores of other injured men and women had been placed and were receiving medical attention. He was later transported to a hospital where, because of the severity of the burns to his leg, he spent the next six weeks.

He found out later that almost three

hundred people died in the fire, and count-less others were injured.

Rebecca's body was never recovered — at least not that they could identify. Two-thirds of the casualties were burned beyond recog-nition and were buried in a mass grave in Green-Wood Cemetery with a giant marble obelisk as a memorial.

Matt finished his dinner and retreated to his living quarters. He sat on the edge of his bed and considered his situation. Thoughts of Rebecca could send him into a deep depression that could last for days, and it had taken him months to learn how to control his emotions. He knew that he needed to focus on today, to force himself to be in the present, so he thought about Tom's predicament.

Matt was convinced that Tom did not kill Curly. He was also convinced that Amos Tolliver was somehow responsible and that Tom was correct in his assumption that this was part of a move by Tolliver to gain pos-session of the Bar-M.

But Matt also believed that Tolliver hid a more sinister secret. But before he spoke to anyone about his suspicions, he wanted to send off two telegrams. That would be his first task in the morning, he thought, as he undressed and climbed into bed.

It was sometime after midnight when Matt awoke with a jerk and sat straight up in bed. Although the night was cool, his pillow was damp with perspiration. He had been dreaming of that awful night fifteen months ago. As he sat up in bed, he could still see the flames and smell the smoke that had tormented his dreams for so long.

Then he heard the sound of men's voices outside his window, followed by the steady cadence of the drumming of horses' hooves as they disappeared down the road.

To his horror, Matt realized that he was awake and that the flames and smoke that filled the schoolhouse were no nightmare.

Matt threw his legs over the side of his bed and stood up. He wasted no time pulling on his pants and boots.

He saw through the windows on either side of his living quarters that flames surrounded that end of the building. Although smoke was creeping into the room, so far, the flames were confined to the outside, but that would not be the case for long. He had to get out.

Reaching for the door latch, he cried out in pain and pulled his hand back. The latch was hot to the touch. Flames were licking at the bottom of the door. He turned and rushed for the door into the schoolroom.

As he stood in the doorway, he looked out over the schoolroom before him. The fire was already inside the schoolhouse. There was an odd pattern to the way the flames crawled across the floors and the desks and up and down the walls. The door on the opposite end of the building was wide open. Matt knew that he had shut it behind him when he came home last night. The windows were all engulfed in flames. The only way out was through that open door. But he would have to run a gauntlet of flames to get to it.

He ducked back into his living quarters for only a few seconds and then reappeared with a blanket tightly wrapped around his head and hanging below his knees. He hesitated only a moment before he rushed through the flames that danced around the schoolroom and bolted out of the open door. Once outside, he doffed the burning blanket and tossed it to the ground.

He stood there doubled over, coughing, as the fire made quick work of the wooden schoolhouse, his home, and his future.

CHAPTER THIRTEEN

That morning, Matt stood to survey the smoldering ruins of the schoolhouse. The entire structure and all of its contents were a complete loss. Matt wondered what they would do now. School was supposed to begin in a couple of days, and it would take weeks to rebuild.

He bent down in the rubble and picked up a board that was only half charred by the fire and held it up to his nose. He sniffed along the edge of the piece of pine. There was no mistake about it. The telltale odor of kerosene still clung to the wood.

Holding the board over his head like a trophy, Matt walked over to where Marshal Guthrie and a handful of other citizens surveyed the burnt schoolhouse. "You want proof, Marshal? Here you go, smell this."

He handed the charred board to Guthrie, who held it up to his nose to have a whiff. The marshal wrinkled his nose and asked,

"What did you do, spill some kerosene when you filled your lamp?"

Matt sighed in disgust. "No, Marshal, I did not. Someone poured kerosene all around the outside of the building and then went into the school and emptied their cans inside. I'd lay odds that we'll find the discarded cans in the rubble. That would explain the strange burn pattern that I observed. Someone used an accelerant to start the fire — with me inside!"

Matt was severely agitated and wasn't about to let Marshal Guthrie pass the fire off as an accident without so much as an investigation.

Guthrie shook his head in disbelief. "Are you saying someone purposely tried to kill you?" he chuckled. "You're just a school teacher."

"I told you, I heard men's voices and horses outside my window when I woke up. The fire was already well under way at that point. Besides, look at this," he said.

He led the crowd of onlookers to the rear of the building, where his sleeping quarters used to be. There, pushed up against what remained of his blackened door, was what had been a huge pile of brush. It had been heaped up against the door and set on fire to prevent him from escaping through that exit.

"What do you make of that, Marshal?"

Guthrie frowned and said, "I'll look into it."

At that moment a black lacquered carriage came up the road, pulled by two beautifully matched black horses. Amos Tolliver was handling the reins, and Katie McCutchen was beside him. As the wagon pulled to a stop, Katie jumped down from her seat without assistance from anyone. Her mouth was open, and her eyes were wide. She saw Matt standing near Marshal Guthrie and ran up to him.

"Matt, thank God you're all right." Then she looked him over from head to foot. He wore only what he had on when he escaped the burning schoolhouse during the night. "You are all right, aren't you? You're not injured?" she asked.

"I'm fine," he assured her.

"Amos and I were on our way to the jail to see Tom when we heard about the fire. What happened?"

"We're not quite sure about that, Miss McCutchen," Marshal Guthrie was quick to reply. "I will conduct an investigation." He gave a sideways glance at Tolliver, who had gotten out of the carriage to stand next to Katie.

"Someone set fire to the school last night," said Matt, matter- of-factly. "They tried to trap me inside." This time it was Matt who cast a glance at Tolliver, who still hadn't said a word.

Katie was still in shock as she looked over the remains of the school that she had worked so hard to establish. She stared at Matt in astonishment. "Why would some-one want to kill you?"

Matt's hands curled into fists as he said, "Maybe you should ask Amos about that."

Tolliver stiffened noticeably. "Are you ac-cusing me of having something to do with this?" He took a threatening step toward Matt, who stepped forward to meet him. The two men stood face to face with only a few inches of daylight to separate them.

"It's quite a coincidence that I start ask-ing questions about you and then someone tries to roast me alive," said Matt.

Katie pushed her hands between the two men to force them apart. "You both need to calm down." Then she turned to Matt and asked, "What do you mean you're asking questions about Amos. Why?"

"Katie, this man is not who he says he is."

"That's ridiculous. Just who do you think he is?"

Matt hesitated and looked sheepishly at Katie, who stood with her hands on her hips. "I can't say right now. Not until I get more proof. But I can tell you that he is not looking out for your best interests . . . or Tom's."

"What does Tom have to do with any of this?" Katie asked.

"Don't you see?" Matt exclaimed. "Who stands to gain with Tom out of the picture?"

Katie's frustration was apparent. She shook her head like she was trying to clear out the confusion and all of the questions that fogged her brain. "I don't understand, Matt. What does any of this have to do with the school burning down?"

Matt turned and addressed Tolliver. "Where were you and your men last night?" Matt's question was as much an accusation as it was an inquiry.

"Not that I need to answer to you, but all my men were with me on my ranch last night. I've instructed them to stay out of town for a while and not stir up any hard feelings about Tom." He placed his arm around Katie and said, "I'm doing my best to see Tom gets a fair trial."

Anger flooded over Matt, and he felt his ears grow hot. Before he realized it, his right arm shot out with a quick jab that landed a punch right on Tolliver's mouth.

The action on Matt's part was totally unexpected, and Tolliver wound up on his backside in the dirt.

Katie gasped. She bent down to see how badly Tolliver was hurt. He had a split lip with a trickle of blood in his beard. She looked up at Matt in shock. "What are you doing? Are you crazy?"

"Katie, can't you see what Amos is trying to do?" Matt's voice was desperate. He knew he shouldn't have hit Tolliver, but the man had asked for it. "You can't possibly believe what he says. He wants Tom to hang. He's only after your ranch."

Katie stood to her feet and faced Matt. Her hat had fallen off when she bent down to check on Tolliver, and her red hair was hanging loosely. It matched the burning color in her cheeks, and her eyes flashed with a fire that was equal to the flames that had destroyed the schoolhouse.

"For your information, Amos has been a good friend to me much longer than I have known you!" she shouted. "He has been a tremendous comfort to me these last few days since Tom was arrested, and I know he would never do the things that you accuse him of."

"But Katie . . ." Matt tried to explain.

"Mr. Gaines," Katie said, as she composed herself and lowered her voice, "We no longer have a school in which to hold classes. Therefore, we are no longer in need of a teacher. As head of the school committee, I am terminating your contract."

Matt stood in shocked silence as Tolliver got to his feet and brushed himself off. He took Katie by the arm, led her over to the carriage, and helped her in. Once in his seat, he gave the reins a shake, and the two blacks started in a walk down the road to town.

Marshal Guthrie and the others who were still there looked at Matt before, one by one, they walked away until only John from the mercantile store remained. He walked over to Matt and put his hand on his shoulder. "Come on with me over to the store. Violet and I will get you fixed up with some new clothes and whatever else you need."

Matt looked one last time at the remains of the schoolhouse and felt relieved that his books and other belongings hadn't arrived yet from Princeton, or else everything he owned might have been destroyed. He still had some money in the bank, enough to carry him for a few months anyway. But it would be difficult to find another position this time of the year.

He had really been looking forward to

teaching school in Mustang Flats and had no idea what he would do from here on out. But one thing he was sure of: he wasn't leaving town until Tom was set free and Amos Tolliver was behind bars.

CHAPTER FOURTEEN

Matt was able to outfit himself at the mercantile with some new clothes and a few personal items. Then he went over to the hotel and rented a room, paying for a week in advance. At first, he thought about the wisdom of paying in advance when someone was trying to kill him. Why waste the money? Then he laughed when he realized that, if he were dead, then the money wouldn't matter anyway.

At the hotel, he was able to shave and take a hot bath. It felt good to get the soot and the odor of smoke off of him and to sit in the tub and soak. He had only had a few hours of sleep last night before he was awakened by the fire, so he closed his eyes while he relaxed in the tub.

When he opened his eyes again, several hours had gone by. It was past noon, and his bath water had become cold. He stepped out of the tub, dried himself off, and got dressed. He still wanted to send those telegrams, and he wanted to stop by the jail and check on Tom, but that might have to wait until tomorrow. He had too much to do yet today, and, even though he had been able to catch a few hours of sleep, he still felt exhausted. He also wanted something to eat.

He went to the telegraph office first. After composing the two telegrams for the agent he said, "I wouldn't want anyone else to find out about these, or about any response I might get."

The telegraph agent, who was an employee of the railroad, was a tall, middle-aged man with a hawkish nose. He wore a visor around his balding scalp and a blue and white pinstriped shirt with sleeve garters under an unbuttoned, black vest. He looked at Matt as though he had been insulted. "All telegrams are confidential," he answered, somewhat annoyed. "That's railroad policy, and I've been a telegraph operator for fifteen years . . ."

"I apologize," Matt interjected. "I didn't mean to offend you. It's just that it's difficult to know who works for whom in this town." Tolliver had his own agents in Mustang Flats, and the telegraph agent might be one of them. He would have to take his chances.

Matt handed the agent the money for the telegrams.

"Mr. Gaines, do you want to check back later to see if you get a response, or do you want me to send it somewhere?"

"As soon as something comes in, please send it to me at the hotel."

The agent agreed, and Matt headed back to the hotel. He wanted to write some letters to inquire about other teaching positions; then he would eat some dinner and go to bed at a decent hour.

When Matt walked into the marshal's office the following morning, Guthrie was sitting at his desk with his feet up, reading the newspaper.

"I see you are hard at work solving the arson and the attempt on my life," said Matt, with an edginess in his voice fueled by the contempt he felt for the marshal.

Guthrie looked up from his paper. "What do you want, Gaines?"

"I want to talk to Tom."

"I'm afraid Tom isn't feeling well. He may not be too talkative." The marshal waved his hand toward the door that led back to the detention area. "Go on, if you want. The door's open."

Matt let himself through the door and walked over to Tom's cell. He was still the only one behind bars. The other two cells were empty. Their doors were unlocked and open.

Tom was lying on his side on his bunk, facing the wall. It looked as though he was sleeping, so Matt called out his name. There was no answer, only a quiet, low groan. Matt called him again. This time Tom rolled over onto his back and Matt could see that there was blood on his face, and both of his eyes were purple and swollen shut.

"Marshal, get in here!" Matt shouted. He hurried back to the door to the marshal's office.

Guthrie took his time folding the newspaper. Placing the paper on his desk, he opened his desk drawer to locate the keys to the cell. He looked up at Matt, who stood anxiously in the doorway. "I told you he wasn't feeling well."

Matt felt the anger rise up in him again like it had yesterday morning when he punched Tolliver. He wanted to do the same to the marshal. "There is a difference between ill and injured," Matt said in a near shout. "What happened?"

The marshal got the keys to the cell and led Matt back to the holding area. He slid the key into Tom's cell door and gave it a turn. The lock clicked, and the iron door swung open with a squeak that made Matt's jaw tighten.

Matt pushed past Guthrie and rushed to Tom's side.

Tom was barely conscious. His face was bloody and bruised, and his breathing was shallow and raspy. His lips moved as he tried to speak. Matt bent down closer. "My ribs . . . broken."

Matt pulled back the blanket and saw that Tom's shirt was torn open. His body was covered with bruises as though he had been repeatedly punched or kicked. His left side, in particular, was swollen and had turned a deep purple in color.

Matt turned to Guthrie so suddenly that the older man flinched. "What the hell happened?"

"I had to lock up a couple of drunks last night. They got into a fight with Tom. I didn't see it, but they said Tom started it."

"Why in the world would you put them in Tom's cell when you have two other cells that are empty?" Matt was incredulous.

"I lost the keys to those two cells. I'm having new ones made."

"Who were the two men?" Matt demanded.

The marshal shrugged his shoulders. "They weren't from around here."

"Were they Tolliver's men?"

"No. I told you, they were drifters. I turned them loose this morning. I'm sure they're long gone by now."

Matt looked down helplessly at his injured friend. He didn't buy the marshal's story one bit. The two men may not have been Tolliver's ranch hands, but Matt had no doubt that they were paid by Tolliver and no doubt that the marshal was in on it also.

Matt bent down and spoke softly into Tom's ear, "Hang in there, Tom. I'm going to get the doctor, and then I'm going to get you out of here."

He looked at the marshal and said, "I'm going to have your badge for this." Then he turned abruptly and stormed out of the jail.

Marshal Guthrie called after him, "I can't watch my prisoners every blasted hour of the day. I'm just one man. What do you want from me?"

Guthrie shut the cell door and went back out to his office. He looked around. He liked it here. He liked his position as town marshal. But things were becoming too complicated for him. He liked to sit back and drink coffee and read the paper. He liked taking fishing trips when Amos suggested that he do so. He liked the discounts he got at the restaurant and at the saloon, for no other reason than that he was Tolliver's man, and no one wanted trouble with Amos Tolliver.

But was it worth it all? Murder, arson, attempted murder, prisoners beaten while in his custody. Now it was more likely than not that Gaines would make good on his threat, and the governor's office would start an investigation. Guthrie knew that any investigation would not end well for him. He would wind up on the inside of a jail cell himself. He knew what happened to lawmen who wound up in jail. He shuddered as he thought about it.

He had some money squirreled away in a jar at his shack. "The hell with Amos Tolliver," he said out loud. "I'm not going to prison for that son of a bitch."

He walked over to his desk and pulled a piece of paper out of one of the drawers. Picking up a pen, he dipped it in ink and scribbled on it. Then he walked back to the detention area and opened the door to Tom's cell.

Tom had passed out, so Guthrie walked over to the injured man, bent down, and shoved the piece of paper into Tom's shirt pocket. Then he turned and walked out of the cell, leaving the door open.

Back in his office, Guthrie removed the badge from his chest and set it on the top of the desk. Twenty minutes later, he had collected his jar of money, packed up his few belongings, and was headed east. His sister lived in Fort Graham, and there was good fishing on the Brazos.

CHAPTER FIFTEEN

A short time later, Matt returned to the jail with the doctor in tow. The marshal's office was empty, so he and the doctor went straight back to Tom's cell. Matt was surprised to see Tom's cell door open, especially as the marshal didn't seem to be anywhere around.

The doctor was a distinguished looking man in his sixties. He had a head full of white hair and a long, walrus mustache. He went over to Tom and pulled the blanket back to have a better look at his injuries. After a moment, he sighed and shook his head from side to side. "Tom has at least three broken ribs, and it looks like his nose is broken also. You say that this happened while he was locked up here last night?"

"That's right, Doctor."

"This is inexcusable," replied the doctor, who was obviously upset by Tom's condition. "That Guthrie is the most incompetent man I know. He's the sorriest excuse for a lawman this town has ever had."

"Speaking of the marshal, I wonder where he is," said Matt as his eyes scanned the jail for clues.

"You'll have to figure that out later. Right now, I need your assistance."

"What do you want me to do?"

"Help me lift Tom into a sitting position so I can wrap his ribs. Fortunately, there doesn't appear to be any internal bleeding or other injuries. He's lucky that one of those broken ribs didn't puncture his lung."

Tom was only semi-conscious, so the two of them worked together to sit him upright. After a few minutes, they had his midsection tightly bound. They found some water and poured it into a basin and used it to clean the blood off of his face and out of his nostrils.

After laying Tom gently back down in his bunk, Matt saw a piece of paper sticking out of his pocket. Removing the paper, he read it to himself, then read it out loud to the doctor.

"Hey, Doc, listen to this. 'Tom Mc-Cutchen is hereby released from my custody, as I find that there is insufficient evidence to hold him for the murder of Curly.' It's signed by Marshal Guthrie. That must be why he left the cell door open, to show that Tom is free to go."

"Well, I imagine that's good news for Tom, but he shouldn't be moved for at least three or four days. You need to give his ribs time to set up a bit and start to heal. Even then, I don't want to see him on a horse for another three weeks."

"All right, Doctor. I think we've seen the last of the marshal, so I'll stay with Tom here at the jail."

"Good." The doctor reached into his bag and pulled out a small brown bottle. "This is laudanum. When he wakes up he will be in a lot of pain. Count out twenty drops of this. It's bitter stuff, so mix it with some whiskey. Then give him another dose about every four hours if he needs it."

"Thank you, Doctor. I appreciate your help."

"Don't mention it. I'll come back and check on him tomorrow." The two men shook hands, and Matt watched as the doctor left.

"What's going on?"

Matt turned in time to see Tom attempting to sit up on his bunk. Tom grimaced in pain and fell backward. "Maybe I should just lay here for a while," he said with a weak, pained grin on his face.

Matt pulled the chair from the hallway into the cell and placed it next to Tom's bunk. He took a seat and said, "You took a bad beating, Tom. Besides some cuts and bruises, the doctor said that you broke your nose and a few ribs. Do you remember what happened?"

Tom closed his eyes for a moment as he tried to recall the events of the past night. "I remember two men coming into the cell. Before I knew what was happening, they knocked me down and began kicking me. I have no idea who they were. I never saw them before."

"It's my guess that Tolliver hired them to rough you up."

"I know he did." For a moment, the pain that Tom must have been feeling from his injuries vacated his eyes and was replaced by a seething anger. "After they beat me down to the ground, one of the men said, 'Amos Tolliver sends his regards.' Then he kicked me in the face. The bastard broke my nose."

Tom tried to sit up again, but Matt urged him to lie back down.

"I never broke any ribs before. This really smarts."

"Hang on a second," replied Matt.

Matt got up and went into the marshal's

office. He went to the desk and checked the drawers. In the bottom one, he found a whiskey bottle that still had about an inch of the amber liquid left in it. He grabbed a coffee cup from off a bookshelf and went back to Tom's cell.

Taking the bottle of laudanum the doctor had left behind, he measured out twenty drops into the cup and poured the whiskey in afterward. "Here, take this. It will help with the pain."

He held the cup up to Tom's mouth until he had drained the contents.

"I have some good news for you if you can believe it," Matt said.

"Did you figure out who it was that killed Curly?"

"No, but you're no longer a suspect."

"What do you mean?"

Matt showed Tom the paper that had been in his pocket. "I think the marshal cleared out. I found his badge on his desk, and when I got here with the doctor, your cell door was open, and he was gone. I found that paper in your shirt pocket. Looks like you're in the clear, but you should stay here for three or four days while you heal up and get some of your strength back. I'll bring you your meals and check in on you from time to time. The doc will be in to check on you also."

Tom smiled. His eyes were heavy. Matt could see that the laudanum was having its effect on him. "As long as that cell door stays open, I have no problem recuperating here. I'll keep this letter from the marshal handy in case someone gets the idea to drag me out of here and lynch me. Could you get word to Katie for me? We had a heartfelt talk yesterday morning, and she doesn't think me a murderer anymore, but she still doesn't see Amos clearly."

"Well, I can promise you that I'll make the effort, but your sister and I aren't on very good speaking terms right now."

"When we talked yesterday, she told me what happened, I mean about the school burning down and you getting fired. She also told me how you knocked Tolliver on his ass. I sure would have liked to see that." Tom laughed, and then winced. "Man, that hurts," he said, "but it's good to laugh for a change."

Tom closed his eyes and, in no time at all, began to snore. He had succumbed to the effects of the laudanum.

Matt wanted something to eat. Afterward, he would head back to his hotel to see if there had been answers to his telegrams.

Tom's situation was better than it was a

day ago. He would recuperate from his injuries, and, most important, he wasn't wanted for murder anymore. No one ever recuperated from a date with the gallows.

CHAPTER SIXTEEN

Matt washed and shaved, got dressed, and headed downstairs. There had been no telegrams for him last night, so he checked with the front desk to see if any had come in overnight. There was still no response waiting for him.

It was difficult to wait patiently for his telegrams to be answered. If he got the answers back that he expected, then things would get exciting in Mustang Flats. Matt wasn't sure that he would be able to handle it by himself. This was a family matter, and Matt wished his brothers were here with him, but he wasn't even sure where Luke was. David was in Cheyenne — at least he had been a few months ago.

Matt walked the two blocks to the livery to pick up his horse. He wanted to stop in and check on Tom. Then he would ride out to the McCutchen ranch to talk to Katie. He hoped that Tolliver wasn't hovering over her. It would be difficult enough to talk to her without having to go through Tolliver.

He got his horse from the livery, and then he stopped at one of the two restaurants in town and picked up some breakfast to take to the jail. He didn't know if Tom would feel much like eating today, but he might have an appetite if he wasn't still in too much pain.

Tom was awake when Matt got to the jail. "How are you feeling, Tom?"

Tom had propped some pillows behind his back and was sitting up in his bunk. "Better, thanks. That laudanum really knocked me out last night." He tried to sit up straighter but winced with the effort and gave up. "I managed to prop myself up a bit, but it still hurts to move around very much."

"Don't worry about that. Remember, the doctor said to stay put for a few days."

Matt handed him the plate of food he had brought. "I didn't know if you would have an appetite or not, but I brought you some food just in case." He pulled a pint of whiskey out of his pocket and handed it to Tom. "I brought you this too . . . to help with the laudanum."

The plate of food was wrapped in brown paper and secured with a string, which Tom removed. The restaurant had packed some leftover fried chicken and potatoes along with a handful of biscuits. "This smells good." He picked up a chicken leg and went to work on it.

"Did you have a chance to talk to Katie yet?" he asked between bites.

"Actually, I'm on my way out to the ranch as soon as I leave here."

"Well, good luck with that. I know what a handful she can be sometimes. When Katie gets her feathers ruffled, she is likely to let you have both barrels before you have a chance to explain yourself. But she generally calms down after a while, and then you can talk to her without taking your life in your hands."

Matt chuckled. "She sounds a lot like my mother. She's a redhead, too."

There was a deep sadness in Tom's eyes when he looked at Matt. "I know I've said this before, but I sure am sorry that you got dragged into all of this."

Matt took a seat and sat with his elbows on his knees. He asked, "Tom, Katie didn't really believe that you killed Curly, did she?"

"No, not really," Tom replied. "She even sent a wire to a lawyer we know over in Austin." He patted his shirt pocket, then reached in and pulled out the pardon that

Marshal Guthrie had left. "I guess I won't be needing a lawyer anymore."

He tossed a chicken bone onto the brown paper wrapping that he had set aside. "You have to understand about Katie; when our folks started this ranch, Texas had been a state for less than a year. I was five years old at the time, and Katie was only a little over a year old. It was no place for a young family, but my folks had come over from Scotland looking for land that they could call their own. They wanted a place where they could raise a few cattle and grow a few vegetables and make a life for themselves.

"My father wasn't afraid of hard work, and he wasn't going to let anyone take away from him what he had built and provided for his family. He fought Indians, and he fought the Mexicans to protect what he had.

"One day when I was about ten years old — Katie would have been five or six at the time — a group of half a dozen Mexicans rode up to the ranch. They rode fine mounts and were heavily armed. Mother was in the house, I was in the barn with my father, and Katie was playing on the porch.

"These men were up to no good. They were bandits, and my father knew it. They had already robbed and killed the Pattersons, our neighbors to the east. Dad never even gave them a chance.

"He had a pair of old Colt Dragoon revolvers. They were the heaviest guns I ever saw. Before the Mexicans could dismount, Dad came out of the barn with a Dragoon in each hand. He dropped three of them before they could get their guns out. Their horses reared up and pranced around the yard in fright, so their aim was off. Dad got down on one knee and took careful aim — bullets hitting the ground all around him. He knocked two more out of their saddles.

"The last bandit fell off of his horse when it reared up. He lay on his back with his arms up over his head saying, *'No dispares. No dispares,'* when my dad walked up to him and shot him."

Tom had managed to finish off another chicken leg, so he tossed the bone aside, next to the first one. "This was a violent land, Matt, and my dad was a violent man. That was difficult for a young girl to witness, but Katie saw it all. It took her a month before she could even look at our father after that, and another month before she would go near him.

"I think that every time she hears me talk about protecting the ranch from men like Tolliver, she hears my dad speaking, so it's easy for her to see me that way. I've never shot anyone in my life, and I hope I never have to.

"When you add to that what Tolliver and his men have been telling her and the rest of the town, it's no wonder that she had doubts."

"I should go," Matt said, rising. "I'm sure that this ordeal has torn her up inside, and that she'll be thrilled to hear that you have been set free and aren't a suspect anymore. The doc will be by later to check on you, and I'll stop in later tonight and let you know how it went with Katie."

The two men said their farewells, and Matt walked out of the jail. Once astride his horse, he guided her to the road heading north out of town and toward the Bar-M.

He hadn't ridden more than ten minutes before he spotted another rider approaching. It only took a few more seconds for him to recognize Katie McCutchen.

He stopped in the road and waited as she approached. She maneuvered her horse alongside his and pulled back on the reins. "Hello, Matt." Her eyes were soft, and her voice lacked the harshness of their last meeting. "I was on my way into town to visit Tom. I was hoping that I would see you."

Matt tipped his hat. "Good morning, Katie. Is there something wrong?"

Katie grimaced. "I am ashamed of how I acted the other day. You had been through a terrible ordeal, and I should have been more understanding. Can you forgive me?"

Matt looked at her high cheekbones and full, red lips. Her beautiful hazel eyes pulled him in like quicksand. Right then, she could have asked him for anything, and he would have made it his mission in life to give it to her.

He smiled. "There's no need for you to apologize. I'm sure that I provoked your reaction when I hit Amos. I overreacted, probably due to a lack of sleep. I believe that I should be the one to beg your pardon."

Katie smiled broadly. "Good, then all is forgiven. Let's put this awful incident behind us. I want you to know that the school committee — that I — want you to stay on in Mustang Flats. We'll rebuild the school, and we'll still need a teacher."

"I would like to stay."

"That's wonderful." Her eyes lit up as she smiled. "As long as I'm riding to town, would you like to accompany me?"

"Actually," said Matt, "I was riding out to see you because I have some news about Tom."

"Is everything all right? Has something happened to him?"

"Tom's all right; at least he's all right now."

His words didn't do much to allay her fears. "What do you mean? What happened?"

"First, let me tell you the good news. Tom has been set free for lack of evidence. He is no longer a suspect in Curly's murder."

Katie was stunned. She sat with her mouth open. Her eyes had a glazed look to them, and she stared straight ahead for several seconds. "You mean that he really was innocent?"

Her question was a rhetorical one, so Matt kept silent as Katie dealt with the revelation on her own.

Katie hung her head. "I can't believe that I actually thought that he could be guilty of murder. I'm so ashamed of myself." She produced a lace handkerchief from inside her sleeve and wiped away the tears that had pooled in her eyes.

Matt waited until she had finished, then he said, "I was just with him, Katie. He understands why you felt the way that you did."

Katie sniffed and dabbed at her eyes again. Turning toward town, she looked expectantly down the road and asked, "If he's free, where is he? Why hasn't he come back to the ranch?"

Matt explained about the beating and injuries that Tom had received. He left out the part of how Amos Tolliver had arranged it. Tom could share that with her if he was so inclined.

"I have to get to town to see him. Will you come with me?"

"Of course."

The two of them turned their mounts toward town and kicked them into a gallop.

Stopping in front of the jail, Matt and Katie both dismounted. Matt said, "I'll let you and Tom have a visit. I've got a few errands, then I'll meet you back here."

Katie took Matt's hand in hers. "Thank you so much for all that you have done for Tom and me. You have been a good friend, even though I have treated you badly." She reached up and kissed him on the cheek, and then she stepped up on the boardwalk and into the jail.

Matt got back in the saddle and turned his horse toward the hotel.

Across the street on the other side of the block, Amos Tolliver and Red were walking their horses up to the front of the bank when they noticed Katie and Matt in front of the jail. There was no way that they could hear what was said, but Tolliver saw Katie kiss Matt on the cheek and then go into the jail.

She hadn't said anything about visiting Tom. He thought he had been successful at keeping the two of them apart. Why was she here, and why so chummy, all of a sudden, with the school teacher? Two days ago she had fired him, and today she was kissing him right out on the street. "What the hell is that about?" he said.

Tolliver turned to Red. "Go on down to the jail. Find out what's happening. Don't let Katie see you; just tell Guthrie to get over here as soon as she leaves."

"All right, boss," Red replied. He started walking his horse toward the jail as Tolliver went inside the bank.

■ ■ ■ ■

PART TWO
THE GUNMAN

■ ■ ■ ■

"He should have told us his real name. If I'd known he was a Gaines, I would have handled him differently. I would have shot him from ambush. I would have shot him in the back. Who knows? Maybe I would have said, 'To hell with the whole mess' and just gotten on my horse and ridden as far as I could from Mustang Flats."

— Red Decker,
Foreman of the A-Bar-T ranch,
Mustang Flats, Texas

Chapter Seventeen

September 1873, Las Cruces, New Mexico Territory

Twenty-four-year-old Luke Gaines dismounted and tied his horse in front of the dry goods store. He paused for a moment as he looked at the lawyer's shingle hanging underneath the dry goods sign: HEINRICH TRABERT — ATTORNEY AT LAW. Luke had an immense dislike for lawyers, but the message had mentioned the possibility of a job, and he was running low on funds.

His boots sounded a cadence on the wooden boardwalk as he walked up to the front of the store and pushed open the door. The Mexican behind the counter looked up when the bell above the door signaled a new arrival.

"Trabert?"

The Mexican nodded toward the back of the store and went back to his newspaper.

Luke made his way past shelves of coffee,

canned peaches, and bolts of cloth to the office in the rear. The door was partly opened, so he pushed on it and let himself in.

Heinrich Trabert was a fat man. At close to three hundred pounds, he looked to be in his mid-fifties. His balding scalp glistened with sweat that beaded on his forehead and trickled down the sides of his face. He used a handkerchief to wipe away the perspiration as Luke walked in.

"Can I help you?"

"Are you Trabert?"

The lawyer hesitated a moment. "I am. What can I do for you?"

"I'm Luke Jensen." Luke used his mother's maiden name as an alias. It was easier than answering questions about his real last name. The name "Gaines" was too well known, and Luke preferred to keep a low profile. "They told me at the hotel that you wanted to see me . . . something about a job."

"Oh . . . Mr. Jensen." Trabert relaxed noticeably. He stepped out from behind the desk and extended one of his beefy hands. "It's a pleasure to meet you. Please, have a seat." He motioned to a chair in front of his desk. Trabert removed a stack of documents that were piled on the seat. He placed the heap of papers on his desk, creating even more clutter.

"Please excuse the mess, Mr. Jensen. I'm in the middle of some important litigation." Trabert walked around his desk and took his seat while Luke sat down in the chair offered him.

"What's this job you mentioned, Mr. Trabert?"

"Ah, right to the point. I like that. Let me tell you about it, and, if you agree with the particulars, there will be two hundred dollars in it for you — half now and half when you finish."

Luke crossed his legs, removed his Stetson, and balanced it on his knee. "I'm listening."

Trabert took a key from his vest pocket and slipped it into the lock in one of his desk drawers. Reaching in, he pulled out a small wooden box. "All that is required is to deliver this box to a man named Tolliver. He owns a large ranch near Mustang Flats in Texas, south of the Llano Estacado. Can you do that?"

Luke's eyes narrowed with skepticism as he considered the proposition. Two hundred dollars was a lot of money for delivering a package. When a deal sounded this good, it usually meant that there was more to it.

Luke nodded at the small wooden container that was about the size of a cigar box. "What's inside?"

Trabert shook his head. "I have no idea what the contents are. You must understand, Mr. Jensen, I'm only a middleman. It's a favor for a colleague of mine who is in the employ of this Mr. Tolliver. My friend asked me to obtain a suitable person to deliver this box to his employer. I asked around, and your name came up on more than one occasion. You have a reputation as someone who can get the job done."

Luke replaced his hat on his head and stood to his feet. Holding out his hand, he asked, "May I see it?"

The lawyer handed the wooden box to Luke. It was made out of cedar and weighed about three pounds. It had a clasp with a small padlock. There was writing on the top. Luke turned the box to read the words:

Amos Tolliver
Mustang Flats, Texas

Luke hefted the box a few times as though testing its weight while he weighed his options. He could use the money. It would take him almost two weeks to make the journey to Mustang Flats, and it could be a difficult trip across the desert. But he had undertaken difficult trips before.

"Two hundred dollars for delivering this box to Mustang Flats — that's it?"

Trabert's face lit up with a smile. "That's all there is to it, Mr. Jensen. The only stipulations are that you deliver it undamaged and unopened and that you have it there by the end of the month. Do we have a deal?"

Luke held out his hand. "You have a deal. I'll leave first thing in the morning."

"Excellent." Trabert beamed.

He dug around on his desk, pulled a sheet of paper from a pile, and handed it to Luke. "If you will sign this receipt that I turned the box over to you and that it was locked and intact . . ." Then he reached into another desk drawer and pulled out a cash box. He counted out one hundred dollars and handed it to Luke. "Good luck on your journey, Mr. Jensen."

Luke signed the receipt, then folded the money and pushed it into a shirt pocket. "Thank you, Mr. Trabert." Tucking the box under his arm, he turned to leave.

Trabert followed Luke into the store and watched him exit through the front door. When the bell above the doorway had stopped its ringing, he walked over to the counter where the Mexican clerk was still reading his paper. "Cesar, I want you to find Buchanan. He's most likely down at the cantina. Tell him to get back here right away. I have a job for him."

Cesar folded his newspaper and placed it on the countertop. *"Sí, Señor Trabert."*

As he made his way out the door, Trabert shouted after him, "Be quick about it!"

Trabert had no idea what was in the box, but he intended to find out. He reasoned that it must be valuable if someone was willing to pay so much to have it delivered. Now that he had turned it over to Jensen, he was no longer responsible for it. If Buchanan could get the box away from Jensen, then no one would be the wiser. A lot could happen to a man on a long, overland trip: Indians, bandits, bad weather, accidents. If the carrier never showed up at Mustang Flats, no one would suspect him. He had a signed receipt showing that he gave the box to Jensen. Buchanan had done similar jobs for him in the past, and Trabert had no doubts that he would be able to handle this job without any difficulty.

He walked behind the counter, reached down, and grabbed a handful of cigars. Striking a match on the rough countertop, he lit one of the cigars, took a long draw, and exhaled the smoke in a series of rings that floated upward, expanded, and dissipated in the sweltering desert heat.

Trabert walked back around the counter toward his office — a smile of satisfaction gracing his fat, sweaty face.

The morning sun was peeking through the window of his hotel room when Luke awoke. Swinging his legs over the side of his bed, he sat there a moment, rubbing the sleep from his eyes. Standing, he stretched the stiffness out of his six-foot-four-inch frame. His pants hung over the back of a chair next to the bed, so Luke stepped into them and buttoned them up.

After pulling on his boots, he crossed the room to the only window and drew the curtains back enough for a look at the street below. The sun had been up for about an hour, and there was plenty of activity on the streets of Las Cruces. He looked first up one side of the street, and then he turned his gaze in the opposite direction. There was nothing unusual or out of the ordinary . . . at least as far as he could see.

He walked over to the dresser and poured some water from a pitcher into a wash basin. He splashed some water on his face and dried off with the towel that was on the dresser. He pulled on a buckskin shirt inlaid with some Navajo beadwork, strapped on his gun belt, grabbed his hat and saddlebags, and was out the door.

Breakfast in the hotel dining room consisted of beef steak, fried potatoes, beans, and tortillas. He took his time and washed it all down with several cups of hot, black coffee. It could be a while before he got another decent meal, so he made the most of this one.

The room only had three other patrons at the time. A man and woman sat a few tables away from Luke. From what he overheard of their conversation, the couple was married and on their way to California to visit her sister.

The other customer sat across the room. He was a man in his thirties with long, stringy, blond hair that hung down to his shoulders. He had pale-blue eyes and a scar on his left cheek that began under his eye and disappeared under a scraggly beard. He was drinking coffee and looking at a newspaper, but the man hadn't turned a page since Luke had entered the dining room. He was either a very slow reader, or only pretending to read the paper. Luke peered at him over his last cup of coffee.

Luke finished his breakfast, slung his saddlebags over his shoulder, and walked across the dining room to stand next to the man's table. The man with the scar put the paper down and looked surprised to see Luke standing in front of him. "Is there something I can do for you?" he asked Luke.

There was a long pause before Luke answered. "If I catch you on my back trail, there's going to be hell to pay."

"I'm sure I don't know what you're . . ."

Luke bent down and placed both hands on the table in front of him, his face inches from the other man's. "I'm warning you, mister. I don't want to see you again."

Luke stood up and reached into his pocket, pulled out a silver dollar, and tossed it onto the table. "The coffee's on me." Turning, he walked out of the dining room without looking back.

Buchanan watched as Luke left the dining room, walked through the hotel lobby, and exited onto the street. He folded the newspaper and placed it on the table next to his empty coffee cup. The blank expression on his face became a scowl as he stood up and started to walk away.

After a few steps, Buchanan stopped. He turned around and walked back to his table

and picked up the silver dollar. He shoved
it into his pocket and continued on his way.

CHAPTER EIGHTEEN

Luke stopped by the mercantile and picked up the supplies that he had ordered the night before. His provisions included tins of Arbuckle's, some hardtack, jerky, flour, salted pork, and sugar. He decided to add canned peaches and tomatoes to his order. He would have to cross some parched country, and these water-rich foodstuffs might come in handy. He also picked up extra weapons: a new Winchester repeating rifle and a Colt Frontier model six-shooter. Both firearms used the same .44-caliber bullet, so he picked up three boxes of cartridges. As a last thought, he added a spare canteen to his purchases.

As he packed his gear into his saddlebags, he thought about the man with the scar in the restaurant. He knew that he was overly cautious, but he had found caution a necessity in his line of work. It had proved prudent more than once. Careless men seldom got a second chance. He would have to keep a watchful eye on his back trail.

What bothered him was if someone was watching him. What were they after? Did it relate to the job he was on? Was someone after the box? He had only accepted this job last night. How could anyone know about it, unless the lawyer, Trabert, had tipped someone off? There was something he didn't like about the man. Crooked lawyers and crooked lawmen — both left a bad taste in Luke's mouth.

His plan was to connect with the route that Captain Marcy laid out about twenty-five years earlier when he led gold seekers to California. It would take him about a day's ride to make the connection. Then he would follow that to the Pecos and then down into Texas. Once he reached Horsehead Crossing, he would head due north. The trip shouldn't take more than two weeks unless something went wrong, and there was plenty that could go wrong, especially if someone was after the box.

Luke had placed the box in the bottom of one of his saddlebags beneath the flour and the Arbuckle's. He pulled it out for another look at the enigmatic container. His examination didn't reveal anything more than he had already known about it. He held the box up to his ear and shook it but heard nothing. Then he remembered that one of the conditions was that he deliver the contents, whatever it is, in one piece. He frowned and replaced the box back in the saddlebag.

While he made a show out of tightening the girth on his saddle, he took a look around. Satisfied that he wasn't observed, he mounted up and turned his mustang north. He took a meandering route through town, first headed in one direction, then another. He would ride for two or three blocks, then turn around and go back in the direction that he had come. Twice he angled around the corner of a building and stopped, dismounted, and peered around the building. Fifteen minutes of this precaution satisfied him that no one was interested in him. With one last look behind him, he turned his horse east and steered him toward the edge of town.

The rest of the day was uneventful. It was warm, but not too hot, not like it was in July or August. Yet, after the sun set, it could be downright nippy.

He stopped every half hour or so to scan the trail behind him. Most of the way so far had been flat desert, with nothing to give him cause for concern.

As sunset approached, Luke led his horse down into a dry wash that cut across his path. He noticed that the sand was damp, and there were tufts of grass that his horse snatched at as he walked by.

Luke turned his blue roan mustang north up the arroyo toward a rocky outcropping that offered the possibility of some shelter for the night.

Riding a little further, he found a small spring of water that had formed a pool no more than three feet across and a foot deep. It wasn't much, but it was enough to slake his thirst and give his horse a drink. The water was cool and sweet. A watering hole in the desert at night was not a safe place to bed down. There could be wolves or mountain lions, or, worse yet, Indians that knew of the spring.

Mounted again, he followed the arroyo until he arrived at the rocky outcropping he had spotted earlier.

He found an overhanging ledge that offered natural shelter, so he picketed his horse, removed the saddle, and placed it under the overhang. Then he spread out his bedroll, took off his boots, and lay down, with his saddle for a pillow. He decided against a fire, so he dined on hardtack and jerky and washed it down with water from his canteen. Within the hour, Luke had fallen asleep.

He awoke sometime later when he heard the mustang snort. Luke sat up and, after giving his boots a shake, pulled them on. He sat there under the rocky ledge for several minutes, listening to the evening sounds of the desert. Luke had spent many nights under the desert stars, so he listened for anything that was out of place. Somewhere to the east, he could hear the yips and yaps of a coyote and the *kildee-kildee* of a killdeer as it swooped in and out of the night in search of insects. Everything sounded as it should.

Darkness had settled over the desert like a curtain drawn over a window. The crescent moon was waning. It cast a diffused silvery glow over the rocky terrain that extended for a hundred yards before it was absorbed by the distant shadows. Even with the luster of the moon, thousands of stars were visible, flickering and dancing in the heavens. They reminded Luke of thousands of campfires viewed from a mountaintop. He even imagined that he could smell the smoke rising from the flames.

The mustang snorted again, and Luke realized that the pungent aroma of smoke in his nostrils wasn't his imagination.

He got up, careful not to make a sound, and walked over to the mustang. He scratched the stallion's forehead, calming him. Someone, somewhere, had a campfire burning. Luke scanned the desert in all directions but couldn't detect the glow of a campfire. There was a slight breeze from the south. He needed to be higher to have a better look.

He turned to examine the rock that had been sheltering him as he slept. It was a small escarpment that jutted up about thirty feet above the desert floor. Composed of layered sandstone that provided natural steps to the top, it would be an easy matter for Luke to scale the rock and have a look around.

Grabbing his new Winchester, he made his way up the side of the rock until he reached the top. With his body low, he searched the horizon again. This time, with the higher vantage point, he could see the glow of a campfire to the south. It had to be almost a mile away, which would put it near the waterhole. Luke was unable to see anyone by the fire, so he couldn't be sure if they were Indians or white men, or even how many there were. He watched for a few more minutes and then made his way back down the rock to his horse.

Careful not to make any noise, Luke gathered up his bedroll, saddled his horse, and mounted up. The bottom of the wash was sand and gravel, and there would be some tracks left behind. Whoever had built the campfire must have gotten to the waterhole after dark and not seen his tracks. But as soon as the sun was up, whoever was back there would have no trouble tracking him. He wanted to put some distance between them.

He didn't believe it was Indians. The campfire looked too big. If that was the case, then he was more than likely being followed, and chances are it was the man with the scar.

Luke led his horse up the side of the wash and then pointed him in an easterly direction at a steady walk.

Anger rose up inside of him with each mile that his horse put between him and his pursuer. Who was the man with the scar? Was he working for Trabert, or was he on his own? What made some people think they could take whatever they wanted?

People who didn't know Luke Gaines tended to judge him by his appearance. With his weathered, rugged looks, he appeared older than he was, and days in the saddle often left him unshaven and dust covered. But what settled most in everyone's opinion was the Colt that hung low and ready on his hip. Luke was aware that he didn't always make the best impression on people, but his friends knew that when Luke used his gun, it was in self defense or in the defense of someone else.

Luke stopped his horse to listen. There were no sounds other than the occasional screech of an owl. The sun would rise soon, and it got quietest before sunrise.

Luke dismounted and walked in front of the mustang. He reached up and rubbed him on the nose. The stallion blew softly, nuzzling against Luke's shoulder.

"You know, Creed, if this guy thinks he's gonna take what isn't his then he's in for a painful lesson in manners. We've got a trick or two up our sleeve, don't we?"

The mustang nickered and nodded his head in response.

There was a hint of a pale-blue light in the east as Luke put his boot in the stirrup and threw his leg over the saddle. With a look behind him, he kicked his heels into the sides of the roan and set him to a trot.

CHAPTER NINETEEN

By the time the morning sun had started to pour over the peaks of the Sierra Guadalupe Mountains, Miles Buchanan had already packed up his bedroll and saddled his horse. He walked over to the fire, which by this time had reduced itself to a pile of ashes with a few embers. He kicked at the sleeping form still wrapped up in blankets beside the extinguished remains of the fire.

"Jake. Get up."

Jake moaned and rolled over on his back. After a few seconds, he sat up and rubbed the sleep from his eyes. "What time is it?"

"It's got to be close to six," Buchanan replied. "It will be light enough soon to pick up his tracks, so get a move on."

Jake crawled out of his blanket and pulled on his boots, first dumping them upside down to check for scorpions or other critters that might have taken refuge inside while he slept. Then he gathered up his belongings and saddled his horse.

Buchanan had known Jake for about five years. They had ridden together on several occasions. They weren't exactly what you would call "friends," but they were occasional partners, and they worked well together. When Buchanan asked him to ride along on this job, Jake had nothing else to do so he agreed.

The sun had risen enough by this time that the ground was visible. While Jake finished cinching up his saddle, Buchanan walked about ten or fifteen yards further up the wash looking for tracks. They had seen where Luke had ridden down into the wash, so they had followed his tracks north. By the time that they had reached the waterhole, it was too dark to see anything else. They made camp for the night, expecting to pick up the trail again in the morning.

Buchanan kneeled down several times to look at the ground, then he walked back to the horses.

"It looks like he continued up the wash. With any luck, he made camp, and we'll be able to catch him sleeping." Buchanan sounded more optimistic than he actually was. He would like to finish this job without having to travel much further than a day or two from town, but he suspected that it might not be that easy. That's why he had asked Jake to ride along with him. He was confident in his own abilities, but, if shooting started, it was better to have someone else along who could take that first bullet.

Both men stood holding their horses' reins and looking up the arroyo. Neither man knew for certain where their prey was, only that he had gone that way the night before. Did Luke Jensen know he was being followed? Buchanan had given him plenty of lead time to throw him off guard. He didn't seem to be particularly careful about his trail. Chances are he had no idea anyone was on his trail.

"How do you want to handle this?" asked Jake.

"Well," said Buchanan, "we're not going to ride right down the middle of this arroyo not knowing where he is. It could be a trap." He took the mesquite thorn he had been using to pick his teeth and tossed it to the ground. "I'll tell you what we're gonna do. Let's get out of this wash. I'll ride up the east side, and you can ride up the west side. Keep quiet and keep your eyes open. Maybe we can trap him instead."

The two men mounted up and rode their horses out of the arroyo up onto the floor of the desert. They rode north, their eyes on the inside of the gulch and out across the sand and rocks that lay before them.

After about a mile, they came to the place where Luke had spent the night. "Over here!" yelled Buchanan to Jake.

Jake walked his horse down into the wash and up the opposite side, where Buchanan had dismounted and was looking at the ground. Buchanan was a far better tracker than Jake, but even he could see the tracks visible in the sand heading east.

"Looks like your boy is an even earlier riser than you are," said Jake.

Buchanan frowned and got back on his horse. "Let's go," was all he said as the two men continued on the trail of Luke Jensen.

CHAPTER TWENTY

On the third day out of Las Cruces, Buchanan grew more uneasy and more irritated. He had expected to be done with this job by now, but here they were, still trying to catch up to Jensen.

He had dismounted and squatted down to examine some tracks in the sand. He stared off in the direction the tracks seemed to be pointing. "That guy must have a hell of a horse," he said out loud to no one in particular.

He had lost the trail several times already and had almost decided to give up the chase. After all, he knew that Jensen was on the way to Mustang Flats. He and Jake could jump ahead and wait for him somewhere on the trail. But that would add weeks to this job. That was time he didn't want to waste. Trabert had offered him half of whatever was in the box. Not knowing what that was, Buchanan wanted to invest as little time in the effort as he could in case the payday wasn't worth it. But every time he felt like that's what he should do, he would pick up the trail again. It was almost like Jensen was taunting him, and that added to his irritation.

Buchanan knew his partner was as frustrated with the chase as he was. Jake was nursing a nasty puncture wound in his thumb from a mesquite thorn that had pierced it the day before. He had managed to dig it out, but his thumb throbbed with pain and had swollen to twice its size.

"I don't understand this guy, Miles. What's he up to? First, he takes us in one direction, then he turns around and goes the opposite way. He's even had us going in circles."

Jake removed the bandana he was using as a bandage on his thumb to examine the wound. "Leading us down into that mesquite thicket yesterday was pure meanness if you ask me."

He rewrapped his thumb and then removed the cork from his canteen. "I hope my thumb doesn't become infected." He tilted his head back and took a long drink.

Buchanan stood to his feet and removed his hat to run his fingers up his forehead and through his hair. He replaced his hat and scanned the country ahead of him as far as he could see. They would be in the Guadalupe Mountains by nightfall.

Gathering up the reins, he saddled up again. "I think it's safe to assume that he knows that he's being followed," he said. "But I don't get him either. If someone was following me, I'd want to put as many miles between us as possible. That wouldn't be much of a problem with that horse of his."

"Well," said Jake, "for a guy who knows he's being followed, he doesn't seem to be making much of an effort to hide his trail."

"No, he's not."

"Why do you think that is?"

Buchanan's eyes narrowed, and Jake could see the muscles in his jaws working as he ground his teeth together. "Because he's playing with us," remarked Buchanan, "and when I do catch up with that son of a bitch, I'm going to take my time killing him."

The two men turned their horses in the direction of Guadalupe Pass, hoping to make camp before it got too dark to see. The tracks that Jensen left were still visible in the remaining light and headed straight for the pass, so Buchanan and Jake set their horses to a steady trot.

As dusk approached, the country began to break up into arroyos and canyons — some with walls stretching upwards a hundred feet. Shadows already darkened the canyons, where the air was discernibly cooler.

They had been climbing steadily for the last few miles. Desert willow grew more numerous, as well as a variety of sunflowers, daisies, silky lupine, and Apache plume. Piñon pines clung to the sides of the canyon's walls.

They followed the tracks to the mouth of a canyon with walls almost one hundred feet high. Buchanan got off of his horse to examine the ground around the entrance to the canyon. Tracks clearly went in, but there were no tracks coming out. The vast majority of these canyons were dead ends; "box" canyons they were called. If that was the case with this one, thought Buchanan, then they had Jensen trapped. But there was no way of knowing without going in.

Buchanan and Jake looked at each other uneasily. The light inside the canyon was dim and growing darker with each step that their horses made. It was only about sixty feet wide at the entrance but narrowed to about forty feet once inside. Thirty yards in, the walls of the canyon curved to the right, so Buchanan couldn't see how far back it went.

Neither man said anything as Buchanan

took the lead walking his horse into the mouth of the canyon. The temperature dropped at least fifteen degrees as they entered the shadows created by the towering limestone walls.

As they approached the curve in the wall, they moved more cautiously. Both men expected at any moment that rifle fire would rain down on them from the ledge above.

After navigating the curve in the canyon, they discovered there were actually a series of curves. First, the trail wound to the right, then to the left, in a snake-like pattern. The width of the canyon had narrowed to about twenty feet. They picked their way around some large boulders. Although they couldn't make it out in the dim light, they seemed to be following some type of defined trail.

They followed the canyon's winding course back about a thousand yards. Buchanan stopped. He saw flickering light against the canyon wall ahead of him.

"Looks like a campfire," he whispered to Jake.

Smiling in triumph, he motioned for Jake to dismount. They pulled their rifles from their saddle boots and proceeded warily on foot, leaving their horses behind.

After several minutes, they reached a huge boulder that seemed at first to block any further progress up the canyon. Darkness had descended, and the flickering light was still visible against the far wall of the canyon to their left on the other side of the boulder.

They made their way along the left side of the massive rock and discovered an opening large enough for a man leading his horse to squeeze through.

As they made their way through the opening past the boulder, they found themselves in an open area inside the canyon about two or three acres in size. The walls of the canyon rose up around on all sides, and stars could be seen in the night sky above. There was a small waterfall where water streamed out of a crack fifty feet up in the canyon wall. The water formed a small pool that watered the grass that grew throughout the oasis.

There was a campfire burning to their right, close to the wall of the canyon, but there was no one in sight. Buchanan and Jake looked around for signs of Jensen, or anyone else, but they appeared to be alone in the canyon.

The two men approached the campfire, dumbfounded as to where Jensen could have gone.

"I'll be damned," exclaimed Jake, staring at the fire. Roasting over the flames were two quail on a spit. The flames danced on the canyon wall behind the fire, revealing scratches in the limestone. Buchanan stepped forward for a better look but couldn't make it out. Pulling a burning stick from the fire, he held it up and read, "Enjoy your meal. — L.J."

CHAPTER TWENTY-ONE

The next morning, Luke lay on the rocks at the top of the canyon's north wall and watched the two men below. He had scouted out the canyon yesterday while it was still light and had found the cleft in the wall that led to a trail up the side of the canyon. The trail was used by deer and other animals to gain access to the water below without having to go the long way around through the canyon's mouth.

The opening in the wall of the canyon that led to the trail was partly obscured by pine trees, and Luke doubted if the two men would find it. He had covered his tracks, so there was no trail that would give him away. His stallion was a desert bred mustang and could navigate these canyons better than any horse he knew. Luke doubted the inferior mounts of the two men would be able to traverse the path without great difficulty, even if they did find the way up. That meant they would have to go back out the way they had come in, and that's what Luke wanted.

As he lay prostrate on the rim of the canyon watching the two men below, he thought about his brothers, David and Matt. The three of them had grown up together in the backwoods of Tennessee. It had been almost three years since he had seen either of them.

His oldest brother, Matt, had been the quiet thinker of the three boys. He was more comfortable with a book in his hands than he was with a hunting rifle or a hoe. Matt was the most responsible of the three and always thought of the consequences. As a result, he was not much fun — at least to Luke as a young boy growing up.

Fun was David's department. David was the middle son, and there were never two boys more different than Matt and David Gaines. David rarely thought about the consequences of his actions. "Tomorrow might as well be a million miles away," he often said. "It may never get here, so why should I worry about it?" This devil-may-care attitude of David's had the sheriff of Monroe County rethinking his reelection plans more than once.

Luke didn't have a problem with responsibility, and he didn't mind having his fair share of fun. He just didn't want anyone telling him that he had to do one or he ought to do the other. In fact, he didn't much care for anyone imposing their beliefs or their authority on him — bosses, lawmen, judges, even the women he had known. Luke wasn't ready for that kind of life. He liked his vagabond lifestyle. He liked the freedom of accepting the jobs that appealed to him and refusing those that didn't.

That sometimes put him on the wrong side of what was popular or even technically legal. But popular usually meant powerful and wealthy, and it was the powerful and wealthy who decided what was legal.

As he watched, one of the men began to prepare breakfast, putting a coffee pot on to boil. Luke knew he ought to ride away. He could easily lose these two, whoever they were. Creed had been riding circles around them for the last three days. But his insides wouldn't let him ride away.

These men were intent on harm. Somehow, they had developed a twisted way of thinking that led them to believe they had a right to do or take whatever they wanted as long as they were strong enough or numerous enough to impose their will.

Luke wasn't motivated by whiskey and

cards like his brother David. He wasn't motivated by academics and a sense of obligation like Matt. But his dander did rise when he saw people try to abuse and take advantage of others. Luke had a strong sense of justice, and he blamed his mother and father for that. These two guys had chosen their path, and, if they chose to continue on it, they would have no one to blame but themselves for the consequences.

Standing from the edge of the canyon, Luke brought his Winchester to his shoulder and levered a round into the chamber. Taking aim at the campfire, he squeezed the trigger and sent fire and embers flying into the air. Jerking the lever, he put four more bullets into the fire.

Buchanan and Jake dove for whatever cover they could find as soon as the first shot knocked their coffee pot off a rock and into the fire.

Luke stepped back from the edge of the canyon to where Creed was waiting. He slid the Winchester into the rifle boot and mounted up. It would be some time before those two worked up the nerve to make their way back out of the canyon. They will be expecting an ambush at every turn. Good, thought Luke. Let them sweat it out.

CHAPTER TWENTY-TWO

Buchanan and Jake lay still for several minutes after the shooting had stopped. Neither man wanted to be the first one to move and draw fire from the rim of the canyon.

"Are you all right?" Buchanan called to Jake, who was hugging the ground behind a clump of prickly pear. Jake was only about ten yards away from where Buchanan had found shelter behind a small pile of rocks that was barely large enough to conceal him.

"Yeah, I'm okay."

Buchanan could hear the frustration in Jake's voice, and it was no wonder. When Jake took cover behind the prickly pear, he plunged in headfirst and wound up with a cactus thorn in the side of his face below his right eye. Blood trickled down his cheek and caked in his beard. "When we catch up with that guy, I'm gonna enjoy gutting him like a fish."

The two men slowly crawled out from behind their meager cover and stood to their feet. Buchanan put his hands on his hips and gazed along the canyon's north rim, where he figured the shots had come from. Taking a step over to the campfire, he kicked the coffee pot out of the coals and sent it flying several feet. "I'm getting damned tired of this myself."

"What do you want to do now?" Jake removed the bandana from around his neck and wiped at the blood on his face.

"Well, we need to get out of this canyon without getting shot. That's the first thing. Let's pack up and get out of here."

The two men gathered up their few belongings and saddled their horses. After they had mounted up, Buchanan said, "I'll take the lead. You hang back about fifty feet. Keep your rifle ready and a sharp lookout on the rim of the canyon walls. If you see anything, shoot. I don't think he wants to kill us, at least not yet. He could have done that already if he wanted to, but he seems to enjoy this game of cat and mouse."

Jake removed his rifle from its scabbard, careful not to bump his sore thumb. "I'd enjoy it to, if I was the cat."

Buchanan took the lead, and Jake followed at a distance as they entered the narrow breach in the wall that would lead them back to the mouth of the canyon. It was slow going. Both of the men were jumpy, expecting an ambush at any moment. Several times, a bird took off from a nest in the limestone wall, and the men would bring their rifles to bear, prepared to fire.

The distance to the mouth was less than a mile from where they had spent the night. Even so, it took half an hour to reach the opening, and that was after running their horses for the last third of the way after the canyon walls widened enough to allow them to put their horses to the gallop.

Buchanan brought their horses out of the canyon at a run, aiming for a small cluster of seven-foot-high cholla. The cactus would offer some degree of concealment while they regrouped and considered their next move.

Safely hidden inside the maze of cactus plants, the two men dismounted. Buchanan looked east towards Guadalupe Pass, squinting and shading his eyes against the glare of the sun. He turned to look at Jake, who had dried blood on the side of his face.

"We've got to change our tactics."

"What do you mean?"

"He's headed for Guadalupe Pass, which means he'll most likely follow Delaware

Creek east until he hits the Pecos. We're not getting anywhere chasing after him, so maybe we can get in front of him."

"How we gonna do that?"

Buchanan knelt down and traced out his plans in the sand.

"If we head south towards the Salt Lakes, I know of an old Indian trail that will take us to the Presidio Mountains." He drew a line in the sand toward the south and then turned it east. He represented the Presidio Mountains on his map with a few pebbles at the proper place.

"On the north side of the mountains is the Saline Creek," he continued. "It runs into the Pecos about a half a day's ride south of the Delaware."

Buchanan stood up and brushed the sand from his knees. "It will take some hard riding, but we should be able to have a nice surprise waiting for him when he gets there."

Jake turned and put his foot in the stirrup, grabbed the saddle horn, and boosted himself up, throwing his other leg over the saddle. "Lead the way," was all he said.

CHAPTER TWENTY-THREE

Luke let Creed pick his way along the trail that led up and over Guadalupe Pass. At about eight thousand feet in elevation, the Guadalupe Mountains offered a good vantage point of the surrounding desert. A few of the peaks lay to the south and crossed the border into Texas. To the north, the mountain range curved off to the northeast and disappeared into the horizon. To the east, about a day's ride, was the Pecos, and across the river was the Llano Estacado — the Staked Plains.

The Llano was a vast mesa of desert prairie that stretched one hundred and fifty miles east from the Pecos, and about two hundred and fifty miles north to south. Mustang Flats lay south of the Llano, and the Canadian River was its northern border. It was about as barren a place as God ever created, without a tree or bush to break the monotony. What's more, water on the Llano was almost nonexistent. Only the Apaches and the Comanches dared to venture out onto it, and then only at certain locations.

Luke had no intention of going into the Llano. His plan was to follow the Pecos south. After about a week's worth of riding, he should make it to Horsehead Crossing. There he would cross the river and make his way northeast to Wild China Ponds. Mustang Flats was three days due north from there. That should put him at his destination in about ten to twelve days.

Luke dismounted and took a swallow from his canteen. Then he poured some water into his hat and held it in front of Creed. The stallion stuck his nose into the Stetson and sucked up the liquid. When he had finished, Creed nuzzled against Luke's shoulder. Luke reached up and scratched the horse between the eyes.

"We're making good time, Creed. We're gonna have to stop fooling around with those two men who are following us, though."

Luke thought about his two pursuers. He hadn't seen any sign of them since he had fired down into their camp in the canyon earlier that morning. For all he knew, they were still there, afraid to venture out where they might be easily picked off by rifle fire.

It didn't matter to him. Creed could outpace them without any difficulty, and Luke didn't intend to waste any more time with them.

Luke made camp that evening on the eastern slope of the Guadalupe Mountains, about a half day's ride from Delaware Creek. He hobbled Creed, then made a small fire and soon had the water boiling for coffee. Then he fried up bacon and mixed together some flour, salt, and baking powder, with water, and made biscuits. He used the biscuits to sop up the bacon grease. For dessert, he cut open a can of peaches.

After dinner, Luke stretched out on his blanket and propped his head on his saddle. He reached into his shirt pocket and drew out the fixings for a cigarette. The sun was already behind the mountains, and the darkness that had settled on the eastern horizon was chasing the daylight from the desert sky. Stars were popping out quicker than Luke could count them, and the nocturnal residents of the desert would soon be about their business.

Luke lay on his bedroll smoking his cigarette and watching Creed munch on some curly mesquite. The stallion was about ten years old, and Luke had owned him for half of that time. He wasn't the fastest horse Luke had ever seen, but he had more staying power than any of them. He could last long past the point other horses gave out and made it look easy.

Lying under the stars Luke often became introspective. A man alone in the desert had a lot of time to think, and it wasn't long before his thoughts turned to home.

Growing up the youngest of four had its challenges, but they were nothing compared to growing up the son of Philo Gaines. People had a certain expectation of Luke and his brothers. When strangers discovered he was the son of Philo Gaines, they mistakenly assumed they knew who Luke was as well, and what he would do and say in any particular situation. It was Luke, more so than his two brothers or his sister, who hated being put in that box. As odd as it might seem, Luke didn't know his father any better than anyone else who could read a newspaper.

Before Luke's birth, his father had already made a name for himself as a fur trapper and mountain man. He had lived with and fought with the Indians and in 1846 had served as a scout under General Zachary Taylor in the war with Mexico. Philo returned home to Tennessee after the war, and

Luke was born the following year.

The next few years, Luke and his siblings only saw their father on occasion. The discovery of gold in California kept Philo occupied with more scouting for the army, and leading several groups of prospectors out to the gold fields.

When Luke was eleven years old, another war beckoned to Philo's sense of duty. He served as a colonel in a division of Confederate cavalry from Tennessee. Philo served throughout the war and was wounded twice.

After the war, Philo became involved in the politics of reconstruction and was appointed to the U.S. Senate in 1868. Luke hadn't seen his father in almost five years.

It was Luke's mother, Marie, who held the family together. It was she who raised the children and schooled them. She nursed them back to health when they were sick. She fed them and clothed them and took them to town every Sunday to hear the preacher. She managed the family's horse ranch, growing it into the largest in Monroe County.

It wasn't as if Philo were completely absent. The times he did spend at home were happy ones for the family. Philo took a deep interest in his sons, teaching them to ride and to hunt. He taught them to have honor and pride, and the joy of making something with their own hands and being productive. It was his belief that they were fashioned in the image of a creator God, so it was part of every man to want to create and build, to conquer and subdue, to make his life count for something.

At some point in the middle of his thoughts, Luke fell asleep and dreamt he was four years old and crying in his mother's arms, pointing down the dirt road in front of their home as his father rode away.

CHAPTER TWENTY-FOUR

Luke arose as the first rays of the sun shot out of the east like giant fingers clawing at the dome of the morning sky. He relit the fire and reheated the leftover coffee.

He looked east toward the sun and the country that lay before him. The desert was beautiful, bathed in the first light of a new day. Many people didn't like the desert because it was harsh and unforgiving. That's what Luke liked about it. The desert tested a man. It challenged him. It showed him what he was made of. The secret, Luke had discovered, was not to resist the desert but to embrace it and learn from it.

He turned to gather up his bedroll and saddle. He hoped to make it to the Pecos by the end of the day.

He reached down to pick up his blanket and felt a sharp sting on the back of his right hand. He jerked his hand back and shook it in an effort to relieve the sudden pain. Examining his hand, he saw a welt forming about an inch in diameter. It was red and swollen, and his fingers were beginning to tingle.

He used the toe of his boot to push his blanket aside and saw a scorpion crawl into a hole under where he had been sleeping.

Scorpion stings could be dangerous. They weren't usually fatal, but they could be painful and could cause other symptoms as well. From what Luke had seen before the scorpion had disappeared down its hole, this was a good sized one. Most of the ones Luke had seen were less than three inches in length, but this one had been close to five inches.

Luke undid the buttons on the front of his Levi's and relieved himself into the dirt and sand. Then he scooped up a handful of the mud and plastered it on the back of his hand. He had never been stung by a scorpion before, but he knew people who had been and had said that something in urine helped to ease the pain. Removing his bandana, he wrapped it around his hand to hold the poultice in place.

Luke took extra time packing up his camp and saddling Creed. The pain and tingling sensation had intensified to the point where his hand was no longer useful. He pulled himself into the saddle and pointed Creed in a direction that would intersect Delaware Creek.

After the first hour on the trail, the tingling had stopped, but his hand had gone numb. This was cause for concern for Luke because he was right-handed. If he needed to draw his gun, he wouldn't be able to. He could shoot well enough with his left hand, but trying to draw his Colt in a hurry would be awkward.

He brought Creed to a halt. Reaching around with his left hand, he managed to work his revolver out of the holster. He tucked it into his waistband behind his back where he could reach it without much difficulty.

The sun was past its zenith by the time Luke reached Delaware Creek. It had been a slow process. Before long, beads of perspiration had broken out on his forehead, even though the morning air was still cool. He had stopped twice to vomit and was feeling dizzy and light-headed in the saddle.

The Delaware wasn't very wide, and Creed jumped across it without getting his feet wet. Luke found a shady spot in a small grove of cottonwoods where he could picket Creed by some grass. He half fell off of his horse and somehow managed to remove the saddle and blanket.

Tossing the saddle on the ground against the trunk of one of the cottonwoods, Luke sunk down to his knees and rolled onto the grass. He felt nauseous again although he hadn't eaten any food all day. The numbness had lessened, only to be replaced by an uncontrollable twitching in the muscles of his hand and arm.

He lay there under the cottonwood for over an hour, waiting for the queasiness to pass. When he was able to sit up, he still felt too dizzy to try to stand to his feet. He managed to remove the canteen off of his saddle, and he found some jerky in his saddlebags. He was able to take a few bites and a few swallows of water.

The sun was past its zenith, but it was still early afternoon. His shirt was drenched in sweat, but Luke was shivering and knew that he had a fever. Crawling on his hands and knees, he managed to find enough dead branches on the ground under the trees to break up for firewood and soon had a fire. He wrapped himself in his blanket and rested with his back against his saddle.

He tried to consciously will his muscles to stop twitching, but it was no use. It was almost as if some other entity had taken over his body, and he could only watch. He hoped that it wouldn't last much longer.

He worried about how much time he would lose while laid up. But what concerned him more was his inability to defend himself in his present condition. So far, the muscle spasms were confined to his right hand and arm, but his fever was also causing periods of intense shaking that would consume his entire body. With the ever-present threat of Indians, wolves, mountain lions, and rattlesnakes, Luke might have to use his gun at any time, and he knew he was in no shape to fire a gun with any accuracy.

Then another thought occurred to him. What if the two men who had been following him were still on his trail? They could catch up with him and overpower him or even kill him in his present condition. He was in a comfortable camp, but it was too exposed. He would have to find a different place to spend the night.

Using the tree trunk, he succeeded in rising to his feet. However, when he bent down to pick up his saddle, he felt a warmth flood over him with a wave of dizziness that caused his vision to black out as if he had closed his lids, but his eyes were still open.

He fell back down on his hands and knees, shaking his head as if he could shake the blinders off of his eyes. It took a moment for his sight to return. Luke remained motionless for several more minutes until he felt steady enough to try again.

This time, Luke took it easy. He threw the saddle blanket over his shoulder, took a firm grip on the saddle, and managed to climb to his feet. He took a few tentative steps. He was still shaking from his fever and felt weak but with slow, deliberate steps was able to reach Creed. It took Luke considerable time to saddle Creed and tie down the rest of his gear.

After that effort, Luke made several attempts to pull himself onto the horse's back, but with no success. Luke made two quick clicking sounds with his tongue, and the stallion lay down on the ground. Luke slumped into the saddle, and Creed got to his feet, first with his front legs, then with his hind legs. Clicking his tongue, Luke gave the reins a shake, and Creed was on his way downstream, walking down the middle of Delaware Creek.

They continued downstream for over an hour before Luke saw a rocky slide he could use to exit the creek bed. He turned Creed north. There was a small hill about a mile away with a growth of pines on the east side that would offer a measure of concealment, and the higher ground was more defensible if the need arose.

By the time he had found a spot inside the trees to make camp, Luke was exhausted. He tied Creed to a piñon pine and removed the saddle. The twitch in his hand and arm had stopped, but he still had the chills associated with a fever.

He dug a small pit behind some fallen logs for a campfire. He struggled with his knife to open a can of tomatoes and, after eating a bit, fell asleep.

When he awoke sometime during the night, the sky was bright with stars. His fever had broken, and Luke felt much better. He guessed that it was after midnight, and that he had been asleep for about six hours.

He added more wood to his fire and soon had a few flames licking at the twigs he had thrown in. The crackle and pop of the flames were like music to Luke who figured that, since he had left home when he was seventeen, he had spent at least five nights out under the stars for every night he had spent inside.

He got to his feet to test his legs and found out that, although stiff and still weak, they were otherwise usable. Luke grabbed his rifle and walked off about twenty yards from his campfire — first in one direction, and then in another — until he had satisfied himself that he was alone on the hill.

Back in camp, he pulled his blanket around his shoulders and fell asleep with his legs crossed and his back against a pine log. The crackling of the fire, the barking of a coyote, and the hoot of an owl in one of the branches above him were the desert symphony that lulled him to sleep.

CHAPTER TWENTY-FIVE

Buchanan and Jake had ridden hard, and, on the second day after leaving the box canyon, they reached the Presidio Mountains and made their evening camp along the banks of Saline Creek.

It had been a gamble taking the long way around to the south in an attempt to get in front of Jensen, but they were confident that they had made it to the Pecos in time to intercept him.

Buchanan had confessed to Jake that this trip had not gone at all the way that he thought it would. It shouldn't have taken them more than two or three days to finish the job. Instead, it had been a week since they had left Las Cruces, and they weren't any closer to catching up to Jensen. Jake wondered if the box was worth all the trouble that they had been through.

Picking up the last sticks of firewood, Buchanan tossed them into the coals. Turning toward Jake he said, "Go gather some more wood. It's going to get cold out tonight."

Jake had already spread out his bedroll and had removed his gun belt and hat. He was tired from the hard ride. He looked at Buchanan with contempt that was barely hidden in the dim glow of the campfire. "I gathered that bunch. It's your turn to get the firewood. I'm tired. I'm going to bed."

Jake kicked off his boots and stretched out on the ground, pulling the edge of his blanket up over his shoulders.

Buchanan reached down and grabbed one of the burning sticks out of the fire and tossed it onto Jake's blanket. It bounced off of Jakes's hip, sending a shower of sparks across his bed.

"What the . . ." Jake yelled as he sprang to his feet. He grabbed his blanket, which had caught fire, swung it through the air, and beat it against the ground. He stood in his stocking feet and stared at Buchanan in disbelief.

"Now that you're up, get some more firewood," Buchanan said indifferently.

Jake wadded up his blanket and threw it to the ground. He kicked it, sending it flying through the air several feet, where it landed in a clump of prickly pear. "One of these days, Miles, you're going to push me too far."

Buchanan faced Jake. Jake could see that Buchanan's hand, backlit by the campfire, was hovering close to his gun. Although he couldn't see his face clearly, he could sense Buchanan sneering at him.

"Any time you think you're up to it . . ." Buchanan replied.

Both men faced each other for a long moment. Jake considered Buchanan's offer until he remembered that he had taken his gun off before lying down.

"There's no need to get excited, Miles. I just wish you'd stop being such a hard case. This hasn't been a whole lot of fun for me either."

Jake sat down on the ground and pulled on his boots. Then he stood up and looked around for more firewood. After gathering several arm loads and stacking them next to the fire, he retrieved his blanket, wrapped it around himself, and lay down next to his saddle and gun belt. This time he left his boots on.

As tired as he was, Jake didn't fall asleep right away. His mind raced over the events of the past week. If he had known what he was getting into, he wouldn't have agreed to partner with Buchanan on this job. Buchanan had said that it would only take a few days, and it would be easy money. This Jensen fellow was supposed to have a hundred dollars on him, and Buchanan had promised him half of it. Jake had figured that there was some other reason Buchanan was after Jensen, but he hadn't bothered to share that information, and Jake hadn't asked. Besides, a hundred dollars was reason enough for him. Buchanan had killed men for less.

Lying in his bed, just outside the ring of light from the campfire, he was close enough to feel the heat, but far enough away to be partially obscured by the shadows. He lay there and watched Buchanan, who still hadn't spread out his own bedroll. Jake could sense Buchanan's frustration, and that made Buchanan meaner than usual. Buchanan was even more dangerous to be around when things weren't going his way. He would have to be careful not to trigger his wrath.

That was the difference between him and Buchanan. Sure, he had been in his share of scrapes. He preferred stealing over working. He liked to brag that when he was a boy, he had stabbed and killed a Mexican in Laredo. What he didn't tell folks was that the Mexican was an old man, a farmer who caught him trying to steal a chicken and came at him with a pitchfork. Jake shoved his knife under the old man's ribs. Afterward, he had gotten sick.

But Buchanan was different. He was the real deal. He had never shed a tear over the people he had killed, and it was rumored that he had killed plenty. He was fast with a gun, but he didn't restrict himself to any particular method. He was equally adept with a blade. It was reported that he had doused one guy with coal oil and set him on fire, for the simple reason that he wanted the man's horse.

After half an hour, Buchanan unrolled his blanket and stretched out on the ground. Jake listened to the sound of Buchanan's breathing until the man had fallen asleep. Then he relaxed some and closed his eyes. Within minutes, he, too, was asleep.

When he awoke early the next morning, it was with a sharp pain in his ribs from someone's foot. He rolled over, expecting to find Buchanan standing over him. What he saw instead was the barrel end of a rifle pointed in his direction with a Comanche brave on the other end.

Jake looked toward Buchanan. There was another Comanche brave holding a gun on him as well. The Indians forced the two men to their feet and bound their hands together in front of them.

He counted three braves: the two that had tied them up and one other who remained on his horse. He seemed to be the one in charge. He appeared to be about thirty years old, older than the others. He had long, raven hair that hung in two braids almost to his waist. He wore a fur cap with a row of eagle feathers sticking straight up down the middle. His chest was bare and showed several tribal tattoos. He sat on a magnificent appaloosa that had feathers and beads braided into its mane.

The one on the horse said something to the other two. One of the braves kept his rifle pointed at them and forced them to sit on the ground together. The other brave ransacked their saddlebags and other belongings.

Jake looked around when he heard the sound of horses galloping. The air was soon filled with a cloud of dust that threatened to choke them as a herd of about two dozen horses came around a bend in the trail pushed by two more braves, who brought their horses to a halt when they saw that the rest of their party had stopped as well.

The leader turned to look at the two new arrivals. He said something unintelligible, then raised his rifle into the air and let out a yell that made the hair on the back of Jake's neck stand up. The other braves lifted their rifles into the air and joined in the celebration.

The leader spoke again, and Jake was forced to his feet. One of the Indians pushed him over to his horse, then grabbed hold of him and hoisted him up onto its back. Jake tried to say something about the saddle, but the Indian either didn't understand him or he ignored him.

As one of the Comanche braves prodded Buchanan over to his horse, Buchanan spat in his face. This earned him the butt end of the Indian's rifle on the side of his head. Buchanan sank to his knees and fell over backward. He had a nasty gash, and blood already flowed.

Two of the Indians picked him up and put him on his horse. He looked limp but managed to grab a handful of the horse's mane and keep his seat as the Indians mounted up and started out at a steady trot in the direction of the Pecos.

The Indian in charge took the lead, followed by the two braves who were leading Buchanan and Jake on their horses. The other two braves moved the herd of horses behind them.

Jake kept his eye on Buchanan, who was

ahead of him. It was hard to tell what kind of condition he was in. He had taken a mighty blow to the head. After about an hour on the trail, it seemed as though Buchanan was sitting straighter on his horse and wasn't being jostled around as much as when they started out.

Jake wished he could talk to Buchanan. Hearing the other man's voice right now would be a comfort to him. He hoped Buchanan was smart enough not to resist. Obeying their captors would make it easier on them, and they would have a better chance of survival if they didn't fight back.

Jake considered their chances as they rode along. Comanches often kidnapped people and kept them as captives until they could sell or ransom them. Then again, it was just as likely they would kill them at their leisure in some horrid fashion.

Jake tried not to think about it, but he couldn't help but remember every horror story he had ever heard about the Comanches, and how they had made death and torture an art form. It made him sick to his stomach to think about it, so he forced himself to think about other things instead.

He noted that the Indians were armed with bows and arrows and carried lances and buffalo-hide shields, but it appeared as though the two that were driving the horses didn't possess rifles. Furthermore, these two looked like they were only in their teens. Chances are they were some young bucks that had gone raiding into Mexico and had stolen some horses. They were out for adventure and prizes and would want to return to their village with many trophies to prove their worth as warriors. That meant they might have a chance if Buchanan didn't piss them off and give the Comanches a reason to kill them.

They continued throughout the afternoon, stopping only once to let the horses water in Saline Creek. The creek, for the most part, was dry this time of year, but there were occasional pools scattered along its length that had not yet evaporated.

The Indians kept Jake and Buchanan separated when they stopped. However, Jake got a look at his partner. The gash on his head now perched on top of an egg-sized purple knot, but the bleeding had stopped, and the blood had dried. Buchanan didn't refuse the drink of water from one of the Indians, and, when it was time to mount up about thirty minutes later, he didn't offer any resistance to the Indian that helped lift him onto his horse.

They continued their pace, and by early evening they had reached the Pecos.

CHAPTER TWENTY-SIX

Luke had reached the Pecos earlier in the day and had followed it southward without any incident or surprises. It had been an easy trip with few obstructions. The weather had been mild, and it had been a downright pleasant ride. He had recovered from his scorpion sting and figured he was on track to arrive in Mustang Flats with at least a week to spare.

He kept Creed on a path parallel to the river, but at a distance of about a mile from its banks. He was more likely to run into someone he didn't want to see if he travelled closer to the Pecos. He made occasional trips down to the water so Creed could drink and rest. Then he would veer away from it again to continue his journey.

It was approaching evening, and Luke began looking for a safe place to bed down for the night. He rode Creed up on top of a mesa that rose about fifty feet above the river. It followed the Pecos for a couple hundred yards and then cut sharply to the southwest, eventually sloping off to river level. It was covered with pine and scrub oak and looked like a good place to spend the night.

Luke sat on Creed, at the edge of the mesa, and looked downriver into Texas. He had actually been in Texas since early morning. He could see the Presidio Mountains to the south, so he knew that the place where Saline Creek emptied into the Pecos was up ahead somewhere. He followed the course of the Pecos with his eyes to see if he could locate the juncture. That's when he saw a cloud of dust about two miles away.

Reaching into his saddlebag, he pulled out a brass spyglass that had belonged to his father during the war. Philo had won it from an officer in the signal corps who, hopefully, had been a better officer than he was a card player.

Luke extended the optics and put it up to his eye, training it in the direction of the dust cloud. He could make out a small herd of horses driven by several mounted riders who looked like Indians. They were most likely a raiding party of Comanches returning from Mexico. In either case, Luke planned to stay out of sight and out of their way.

He unsaddled Creed inside the trees and decided against making a fire for the night. There were still plenty of canned goods and jerky, and his canteens were full, so he sat down and got comfortable. Luke rolled a cigarette and had a smoke. Afterward, he took his spyglass and walked back over to the edge of the mesa to have another look. If trouble was in the area, it would be good to know where it was at all times.

He kept up this routine about every fifteen minutes until it got too dark to make out the herd any longer. Luke thought they might camp by the river for the night, but, after stopping to rest and water the herd, they drove the horses across in a northeasterly direction into the Llano Estacado. Luke stood on the edge of the mesa and watched until they disappeared into the distance and the darkness.

Luke slept soundly that night. Creed would notify him of any danger that might appear on the mesa.

He woke up early the next morning but lay in bed and waited until the sun was full up in the east before rising and pulling on his boots. He strapped on his colt, grabbed his rifle and spyglass, and stood on the edge of the mesa to have a look around.

For as far as he could see in every direction, he was the only person who occupied this section of Texas real estate.

An hour later he had eaten and packed up his camp and was walking Creed down the last few yards of the slope that took him off of the mesa. He took his time covering the next couple of miles to Saline Creek. He had checked the surrounding country before leaving the heights of the mesa, and he hadn't seen signs of anyone else in the area. But where there was one group of Indians there could be others, and they were seldom as easy to spot as a herd of horses.

It wasn't difficult to spot the tracks of so many horses when he came upon them. Luke dismounted from Creed for a better look. He was fifty or sixty yards from the river, and the ground here was loose sand with tufts of bunch grass scattered every few feet. The horse's tracks through the sand were visible, but not distinct.

Leading Creed by the reins, Luke walked towards the Pecos. The ground along the banks was muddier than it was further back, and the horses' tracks would be better outlined.

He scoured the ground carefully for the next five minutes. As near as he could tell, it was as it had appeared through his spy-glass — a group of five or six Indians driving a herd of a couple dozen horses. They had come from the southwest, following Saline Creek, and were headed into the Staked Plains.

He was about to mount up when a hoof-print caught his eye. He bent down to look at a track partly obscured by another track that overlaid it. The top track was of an unshod horse and was like all the other tracks he had seen. But the track beneath it was of a shod horse, and Luke had seen the track before. There was a distinctive nick in the toe of the horseshoe that had made the impression in the mud. Lucas recognized it as belonging to one of the horses of the two men who had been following him several days ago.

He widened his search and found a few more tracks from a shod horse. The tracks he found were always partly obscured by other tracks, which meant that these riders, if they were the two men that had been following him, were riding in front of the bulk of the herd.

Luke patted Creed on the side of the neck. "Well, it looks like we won't have to worry about those two good-for-nothings any-more."

Creed stomped his foot and bobbed his head up and down.

Climbing onto Creed's back, Luke gave a tug on the reins to point him south. He set him to a fast walk as he followed the flow of the river towards his destination. Horsehead Crossing was three or four days away, and then another three days to Mustang Flats. Without his two pursuers, he would make better time than he had thought.

It was nearly four hours later when Luke and Creed stopped to rest in the shade of some willows. The sun was almost directly overhead. It was considerably warmer than it had been the last couple of days, and sweat trickled down Luke's temples and under his arms. He uncorked his canteen and took a long, satisfying drink, emptying the contents. Then he stooped down to refill it from the river as Creed drank his fill.

An uneasy feeling had been building up in him throughout the morning, and, for some reason, he thought about his mom and heard her voice inside his head, although the words were not clear. This had happened a few times before, and it frustrated the hell out of him. It was like his mother was his conscience, prodding and scolding him. The voice urged him to do something that he didn't want to do, even though he knew it was the right thing. Eventually, her words became clear in his head.

"You know what you should do, Luke."

"But why should I? It's none of my business."

"Luke, you are the only one who knows that those men are in trouble. If you don't help them, there is no one else. You know what Indians do to captives. Do you want that on your conscience?"

"Those men were planning to rob me, maybe even kill me."

"Let their consciences worry about that. I raised you better."

"Well, whatever the Comanches do to them, I'm sure they deserve it."

"Lucas Michael Gaines," the voice became more frustrated, "those men need your help!"

Luke finished filling his canteen, draping it over the saddle horn. He stuck his foot in the stirrup and pulled himself up onto Creed's back.

He looked downriver in the direction he had been traveling. He had a job to do. Why complicate it? Why borrow trouble?

Then he looked upriver in the opposite direction. "Creed, do you suppose every man's conscience comes to him in the voice of his mother?"

Creed snorted and nodded his head.

Luke turned the horse back upriver and kicked him in the sides.

"Well, then damn it all to high heaven."

"Watch your language, Luke. You know I don't like it when you curse."

"Sorry, Ma."

"You're a good son, Luke."

CHAPTER TWENTY-SEVEN

For two days, Luke trailed the Comanches through the Llano Estacado. Trailing a herd of horses through the grasslands was not difficult. The difficulty was not letting the Indians know that they were being followed.

He was careful because the Llano was flat and unremarkable, with nothing to distinguish one square mile of the massive plateau from the next. There were no trees, no shrubs, no rocks, not even a depression anywhere to break the monotony. Consequently, it was impossible to sneak up on anyone. Luke had no idea how to rescue the two captives once he did get close enough.

He knew that the two men were still alive, because he hadn't found their bodies anywhere along the trail. He had found boot prints at the places they had stopped to rest, but he had no idea what kind of shape they were in. The Comanches could be sadistic with their prisoners, keeping them barely alive until they reached their village. There they could be killed, turned into slaves, ransomed, or, if they found some redeeming quality in a person, they might adopt them into the tribe.

Luke doubted that there were any redeeming qualities in the captives and wondered again for the hundredth time why he was risking his life for them. He was only one man against five or six Indians in a land that offered no cover for a fight. He was attempting to rescue two men who had tried to kill him. And, to top it all off, there was no water anywhere in this godforsaken land. He had enough water in his canteen for one more day, yet it was a two-days ride back to the Pecos. Whatever he was going to do, he would have to do it soon.

To the east, a dark, blue-black sky was building as the sun dipped below the western horizon. Luke pulled back on the reins, and Creed came to a stop. Retrieving his spyglass from his pack, he scanned the horizon in front of him. He had halted Creed several times to keep him from riding too close to the Comanches. Thank God he had the spyglass. With it, he was able to see the Indians without them spotting him.

He was close enough to make out the

figures of the Indians. One . . . two . . . three . . . he counted five. They appeared to have stopped for the night. He could see them moving around and could make out the two white captives who sat on the ground next to each other. That's good, thought Luke. That will make it easier.

At one time, tens of thousands of buffalo had wandered the Llano. The herds had diminished drastically over the past decade, but there were still plenty of buffalo chips scattered across the mesa. The Indians had been collecting them and used them now to build a small fire.

Luke dismounted. He didn't want his silhouette outlined against the setting sun. Holding onto the reins he clicked his tongue. Creed responded and lay down in the grass. This would better conceal the horse — at least until the sun had gone down and darkness had settled in.

He got some jerky out of his saddlebags and sat down in the grass next to Creed to make his plans.

The previous evening, Luke and Creed had accidentally come to within thirty yards of where the horses had spent the night. The Comanches had not been very cautious, and they weren't paying much attention to the horses after sunset. Luke could have gotten closer if he had wanted to, but he didn't want to spook the horses and alert the Indians. He had considered making a rescue attempt then, but the Indians had kept the captives separated at opposite ends of the camp. Apparently, the Comanches felt secure out on the Llano and were relying on the horses to alert them of any danger.

Luke hoped that they would be as lax tonight. He could use the cover of darkness to get in close and spook the horses. If he fired a few shots into the Indians' camp, they might scatter. In the confusion, he could rush in and free the captives — if they stayed put, and if they stayed together so he didn't have to look for them. And *if* the Indians didn't decide to post a guard, and *if* he could get close enough to the horses before they spooked, and *if* . . . Luke thought of about a dozen things that could go wrong.

He lay down with his head against Creed and pulled his hat over his eyes. "Might as well get a couple hours of sleep, boy. Tomorrow, if we have any luck, we'll be too busy running."

Luke awoke a little past midnight. There was a sliver of a moon casting just enough light to see a few yards in front of him. This is perfect, thought Luke. If he could catch the Comanches by surprise and managed to free the hostages, the darkness would help cover their escape and give them a few hours head start if the Indians chose to pursue them.

He checked his Winchester and then his Colt. He also checked that his Bowie knife was in its sheath. He took a drink and then gave one to Creed. He tugged the cinch, then put his foot in the stirrup and threw his leg over the saddle.

Before going to sleep, he had taken two lengths of rope and fashioned two hackamores. He was going to have to get his hands on a pair of the horses so the two captives would have horses to ride if he could get them out of the camp. He checked that the hackamores were still draped over the saddle horn where he had put them. Satisfied that everything was in place, he sat for a moment and thought about what he was planning to do.

"Creed, if we had any sense at all, we'd turn around right now and head back to the Pecos."

Luke could feel the horse's muscles quiver beneath him. The stallion sensed Luke's coiled tension and was eager for whatever was about to happen.

Luke got out his spyglass and aimed it in the general direction of the Indian camp. It took him a few seconds of scanning the horizon to locate the campfire. Nothing else showed through the eyepiece anywhere on the Llano, nothing but never-ending darkness in every direction.

He walked Creed slowly toward the campfire, stopping after twenty minutes to look through the spyglass once more. The campfire looked larger through the lens this time. He tried to estimate how far away the camp was, but it was difficult to tell in the blackness of the barren mesa without anything for reference. It could have been a mile away. It could have been two miles. It could be a hundred yards. He might stumble upon it at any time, walking Creed right into the middle of the camp.

He couldn't rely on his eyesight alone, so he tried to engage his other senses as well. He stopped and listened for any sound from the camp. He listened for any movement from the herd of horses — any stomping or snorting or swishing of tails. He sniffed the air to discern any scents or odors, like smoke or the smell of horses, which would tell him he was near. There was virtually no breeze tonight, so odors would not carry far.

After almost two hours of carefully making his way toward the Comanche camp, Luke brought Creed to a halt once again. He knew he must be near. The campfire was visible and appeared to be close.

Creed's ears pricked up and pointed forward. To his left, Luke heard a horse snort. Then another horse on his right answered. Creed snorted in return.

Luke bent forward in the saddle and rubbed Creed's neck. "Shhhhhh," he whispered.

Luke could sense movement around him and could make out the shadow of other horses. Apparently, Creed had taken him right into the middle of the herd of horses that grazed outside the Indian camp. So far, so good.

Luke was startled when a horse bumped against Creed and began nuzzling with him. Then a second horse appeared. To his amazement, Luke realized that these must be the two horses belonging to the captive men. The horses must have felt some familiarity with Creed after following him for the past week.

Luke slipped the hackamores off of his saddle horn and onto the two horses, who offered no resistance to the makeshift bridles.

Holding the reins for Creed, as well as the leads for the other two horses, in his left hand, Luke removed his revolver with his right hand and pointed it toward the sky. Firing two shots into the air, Luke yelled, "Heyahhh!"

The loose horse that was closest reared up. He squealed and bolted away. The herd took off in different directions with a thunderous pounding of hooves that shattered the silence of the mesa. Yet, at least half of the horses stampeded in the direction of the campfire. Luke ducked low in the saddle and spurred Creed in behind them.

The horses charged into the camp, catching the sleeping Indians by surprise. One young brave jumped up and stepped in front of the lead horse, waving his arms. The horse reared up, and a hoof crushed the Indian's head.

Luke spotted the two white men, who had been lying next to each other. At first, they looked dazed and confused, but in a matter of seconds they were sitting upright and were trying to free themselves from the ropes that bound their hands and feet.

Luke holstered his gun and jumped from Creed's back. Sliding his knife out of its sheath, he bent down in front of the prisoners and sliced through the ropes that bound one of the men. Then he handed him the knife so he could free the second man.

An Indian about ten feet from the prisoners took aim at Luke and pulled the trigger, but the rifle misfired. The Indian threw the rifle aside and pulled a knife from a sheath at his waist. He rushed toward Luke.

Luke straightened up in time to see the brave with his knife raised. Drawing his revolver, he fired at the charging Comanche. The bullet hit the Indian in the chest. His body fell forward and landed at Luke's feet, dead before he hit the ground.

Luke turned to face the two men who had finished freeing themselves and were standing to their feet. "Grab a horse, and let's get going!"

"I'm not leaving without my guns," said Buchanan, as he started rummaging through a pile of belongings that the Indians had stacked not too far from the fire.

Luke and Jake were already on their horses.

"Come on, Miles," said Jake, "let's get the hell out of here."

Buchanan located their guns in the pile. Grabbing them, he threw his leg up over the waiting horse. "Now I can go."

Luke took the lead as the three men

kicked their horses into a fast gallop and disappeared into the darkness. There was nothing for their horses to run into out on the Llano, but it was still unnerving running the horses in the pitch darkness with just a sliver of moonlight to light the way.

After about a mile, they slowed the horses and changed directions. They had started west when they left the Indian camp, so they turned south and let the horses trot at a steady pace.

They were two days from the Pecos. Luke didn't know if the Comanches would choose to pursue them or not. At least two of the Indians were dead. Chances were that their priority would be to catch the scattered horse herd and round up as many as they could find, then cut their losses and return home.

If they did pursue, it would be a while before they could get started. Luke had every intention of putting as much distance between him and the Indians as he could.

Using the North Star as a guide, they continued riding south for the next hour before stopping to rest the horses.

It wasn't until they had come to a halt that anyone said anything. Buchanan took the opportunity to hand Jake his gun belt, then buckled his own gun in place.

"I don't know why you came after us, Jensen, but I'm sure glad you did."

"Yeah, I'm still pondering that one myself," said Luke.

In the dim light on the mesa, the three men brought their horses in close enough to see each other. Jake held out his hand for Luke. "That was really something back there. I don't know what to say except that I owe you a debt of gratitude. My name's Jake."

Luke hesitated a moment, then shook Jake's hand.

Luke and Buchanan looked at each other and held their gaze for a good long moment. Buchanan was the first to speak.

"I think that whatever differences we have had in the past should stay in the past." He extended his hand. "My name's Miles Buchanan."

The two men shook hands.

"Now that we are all old friends," said Luke, "we should keep riding. You gents are welcome to go your own way, but it might be advantageous for us to stick together until we reach the Pecos, just in case the Comanches decide to come after us."

"The Indians left our saddles where they captured us, about a day's ride south of the river," said Buchanan, "That's where we're headed. I reckon we can stick together until we reach the river."

The three of them moved out again, this time riding side by side. Luke had heard of Miles Buchanan. There was no way he was letting this guy behind him with a gun.

CHAPTER TWENTY-EIGHT

The three men rode their horses hard that first day out from the Indian camp. Luke stopped every couple of hours and took his spyglass out to scan their back trail. So far he hadn't detected any sign of pursuit.

Luke considered their situation. He had enough food in his packs to go around, but they only had one canteen of water between the three men and their horses. Even rationing it, the canteen would be empty by the end of the day. Tomorrow will be a dry one, he thought, but they should make it to the Pecos by early evening, so it could be worse.

The three men rode in silence for the most part. They didn't have much to say to each other. Jake and Buchanan were not his friends. At best, they were enemies in the midst of an uneasy truce. Luke recognized that they could turn on him at any moment.

That evening, when they stopped to bunk down for the night, Luke kept his saddlebags next to his bed, and he slept with his colt under his blanket. Even so, he slept uneasily that night. Every time one of the other men rolled over in his sleep, Luke woke with a jolt and swung his gun to bear on the sound.

Of the two men, Buchanan gave him the most cause for concern. Luke had caught the man staring at him several times, as though he were sizing him up, looking for an opportunity to make a move against him. He had also caught him staring at the saddlebags. If he was after the box, then this is as close as he had come to it in the past week and a half. If trouble was going to develop, it would come from Buchanan.

Jake was more difficult to figure out. He didn't seem to have the same intensity as Buchanan. Buchanan seemed always on edge. Jake was more laid back. Luke had heard him humming to himself. Luke believed Jake was probably a thief. He had more than likely rolled a few drunks in his day, but he didn't have the look of a gunfighter.

The question that nagged at Luke, as they continued south toward the Pecos on their second day, was when Buchanan made his play, would Jake remember that Luke saved his life, or would some misguided sense of puppy-dog loyalty make him back Buchanan?

It was past noon on their second day, and despite their parched lips and dry tongues, they were making decent progress toward the Pecos. Buchanan had been staring at Luke, and he looked as though he had something to say.

Luke rode with the reins in his left hand and his right hand resting on his thigh close to his gun. He looked at Buchanan and asked, "You got something on your mind?"

"As a matter of fact, there is something that's been eating at me."

Luke was riding to the far left of the group. Buchanan was next to him, and Jake was on the right flank. Luke glanced at Jake, who was wide eyed and sitting straight on his mount, his muscles tense with anticipation. If Buchanan was going to make a move now, it seemed to have caught Jake by surprise.

Luke had slowed Creed's pace. The other riders followed suit. The sun had embarked on its descent toward the west. Luke had to keep his head lowered slightly so that his hat brim shaded his eyes from the glare. He silently cursed himself for not thinking about the position of the sun.

"If you've got something to say, say it,"

Luke said.

Buchanan looked at him with a grin that was half curious and half mocking. "I heard about you."

Luke rode on without replying.

Buchanan continued to stare. "I heard about that business up in Trinidad last year."

Luke continued to look straight ahead as he rode. "Don't believe everything that you hear."

"I heard those three miners killed that whole family of Mexicans, and that you dropped all three of them before they could get a shot off."

Luke looked at Buchanan. The outlaw was sizing him up. Sooner or later, they were going to lock horns. "That's not exactly how it happened."

Buchanan huffed and sneered derisively. "I didn't think so."

Luke grinned as though remembering a private joke. "What I mean is it's not true that they never got off a shot. One of them did." He reached up and pulled the collar down on his shirt to reveal a three-inch scar on the side of his neck.

Buchanan stared at Luke for a moment and then replied, "I ain't no Mexican." Kicking his heels into the side of his mount, he trotted ahead of the others.

They rode on in silence throughout the rest of the afternoon and into the early evening hours. By the time the sun had touched the horizon, they were walking their horses knee deep into the waters of the Pecos River.

They walked their mounts to the other side and dismounted before allowing the horses to drink their fill from the river. The men squatted down in the shallows to quench their thirst as well.

While Luke refilled both of his canteens, Jake lay down in the river and let the cooling waters flow over him. Buchanan washed his face and hands and wet his hair, slicking it back on his head before putting his hat back on.

"Damn, this feels good! I could spend the night right here," Jake said. He stretched out in the river with his backside brushing the sandy bottom with only his face above the water.

"You can stay there floating like a turd in a trough if you want to," said Buchanan, "but I'm going after our saddles."

Jake sighed and got to his feet. Walking to the shore, he picked up his hat and gun belt, which he had discarded prior to his bath. As he buckled on his gun, he looked down-river. Then he turned and looked in the opposite direction. Turning to look at Buchanan, he reached up and scratched the back of his neck. "Where do you reckon we are?"

Buchanan stood with his hands on his hips, looking upriver, but didn't answer Jake.

"We're about half a day's ride south of Saline Creek," Luke replied. He had intentionally steered their course back to the Pecos to a place that was downriver from where the two outlaws had been captured. When they parted ways, Luke wanted them traveling in the opposite direction. As he spoke, he was transferring some of his foodstuffs from his pack to an empty flour sack.

Jake walked up to Luke and extended his hand. "I want to thank you once again for what you did, coming after us. I don't know anybody that would have done that for me."

Luke saw the sincerity in the man's eyes. Smiling, he took Jake's hand and said, "Maybe we'll cross paths again sometime. If we do, I'll let you buy me a beer." He handed the sack of provisions to Jake, who looked humbled and grateful for the gift.

"Drinks will be on me, partner," Jake replied.

He turned to walk back to his horse but stopped to scratch Creed behind the ears.

He looked at Luke and said, "You've got some kind of horse here." Jake returned to his horse. Hopping up on its bare back, he waited for Buchanan.

Luke grabbed one of the two canteens that he had filled and walked over to where Buchanan was standing.

The two men stood face to face about two feet apart. Buchanan was a good five inches shorter than Luke, but he wasn't intimidated by Luke's size. Buchanan was about ten years older, and, although he wasn't as tall, he had a stocky build and outweighed Luke by twenty pounds.

"I've had hell to pay this past week and a half. I'd just as soon let bygones be bygones if it's all the same to you," Buchanan said. Then he added with a wink, "And if you want to call yourself 'Jensen,' your secret is safe with me."

"As long as you go north and I head south, I'll have no hard feelings," replied Luke.

Buchanan smiled and held out his right hand.

Luke, who was already holding the canteen in his left hand, reached out with his right hand to shake with Buchanan. As they grasped hands, there was a flash of triumph in Buchanan's eyes. Jensen had made a fatal mistake. Buchanan was left handed, and he went for his gun.

Luke tried to pull away, but Buchanan's grip was too strong. As Buchanan's gun cleared the holster, Luke dropped the canteen from his left hand and leaned into a left jab to Buchanan's nose that snapped his head backward.

Buchanan was caught by surprise. He had expected Luke to try to escape, not to attack. He brought his gun up and tried to aim it at Luke's chest, but Luke's left hand chopped down on Buchanan's wrist, and the gun fell into the sand.

Buchanan had let go of Luke's hand. He threw a quick right hook that left a cut on Luke's cheek below the eye. He followed with a jab to the gut that had Luke doubled up. A right uppercut knocked Luke on his back, sprawled in the sand.

Buchanan lunged at Luke as he attempted to stand. Luke fell backward, bringing his legs up as Buchanan dove on top of him. Kicking upwards at the same instant, he sent Buchanan flying over him, landing on his back, half in the river and half on shore.

Both men rolled over and got to their knees, but Buchanan was slower getting up after having the wind knocked out of him. Before he could stand up straight, Luke charged, barreling into him and knocking him further into the Pecos.

Both men did the best they could — pushing, shoving, exchanging blows while trying to keep their footing on the slippery river bottom.

The two combatants had worked their way out to where they were waist deep in the river. Luke had a longer reach than Buchanan and landed more of his punches than the shorter man.

Luke forced Buchanan to move backward through the water. Buchanan was breathing heavier as Luke connected with punch after punch. Buchanan stumbled over something on the river bottom and fell over backward, disappearing beneath the muddy waters that they had churned up with their struggle.

Luke waited, but when Buchanan didn't reappear after a few seconds, he lunged forward, kicking his legs through the water where Buchanan had sunk below the surface, reaching into the muddy Pecos, trying to find Buchanan's body.

Then he heard a commotion behind him. Turning, he saw Buchanan about five yards away. His arms and legs pumped hard as he splashed his way toward his gun on the bank.

Luke reached down to draw his revolver

and was horrified to discover that his holster was empty. He looked over at the bank and saw his Colt lying on the ground. It had fallen free of its holster when he had been knocked on his back.

Luke plunged toward the shore in a desperate effort to reach his gun before Buchanan could reach his. Luke had a longer stride, but the other man had more of a head start.

Buchanan made shore seconds ahead of Luke. He stumbled forward, picked up his revolver, and aimed it at Luke as he waded out of the water.

Luke saw Buchanan dripping with water, with his legs spread apart, smiling and taking deliberate aim at him.

As he made a dive for his own gun, he heard the explosion of a revolver. He expected to feel the red-hot searing pain of a bullet ripping through him.

As he hit the ground, his fingers curled around the handle of his revolver. He rolled to his left, coming to rest sprawled on his stomach in the hot sand, and brought his gun up to return fire.

Miles Buchanan was lying motionless, face down on the ground.

Jake sat on his horse, revolver in hand, smoke wafting from the barrel.

Luke got slowly to his feet. He slid his Colt into his holster and walked over to where Buchanan was lying in the wet sand. He bent down to examine the body and found a hole in the side of his head.

Luke turned and faced Jake, who still had his revolver in his hand. "I guess that makes us even now."

Jake smiled and let his gun fall back in its holster. "I guess we are." He reached down to grab the reins on Buchanan's horse, which was standing next to him. "Miles won't be needing a horse anymore, but I might need an extra if I run into any more Indians." He turned his horse upriver and started to ride away. Stopping, he turned and said, "That doesn't mean I can't buy you a beer next time I see you."

"I look forward to it," Luke replied. He watched as Jake kicked his heels into the sides of his horse, which broke into a fast trot and disappeared around a bend in the river.

CHAPTER TWENTY-NINE

Red knocked on the door to Tolliver's office, then pushed the door open and stuck his head inside. "Boss, there's a man here to see you. He says he has a package for you."

Tolliver looked up from his desk. "What's his name?"

"He says his name is Luke Jensen."

"Luke Jensen!" Tolliver's eyes widened when he heard the name. "Send him in."

Red stepped aside, and Luke walked into Tolliver's office. He removed his hat as he stepped up to the huge oak desk. Under his arm, he carried the box that he had been protecting with his life for almost three weeks.

"You must be the courier from Las Cruces," said Tolliver.

"I am." Luke held out the box.

Tolliver took the box from Luke. Removing a small key from his vest pocket, he slid it into the padlock on the clasp of the box. He gave the key a twist, and the lock popped open. He lifted the lid of the box enough to have a look inside. He seemed satisfied that the contents were safe, so he closed the lid and placed the box on top of his desk.

"I was beginning to think you would never get here."

Luke's eyes narrowed, and he caught himself grinding his teeth. "I was told to have it here by the end of the month, which is still three days away."

"I don't mean to sound unappreciative, Mr. Jensen. I know you've had a long, hard trip. It's just that I've been anxious for this delivery. It's important to my plans."

Luke, of course, was curious to know what he had agreed to deliver; he had been since the first day. But it wasn't his business to ask if Tolliver didn't offer to tell him. He had done his job. He just wanted to get paid and find a hotel where he could have a bath and a hot meal.

Tolliver stood up from behind his desk and walked across the room to the liquor cabinet. "Where are my manners?" he said. "Can I offer you a drink?"

"I wouldn't turn it down," Luke replied.

"Good. Have a seat, Luke. Tell me about

your trip. Did you encounter any difficulties?"

Luke sat down in an overstuffed chair, sinking down so far he thought the chair was going to swallow him. He had to admit, though, it sure felt good on his saddle hardened backside. It was then that he noticed the dog lying in the corner of the office, apparently asleep. Luke was fond of dogs.

Tolliver poured him a glass of bourbon, which he readily accepted. Then he opened a box of cigars and handed one to Luke. He lit both of their cigars and took a seat next to him.

"There was a little trouble," Luke said, "but nothing I couldn't handle."

"Don't hold back," Tolliver said. "After all, you were in my employ at the time. You owe me a full report."

This guy has had some military experience, thought Luke. The way he holds himself, the way he gives orders and demands reports. No doubt he had been an officer.

Luke gave Tolliver an account of his trip from Las Cruces but didn't add any details. "For the most part, the trip was uneventful," Luke lied.

After Luke had finished with the account

of his trip, Tolliver sat in silence for a long moment. Luke could see that the man was sizing him up.

At last Tolliver said, "I owe you some money, don't I?" Tolliver reached into his coat and pulled a leather wallet out of the inside pocket. Removing the money that was owed, he handed it to Luke, who took it and shoved it into his shirt pocket.

"Tell me, Luke, have you seen much of Mustang Flats yet, or did you come straight here?"

Luke wasn't sure why Tolliver was asking him this question. "I came up from the Pecos, so I rode through town to get here. But that was early this morning. I didn't really see much of the town, but I plan to stick around for a few days."

"Did anyone see you?"

"I stopped at the livery to get directions to your ranch. Why are you asking?"

"If you're the Luke Jensen I've heard of, I could use you on another job, if you're interested."

Luke still wasn't sure what to make of Tolliver. He was obviously a wealthy rancher. He seemed like the ambitious type who kept a lot of irons in the fire. He had seen Tolliver's foreman, Red, and some of the other hands when he rode up to the ranch. They looked less like cowhands and more like gunfighters.

That wasn't necessarily bad. After all, a man works hard to build a ranch into a paying proposition. He has a right to protect it any way he sees fit. Might as well hear what he has to offer.

"I'm listening," Luke said.

Tolliver leaned forward in his chair. "I paid you two hundred dollars to deliver that box to me," he said. "I'll pay you another two hundred for this job."

"If you're headed where I think you're headed with this, Mr. Tolliver," Luke replied, "I saw some of your hands when I rode up to the ranch. Isn't this something they can handle for you?"

Tolliver sat back in his chair and took a long draw on his cigar. "Normally, the answer to that would be 'Yes,' but my men and I are already too close to this situation. Unfortunately, the job has already been bungled once, and, as a result, my men and I are under suspicion. This requires someone not known to be connected to me or to the ranch."

The man had some dirty work to be done, but he wanted someone else to do it for him. He wanted to remain untouchable if something went wrong.

Tolliver was showing himself to be scheming and unscrupulous. Luke's first instinct was to get up and walk away. Prompted by an internal warning mechanism that Luke had learned not to ignore, he waited to hear the rest of Tolliver's offer.

"I can't make you any promises," Luke said. "Give me the details, and I'll give you my answer."

Tolliver smiled. "There's a man in town that has been making life difficult for me of late. He has been asking questions — embarrassing questions — casting suspicion on me and my operations."

Tolliver stood up and walked over to the liquor cabinet. Returning with the bourbon decanter, he refilled Luke's glass, then his own. He continued, "I've got the largest ranch in this part of the state, and I own several other businesses in town. I have a lot of plans that could all be upset if this man is allowed to continue to create misgivings about my character."

He put the decanter on the corner of his desk and stood over Luke, looking down on him. He sipped his bourbon and took his time before he said, "I'll give it to you straight, Luke. I want you to kill him for me. Goad him into some kind of argument and then kill him. The law in town is on my payroll, so, if you make it look like a fair fight, you won't have anything to worry about. What do you say? Will you take the job?"

Luke had to fight back the revulsion he felt for Tolliver. What was it about some men — most men, as far as Luke was concerned. They get some money, they get some power, and then they start making up their own rules. The rules that govern the rest of society don't seem to apply to them anymore. They think that they can act with impunity, walk over other people, take what they want. This is why he avoided people, why he worked alone and rode alone.

It was all that Luke could do to control himself. But his instincts warned him to hear Tolliver out.

He fought back his urges and asked Tolliver, "Who is this guy you want me to kill? What's his name?"

"His name is Matthew Gaines. He's the school teacher in town."

The shock of hearing his brother's name was like a slap in the face. Could it be Matt? As far as he knew, his brother was in New Jersey, but it had been over a year since they had been in contact. He composed himself and stood to his feet. "You pay me up front,

Mr. Tolliver, and you can consider the job done."

Smiling broadly, Tolliver removed his wallet for the second time and counted out two hundred dollars. "I wouldn't normally pay the full amount before the job is done, but with your reputation . . ." Handing the money to Luke, he slapped him on the back and said, "Take care of this to my satisfaction, without it pointing back to me, and I may have other work for you as well."

Luke pushed the money into his shirt pocket with the other bills.

Tolliver walked him out to the porch of the ranch house, and the two men shook hands. "Don't come back to the ranch. I don't want anyone to be able to connect us. Get yourself a room at the hotel, and, if you need to contact me, leave a message with the marshal."

Luke mounted up and said, "I've been in the saddle for three weeks straight. Once I do the job, I'm gonna have to ride the trail again. I could use a couple days of rest first. It might take me that long to find this guy and goad him into a fight anyways."

"I'll give you forty-eight hours, but don't take any longer than that."

Luke tipped his hat and turned Creed up the road and through the gate that led to the main road to town. What in the hell had his brother gotten himself into?

CHAPTER THIRTY

Matt dismounted in front of the hotel and went inside. There was no one behind the check-in desk, so he rang the bell sitting on the countertop. The clerk stuck his head out of a back room, then walked up to the check-in counter and stood dutifully with his hands folded on the countertop. "Good morning, Mister Gaines. What can I do for you?"

"Did any messages come in for me while I was out this morning?"

The clerk turned to examine the cubby holes behind the counter. Reaching into the compartment with Matt's room number stenciled above it, he pulled out two small envelopes. "It looks like you have two messages," said the clerk, handing the envelopes to Matt.

Matt took the envelopes from the clerk and thanked him. Now that he had a response to his inquiries, he was too excited to go up to his room. Finding a comfortable chair in the lobby, he sat down and ripped open the first envelope. It contained a telegram from the president of the Colorado Cattlemen's Association. He read the contents to himself. Smiling, he nodded his head and said, "I knew it!"

He repeated his actions with the second envelope. It contained a response to his inquiry to a gentleman he knew who worked at the Cotton Exchange in Mobile, Alabama. "I've got you now," he said under his breath.

Rising, he shoved the envelopes into his pocket and climbed the stairs to his room.

Slipping the key into the lock and giving it a twist, Matt stepped inside and closed the door. He had left the curtains closed, so the room was bathed in a dim light that required his eyes to refocus when he entered from the brightly lit hallway.

He walked over to the window and threw the curtains back, allowing the sunlight to flood in, filling the room. There was a nice breeze outside, so Matt opened the latch on the window and pulled it up a few inches.

"How's a guy supposed to get any sleep with all that sunlight shining in?"

Startled by the voice behind him, Matt turned to see the figure of a man stretched out on his bed. When he recognized his brother, he smiled broadly and exclaimed, "Luke, what are you doing here?"

Luke swung his stocking feet over the edge of the bed, stood up, and stretched. Then the two brothers embraced.

"It sure is good to see you," said Matt, "But what are you doing here in Mustang Flats?" Matt sat down in a chair next to his bed and waited for Luke to explain.

Luke sat down on the edge of the bed and pulled on his boots. Then he stood up and walked over to the washbasin and splashed some water on his face. Returning to have a seat on the edge of the bed, he said, "I was hired to deliver a package to a rancher outside of town. I got in early this morning, but you were already gone. I saw your name on the register when I checked in. We need to talk." Luke yawned and stretched for a second time.

"I'm glad to see you keep your lock-picking skills honed," Matt teased.

Luke leaned forward and put his elbows on his knees with his fingers interlaced in front of him. "So, tell me, big brother, what kind of trouble have you gotten yourself into?"

Matt grinned. "What makes you think that I'm in any kind of trouble?"

"Well, when a man pays me two hundred dollars to put a bullet in you, that makes me think that maybe you've stepped into something you shouldn't have."

Matt rubbed his chin and said, "Hmmmm . . . two hundred dollars, huh? I've never had a price on my head before. Is that the going rate for school teachers? It doesn't seem like very much money."

"Believe me, it's more than enough to tempt a lot of men. Men have been killed for a lot less. It's a good thing that he offered the job to me first. I'm still using Jensen instead of Gaines, so he had no way of knowing that we're brothers."

"So you told this man that you would do it?"

"Of course," replied Luke. "If I had turned him down he would have given the job to someone else. This way we've got some time to sort this out."

"That man's name wouldn't be Amos Tolliver, would it?"

Luke nodded his head. "Why don't you tell me what's going on."

For the next fifteen minutes, Matt told Luke everything that had happened since his arrival in Mustang Flats, from his first run-in with Tolliver's men, the burning down of the school, and the killing of Curly and the attempt to frame Tom McCutchen for the murder.

"But why does this guy, Tolliver, want to see you stretched out so bad?" asked Luke.

"I guess it is because I've been asking a lot of questions about him," answered Matt.

"And why are you so curious about him?"

Matt leaned forward with his face only inches from Luke. "Because I don't think his name is Amos Tolliver. I think he's Morgan Burnett."

Luke almost jumped to his feet when he heard the name. "Are you kidding me?"

"I wasn't positive until a little while ago when I received these two telegrams." Matt removed the two envelopes from his pocket and handed them to Luke.

Luke looked at the first telegram and then read the second one. He looked at Matt and shook his head. "I don't understand. What are these?"

"Before I explain those, let me tell you what I've found out about Amos Tolliver so far." Matt got to his feet and paced back and forth across his rented room. He had slipped into the role of teacher, pacing the front of the classroom as he lectured his students on the finer points of the lesson. He stopped periodically and shook his hand — which held an imaginary piece of chalk

— to emphasize a point.

"Amos Tolliver appeared in Mustang Flats about six years ago. He had half a dozen men with him, including two named Curly and Red. Those are the same names of two of the men who were with Burnett.

"When he got here, he started buying up the smaller ranches and then some of the businesses in town — and he paid cash for all of it."

"That sounds like a lot of cash," Luke replied. "Does anyone know where he got his money?"

"Supposedly, he had a ranch outside of Denver that he sold before he came to Texas. Before that, during the war, he claims to have made a lot of money as a cotton broker."

"Oh, I see," Luke exclaimed. "That's where these telegrams come in, isn't it?" He held the envelopes over his head and waved them in the air as he spoke.

"That's right," Matt said. "As you can see, the first telegram is from the president of the Colorado Cattlemen's Association. He says that he has never heard of a rancher named Amos Tolliver or his brand, the 'A bar T.'

"The second telegram," Matt continued with his lecture, "is from a friend who works at the Cotton Exchange in Mobile. He's been there for thirty years, and he knows everyone in the business. He has never heard of Amos Tolliver."

Matt stopped his pacing and sat back down opposite his brother. "Amos claims that he has never been in the army, but the day I first met him, his man, Curly, let it slip and referred to him as 'major.' Then, the next day, Curly is gunned down. I know that this is Burnett." Matt was visibly excited as he waited for Luke to respond.

There was a long pause in the conversation before Luke spoke up. "I think you're right. I think after all these years, we've got the son of a bitch. What do you want to do next? I've been to his ranch. I've seen some of the men he has working for him. We're going to need some help."

Matt grinned and asked, "Do you know if David is still in Cheyenne?"

"I believe so. At least he was there last month."

"Good," said Matt. "There's a telegraph station on the west side of town. You get a telegram to him and tell him to get here as soon as he can. I don't know if the telegraph operator can be trusted, so don't be too obvious with the wording of your message."

"All right, but what are you going to do?"

Matt got to his feet and grabbed his hat from the top of the dresser where he had deposited it. "I'm going back to the jail to check on Tom and Katie. I want to tell them what I know about Tolliver. Katie isn't going to want to hear it, but she needs to know what kind of a man he is."

"All right," said Luke. "I'll meet you at the jail after I've sent the telegram."

The two brothers made their way downstairs and out the front door of the hotel. Once outside, they went their separate ways.

Back at the bank, Red had just returned from the jail. He walked into the bank lobby and straight for Tolliver's office.

"Boss, we have a problem," he said as he stepped in and closed the door behind him.

Tolliver had been reading the newspaper. He folded it and laid it on the desk. "What kind of problem?" he asked.

Red knew that his boss wasn't going to take what he had to tell him very well, but there was no way to avoid being the bearer of bad news. "When I got down to the jail, Guthrie was gone. His badge was on his desk, and it seems like he's cleared out. Not only that, but before he left, he gave Tom McCutchen a note saying that there isn't enough evidence to hold him for Curly's murder, and he set him free."

Red saw Tolliver's teeth clench and his jaw tighten. Tolliver slammed his fist down on the top of his desk. Then he swiped his arm across his desk, sending the newspaper, as well as a ledger and pen and inkwell, flying across the room.

"That spineless sack of shit," he hissed through gritted teeth. "Where's Tom now?"

"He's still at the jail. Those two guys you hired to work him over did a good job. Doc said he has to stay put for a few days. Katie and the school teacher are looking after him."

"All right, it sounds like we don't have to worry about McCutchen for a while. This is what I want you to do: Search the town for any sign of Guthrie. Check his shack. Check the saloons. Check anyplace you can think of. If I get my hands on him, I can make him change his mind. See if you can find that Luke fellow from this morning. He should be around town somewhere. Tell him I need him to move his schedule forward. I want Gaines dead! I'm tired of him sticking his nose into my business."

"Sure thing, boss," Red replied as he turned the knob on the door and headed back out of the bank.

CHAPTER THIRTY-ONE

When Matt walked into the back room of the jail, he could hear the sound of laughter in the holding area. Tom was sitting propped up in bed like he had been when Matt saw him earlier, and Katie was sitting in the chair next to his bunk. The two had obviously reconciled and were enjoying a private joke together.

Matt stuck his head into the open cell door. "How are you feeling, Tom?" he asked.

"I'm much better now that Katie is here."

Katie leaned forward and placed her hand on her brother's arm. "And I'm going to stay right here until you are ready to come back home. I'll ride back to the ranch and pick up a few things and let Ben know what's going on. He and the other hands can watch the place while I'm away."

Matt sat down on the edge of Tom's bunk. "I was glad to hear the two of you laughing when I arrived. I have something to tell both of you." He fidgeted with his hat while he searched for the right words. "I know you're not going to want to hear what I have to say, Katie, but please let me finish before you say anything."

"If it's about Amos," Katie interrupted, "you can set your mind at ease. Tom already told me that the two men who beat him up were hired by Amos. I can't believe that I ever let that man touch me!" She was furious as she spoke, and Matt thought that if anything had been handy, she would have thrown it across the room.

Matt sighed. "Well, that certainly makes the rest of this conversation a lot easier, but there is more that you should know."

Tom and Katie both looked eager to hear what he had to say. "As you both know, although I don't have any proof, I believe that it was Amos's men who set the fire at the school. I just found out a while ago that he has hired a man to kill me."

Katie put her hand to her mouth but kept silent. Tom asked, "How did you find that out?"

"Because the man he hired told me so."

Matt saw the looks of confusion on their faces, so he added, "Amos didn't know it at the time, but the man that he hired is my brother Luke. He got into town early this morning and was waiting for me at the hotel."

Both Tom and Katie sat with their mouths open, stunned. Katie spoke first. "Why has Amos taken such a dislike to you? Why does he want you dead?"

"Amos wants me dead because he has a secret that he doesn't want anyone to know, but I know what it is."

"What secret?" they asked in unison.

Matt stood up. Storytelling was like teaching or preaching; he preferred to do it on his feet where he could move around. "I'll have to ask you to keep this to yourselves for the time being until I'm ready to act on it."

They nodded in assent.

"I haven't told either of you much about my family, but I have two brothers, David and Luke, both younger than me. I also have an older sister, Hannah. She was married to a man named Linus Walker, who served in the Confederate cavalry under a major named Morgan Burnett."

Tom and Katie sat quietly as Matt continued with his story.

"A few days before Lee surrendered to Grant, Major Burnett called together a few of his most loyal men, including my brother-in-law, Linus. Burnett knew that it was a matter of time before the Confederacy would be forced into submission. He outlined a proposal to desert from the army. His plan was to rob northern banks, make their way West, buy a ranch, and start over.

"Burnett's men were excited to go along with him, all except Linus, who had a wife and daughter waiting for him back home. When he tried to ride away, Burnett shot him in the back and left him for dead. However, Linus didn't die . . . well, at least not right away. He was discovered by some Confederate infantry. When he woke up, he was in an army hospital in Nashville. He lingered there for over a month before he died from his wound.

"In the meantime, my sister, Hannah, arrived at the hospital. Before he died, he told her about Burnett and his plans, and she told my brothers and me. Ever since then, my two brothers have been looking for any sign of Burnett wherever they went."

Matt chuckled as he added, "It's ironic. David and Luke have been traveling throughout the West for years without finding any clue to Burnett's whereabouts. Then the first time I set my feet west of the Mississippi, to a tiny west Texas town in the middle of nowhere, I'm the one who finds him."

Katie's eyes were wide with shock. "I knew that Amos was ambitious, even ruthless, as Tom had often described him. But he is also very charming and intelligent. I had feelings for the man. How could I have been so deceived?"

"Don't be too hard on yourself," said Matt. "He's fooled a lot of people for a long time."

"So, you're telling us that Amos is this man, Burnett?" she asked, already knowing in her heart that it was true. "Are you sure?"

"I knew that he was no good," Tom almost shouted, victoriously.

Matt went through the evidence that he had, giving the same account that he had given to Luke earlier.

When he had finished, Tom asked, "What are you going to do? Are you going to contact the authorities?"

Matt shook his head. "No, this is family business. I may have a Princeton education, but my family is from Tennessee. That's where I grew up. My brother, Luke, is here now. We're sending for David, who should be in Cheyenne. If he can get on a train today, he should be able to be here by tomorrow night. Once David is here the three of us will confront Amos and his men. We'll take care of it 'Tennessee style.'"

Matt felt a strange exhilaration as he contemplated the approaching showdown with Amos Tolliver. Although he had only known the man for a short time, he had known about him — as Morgan Burnett — for years. He was the man that his family had been hunting for, the man who had turned his sister into a widow and deprived his young niece of her father. And he had done it in a cowardly fashion, shooting Linus in the back and leaving him to die. He had robbed who knew how many banks in the North to settle in Mustang Flats and finance his new identity as Amos Tolliver. He had made a respectable name for himself, buying up ranches and businesses. But a man can only run for so long before his past catches up with him. Sooner or later, Amos Tolliver was going to pay for the sins of Morgan Burnett.

With any luck, tomorrow's evening train would bring David to Mustang Flats. Then the three brothers — the three sons of Philo Gaines — could confront Burnett and exact payment from the man who had taken so much from their family.

Matt realized that Burnett had spent over eight years running from his past, trying to bury the old under the new. He also realized that, unlike Burnett, he had been clinging to his past, trying to hold onto something that he should have let go of over a year ago.

Rebecca's death had left him with a pain that was deeper than the burns to his leg. He had avoided dealing with the pain, and, as a result, he hadn't healed.

He hadn't been able to attend her memorial service because he had been recuperating in the hospital. After he had been released from the hospital, he never went to visit the cemetery. He had never said goodbye. He had convinced himself that he could go on with his life, continue living from day to day without facing the fact that she was really gone and that she wasn't coming back.

In one respect at least, he and Burnett were alike. Neither one of them was going to be able to have a future unless they were able to exorcise the ghosts from their pasts — Matt to let go of the pain that he carried, and Burnett to take responsibility for the pain that he had caused.

Luke had finished sending the telegram to his brother in Cheyenne and was on his way to meet Matt at the jail. He stepped around the corner of a building and almost ran headlong into Tolliver's foreman, Red, who was coming out of a saloon.

"Luke." Red was surprised at having run into him so abruptly. "You're just the man I want to talk to." He glanced up and down the street. Tolliver wouldn't want them to be seen together out in the open like this.

Red brushed past Luke, indicating for him to follow, and stepped into an alley where they could talk in private. He lowered his voice. "Mr. Tolliver has a message. He wants the job done right away. He can't wait any longer."

Luke stood only inches from Red, and, when the foreman had finished speaking, Luke whispered back, "I have a message for Mr. Tolliver, if you wouldn't mind passing it along."

"What is it?" Red asked, leaning closer and cocking his head.

Luke's arm was like a coiled rattlesnake when he drew it back and struck out, landing a solid blow to Red's jaw that spun him around and flung him into the dusty alleyway.

The look of shock on Red's face was replaced by blind rage. He went for his gun, but it wasn't easy to draw from his position. By that time it didn't matter anyway. Luke already had his gun pointed at Red.

Red removed his hand from his gun and moved it up to his face to massage his throbbing jaw. "What the hell was that for?" he asked.

Luke kept his gun pointed at Red as he reached into his shirt pocket and pulled out the two hundred dollars that Tolliver had paid him to kill Matt. He tossed the money on the ground next to Red. "Tell your boss that Luke Gaines decided not to take the job after all."

"Gaines?!"

"That's right," Luke said. A crooked smile parted his lips as he added, "The school teacher is my older brother."

Red picked up the money and shoved it in his own pocket, then started to get to his feet.

Luke waggled his gun and said, "You stay right where you are for a moment or two."

He had started to back away toward the street when he had an idea. He walked back to Red, who was still sitting in the dust, and said, "Peel off fifty dollars of that money and hand it over."

Red was confused but did as Luke instructed.

Luke took the fifty dollars and put it back in his shirt pocket. "My brother's gonna use this money to replace some of the clothes and other personal items that he lost when the school burnt down. You can thank Mr.

Tolliver for his donation."

With that said, he backed up and ducked around the corner of the building and disappeared.

Red got swiftly to his feet and drew his gun, but when he got out to the street, there was no sign of Luke Gaines.

■ ■ ■ ■

PART THREE
THE GAMBLER

■ ■ ■ ■

"When I first met David Gaines on the road north of Horse Creek, I thought that he was there to rob me. Of course, the joke would have been on him, 'cuz I didn't have two nickels to rub together. When I found out what he had in mind for me, you could have knocked me off ol' Harley's back with a feather. As I was soon to find out, there wasn't a better man anywhere for the job ahead of us."

— Lloyd Barta,
Mountain Man, Stage Robber,
Cheyenne, Wyoming Territory

CHAPTER THIRTY-TWO

David Gaines walked across the lobby of
the Rollins House and stepped out into the
afternoon sun. It had been a cool night, but
it had already warmed up outside and had
all the earmarks of a beautiful day.

The cards had been good to him over the
past few nights. He had a wallet full of win-
nings and an emergency one-hundred-
dollar bill folded up inside the sweatband of
his bowler hat.

He lit a cigar and stood outside the hotel
for a while, watching the traffic on Sixteenth
Street. Everything from freight wagons to
fancy carriages traveled the east-west corridor through the center of town.

He stood there for a few minutes and
closed his eyes, feeling the sun on his face
and listening to the sounds of the city
around him. He removed a silver flask from

his coat pocket, unscrewed the cap, held it up to his lips, and tilted it back. The bourbon inside slid down his throat with a burn that was more like the greeting of a close friend than a discomfort to the gambler. He had once been caught in a wildfire out on the Kansas prairie and had had to light a backfire to avoid being roasted alive. He understood fighting fire with fire, just as he understood fighting his hangover with another draw from his flask.

Dusting the ash from his cigar, he pocketed the flask, then he turned to his right and walked to the corner. Taking another right, he strode north up Eddy Street. It was almost two o'clock, and Frenchy's Saloon was a good place to do something about the empty feeling in the pit of his stomach.

As he approached the saloon, he saw a group of men unloading barrels of whiskey from a wagon. One man, in particular, stood out from the rest. At six feet, six inches and weighing over three hundred pounds, the man was as big and as strong as an ox, so that's what people called him. No one knew his real name. Ox didn't know what it was. He was slow of thinking and had the mentality of a child. Most of the time he was as gentle as a child as well, but when he was angry, he could be dangerous. David watched as it took two men to unload one barrel. Ox, on the other hand, carried one barrel under each arm.

David saw Ox stop and look in his direction. He let the barrels he carried fall to the ground, where they shattered, flooding the street with the pungent smell of cheap whiskey and littering it with oak staves. His eyes narrowed, and his knuckles turned white as he clenched his fists and advanced straight toward David.

David saw the look on Ox's face as he crossed Eddy Street and knew that there was about to be a lot more trouble than he could handle. At five foot, seven inches, twenty-nine-year-old David Gaines weighed about one hundred fifty-five pounds. He was no kind of match for Ox in any physical confrontation.

David waited, puffing on his cigar, while Ox stepped up on the boardwalk and stood in front of him. "Good afternoon, Ox. It's a beautiful day today, wouldn't you say?"

Ox towered over David and cast a shadow he could have parked a wagon under. "Davey, I heard you was with Crystal last night, and I heard you kissed her, too." Crystal was one of the girls at Frenchy's. Ox had a crush on her and sometimes got overprotective, not understanding the nature of her relationship with her "special" friends.

David furrowed his brow and looked as though he were deep in thought. "I do believe you're right, Ox. I did run into Crystal last night."

Ox bent down until his face was inches from David's. "Did you kiss her?"

David assumed his former expression of deep deliberation. "Now that you mention it, Ox, I believe that I did kiss her. But I assure you, my friend, that the kiss was purely platonic."

"Pla . . . what?"

"Platonic, Ox. It means Crystal and I are merely friends." If Ox only knew the half of it, he'd have been a dead man weeks ago.

Ox hung his head in grief and sighed. "I wish you hadn't a done that, Davey. Now I've got to pound on you for a while."

"Don't fret about it too much, Ox." David put his hand on Ox's shoulder in a gesture of consolation. "It's something that has to be done. I mean a guy can't go around kissing another guy's girl, can he? Even if it is platonic."

"No," Ox agreed, "I don't reckon he can."

"And Crystal is your girl, isn't she, Ox?"

Ox's eyes rounded, and a smile jumped out of his face. "Yep, Crystal is my girl, and she baked cornbread once and gave me some."

"And I kissed her, didn't I, Ox?"

Ox hung his head and pouted again. "Yeah, you kissed her, Davey."

David threw his arms up in a gesture of frustration and defeat. "Well, there you have it, Ox. You have to pound on me. You don't have a choice in the matter."

Ox nodded his head in agreement. "OK, Davey, if you say so." He reached out with his left hand and grabbed David by the shirtfront. "I'll try not to kill you too hard, Davey, cuz you're my friend." His right hand drew back like a twelve-pound sledgehammer about to make contact with a railroad spike.

David threw his hands up at the last moment. "Wait a minute, Ox. I just thought of something."

Ox paused. "What is it, Davey?"

David sighed. "That was a close one, Ox. You were almost guilty of a very serious breach of protocol."

Ox was dumbfounded. "What's a pro-to-col?"

"That means the rules, Ox. You almost broke the rules."

Ox's eyes widened, and his mouth hung open. "Ox always plays by the pro-to-col,

Davey. What do I need to do?"

David reached up and put his arm around the big man's shoulders. "Don't worry, Ox. We're friends. I wouldn't let you commit such a heinous oversight. The thing is, a boxing exhibition, such as we're about to put on here, could be considered a sporting event. Do you have a license to have a sporting event?"

Ox shook his head. "No, I don't got no license."

David's jaw dropped, and his eyes looked to jump out of their sockets. "No license? Ox, don't you know that without a license you could" — he lowered his voice to a whisper — "you could go to jail?"

Ox's eyes were twice their normal size. He had been to jail on occasion, and David knew that Ox had had a miserable time behind bars. The prospect of going back to jail terrified the giant man. "What do I do, Davey? Will you help me?"

"Don't worry, Ox," David reassured. "This is an easy fix. All you need to do is go down to City Hall and ask them for a license. They will know what you need. They issue them all the time."

The big man's sigh sounded like the wind blowing through the valleys of the Medicine Bow Mountains to the west. "Then once I get the license I can pound on you?" he asked anxiously.

"That's the protocol, Ox. Once you get the license you're free to pound on me."

Ox's meaty hand engulfed David's as he shook it vigorously. "Thanks, Davey, for not letting Ox go to jail. You're a good friend."

"That's what friends are for, Ox."

Ox began walking in the direction of City Hall, turning once to smile at David and wave goodbye.

CHAPTER THIRTY-THREE

Inside Frenchy's, David had just finished his lunch when Gabe Brockman walked in. Gabe was the stage agent for Wells Fargo. He walked over to David's table and stood facing him. He looked like a man on a mission, but Gabe always looked that way — high strung and anxious. Probably caused by all the responsibilities of managing the stage line.

"Good afternoon, Gabe. Have a seat, won't you?"

Gabe sat down while David called for Frenchy to bring over another coffee cup. Pouring a cup for Gabe, he pushed it over in front of him. "What's new with you?"

"Dave, do you have any plans for the next few days?"

"Nothing urgent, I suppose. Why? Do you need a hand with something?"

Gabe picked up the coffee cup in front of him and raised it to his lips. The steam rising from the cup burned the inside of his nose and left condensation on his mustache, which he absentmindedly wiped away with the back of his hand. He blew across the cup a bit before taking a sip. "This is my first cup of coffee today. I've been too dang busy to sit down and enjoy any of the stuff."

"Well, take your time and relax for a few minutes. Tell me what's on your mind when you're ready." David sat back and waited.

Gabe took another sip and then put the cup down on the table in front of him. "I need your help with something. You don't advertise it, but I know you're pretty good with that Colt you have under your coat."

David waited for Gabe to continue. He was hoping that the stage agent wasn't going to ask him to do what it sounded like he was working up to ask him. He didn't do gun work. He preferred making his living with cards. Poker and Faro were more fun and a lot less dangerous than slinging lead, although, there was a time in his life when he could have chosen that path. That path, though, was often a winding one that zigzagged its way across either side of the law and too often ended in an early retirement of a permanent nature.

Gabe continued, "I'd like you to ride shotgun on the morning stage to Fort Laramie. Two days there, two days back, and you're done."

"Why do you need a shotgun rider?"

"Have you ever heard of Lloyd Barta?"

David thought for a moment. "I can't say the name rings any bells for me. Who is he?"

Gabe frowned and looked a little sheepish. "He's the man suspected of trying to rob our stage twice now."

"Trying?"

"Unsuccessful both times. I'd like to stop him before he becomes successful."

"How do you know he will try to rob this stage?"

"Both attempts have been on the Fort Laramie stage, and each time it took place on the same spot on the road."

David thought for a few moments before speaking. "Gabe, you can go outside right now and in the next two minutes find a dozen guys who can shoot well enough to ride shotgun for you. Why are you asking me?"

Gabe sat with his elbows resting on the table. He bent closer as he answered. "Because I don't need someone who will shoot first and ask questions later. I need someone who will *refrain* from shooting unless it's absolutely necessary."

David's eyes narrowed as he looked at the

stage manager. Gabe's fidgeting told him that Gabe was holding something back. "That's a magnanimous attitude you have, considering this guy is trying to rob your stage."

Gabe looked around. "This is embarrassing for me, Dave, me being the stage agent and all." He paused for a moment and then continued, "Barta is my wife's uncle."

Dave chuckled and leaned forward to better hear what Gabe had to say. "That's interesting. Go on."

"He's not a bad guy. Hell, the old coot is sixty-eight years old. He was a hell of a mountain man in his day. He even knew that negro Crow war chief, Jim Beckwourth."

"It sounds like he led an interesting life. How did he take to robbing your stage?"

"You mean *trying* to rob my stage," Gabe corrected.

"All right, *trying* to rob your stage."

Gabe tested his coffee, which had cooled enough for him to take a gulp. "I think that he got bored. He's been living with us out at the ranch for the last year or so. Most of the time he sits on the front porch, rocking and telling his stories to anyone that will slow down long enough to listen.

"One day, about three weeks ago, he got

up off of his rocker, went to the barn, and saddled up that old mule of his and rode off without saying a word. Maggie's worried sick about him.

"Then, two weeks ago, our Fort Laramie stage was stopped about halfway to the home station by an old man on a mule. The driver's description fits Lloyd. He says that he carried a long barrel .50 caliber Henry, which is the same rifle Lloyd carries. He demanded all the 'money and jewels' on board. The driver thought that was kind of funny." Gabe drained his coffee and poured another cup.

"You said that the robbery was unsuccessful. I take it your driver refused to follow his demands."

"He didn't need to. After Lloyd made his demands, a jackrabbit darted in front of that old mule, and he starts bucking and kicking. It was all Lloyd could do to hold on, so my driver simply drove away. He said he was half a mile down the road, and he could still hear Lloyd cussing out that mule."

"What happened the second time he tried to rob you?"

"That's an even stranger story. He stopped the stage and made the same demands. Well, there were no passengers that time, only a mail pouch, so the driver told him that there wasn't any money. Then Lloyd says, 'No money, huh? Well, do you got anything to eat?' The driver says that he has some jerky and biscuits. 'Oh, I ain't had a biscuit in a coon's age.' Lloyd says. So my driver pulls out his lunch, and Lloyd pulls out a bottle of whiskey from his saddlebags. Before you know it, the two of them are chatting, sharing lunch, and reminiscing about the old days."

David sat back in his chair and smiled. The old guy sounded harmless enough. "I think you're right. It sounds like he just wants some excitement in his life."

"If you could talk to him," Gabe implored. "You have an easy way of talking to people. I think he would come back home. It would sure mean a lot to Maggie and me if you would try."

David could hear the desperation in his voice. He didn't have any other pressing business. The thought that some gun happy passenger might put a bullet in the old guy didn't set right with him. But David had a feeling Gabe was still holding out on him. There was something else going on. "That still doesn't explain why you need a gun. Tell me what you aren't telling me."

Gabe looked nervous. "All right, but you have to keep this between the two of us.

I've got the fort's quarterly payroll on this stage — close to twenty thousand dollars."

David whistled. "That's a tempting payday for a holdup man."

"That's the way I see it, too. And I have been hearing rumors that Cain Mason is in the area."

David was in the midst of taking a sip from his cup when Gabe mentioned Cain Mason. He stopped with his cup frozen halfway to his mouth. The two men sat in silence for a long moment before David put his cup back down and spoke. "Where have these rumors been coming from?"

"I don't know, but there's been talk of him for about a week now. Some say he robbed a Denver stage last month. He killed everyone on board, including two women passengers. I can't have something like that happen on my stage." The stage agent was visibly worked up. "Having your stage robbed is bad enough for business, but people getting killed . . ." Gabe's hand shook as he tried to take another sip of his coffee, so he set the cup back down on the table. ". . . well, that's a whole other kind of bad."

"Doesn't the army usually send an escort to accompany their payroll? Shouldn't that be protection enough?"

"That's usually the case, but the fort is stretched thin right now. It seems the Sioux are making some unfriendly gestures to the north and east of the fort."

"All right, Gabe, you've got yourself a shotgun rider."

Gabe finished his coffee and stood to his feet. "I really appreciate this, Dave." Gabe looked relieved, as though a heavy burden had been lifted from his shoulders. He smiled as the two men shook hands. "The stage pulls out at six a.m. sharp."

David moaned. He didn't even know there was a six in the morning. "All right, I'll be there."

Gabe left, and David settled up his bill with Frenchy. He was about to turn and leave when the front door burst open. There stood Ox, grinning from ear to ear and waving a piece of paper. "He gave it to me, Davey. The man at city hall gave me the license."

"Damn," David whispered. "How in the hell did he do that?"

Ox walked over, grinning like a mule eating briars, and handed David a piece of paper he clutched proudly in his meaty hands. David read the paper out loud.

"This license is issued to Ox for the purpose of beating the tar out of David

Gaines, who bluffed with a pair of eights and took twenty dollars from me in poker last night. I hope you break his nose."

It was signed, Harold Smoot, City Clerk.

David had forgotten that Smoot worked at City Hall and that he was a poor loser at cards. He made a show of reading it over carefully. "*License* . . . that's good . . . *issued to Ox* . . . that's all in order."

A look of concern crossed David's face. "What's this?"

"What's wrong, Davey? I got the license like you said."

"Indeed you did, Ox. You did an outstanding job. The best license I've ever seen."

Ox smiled. "Can I pound on you now, Davey?" he said, eager to get on with the fight.

"Almost, Ox. There's just one more thing that needs to be done."

"What's that?"

"Well, this license isn't notarized, Ox. You have to get it notarized before it is official and legal."

The corners of Ox's mouth turned down in a frown. Then his eyes narrowed. "Are you pulling Ox's leg, Davey? Do I really got to do that?"

"It's protocol, Ox."

"Oh, all right then." Ox snatched the paper out of David's hands, clearly frustrated. "This here pounding is sure taking a lot longer than I thought it would."

David tried to console the big man. "That's always the case when dealing with city government, Ox. It's easy to get bogged down in all the red tape. But don't be discouraged. Keep your chin up. The wheels of government bureaucracy grind slowly, but they do indeed grind."

"But how do I get it notarized, Davey?"

David walked Ox to the doorway of Frenchy's, and the two of them stepped outside into the afternoon sun. "You take this license back to City Hall and tell them that you need to get it notarized . . . just don't go to the same man as before," David added. "He only issues licenses. He doesn't do the notarizing."

"Then we will be able to have our fight?"

"Then we will be able to have one hell of a pounding."

"All right, Davey." Ox was his usual chipper self as he walked away down Eddy Street toward City Hall for the second time that day.

CHAPTER THIRTY-FOUR

David woke early with the taste of stale bourbon still in his mouth. He sat on the edge of his bed and waited for the fog in his head to clear. He sat with his elbows on his knees, cradling his throbbing head in his hands. It felt like a mule was trying to kick its way out of his skull. He spotted a bottle on the floor next to his bed where he must have dropped it sometime during the night. A mouthful, or two, of the amber liquid still remained, so he picked up the bottle and tilted it back, draining the contents. Ten minutes later, he was walking through the lobby of his hotel, on his way to the stage station, wishing he could turn around and sleep for about six more hours.

He stuck his head carefully out the front door of the Rollins House and looked around. Somehow, he had managed to avoid running into Ox the previous evening after he had sent him back to City Hall to get his "license" notarized. He was hoping to slip out of town on the stage without a confrontation with the big man. Satisfied Ox was not in sight, David stepped out and proceeded to make his way up Sixteenth Street toward the stage station.

The sun had barely broken the plain of the eastern horizon. The air was cool on his face, but, this time of the year, David had seen it snow at night and reach the eighties during the day. He yawned, trying to recall the last time he had been up this early.

He carried his carpet bag, which contained a fresh shirt and a change of underclothes, as well as some jerky and a copy of the book *Roughing It.* David had met the author — a man named Clemens — in Nevada a few years back.

It took him about five minutes to walk to the Wells Fargo station. There were two men and a woman boarding the stage. Gabe Brockman stood to the side talking to the driver. David walked up to the pair, set his bag down on the boardwalk, stretched his arms, and yawned. "Good morning, Gabe. I can't believe I let you talk me into getting up at this ungodly hour."

Gabe smiled. "Not much of an early bird, are you, Gaines?"

"I thought the only six o'clock was in the

evening. I didn't know there was another one for the morning."

"I appreciate you riding along on this trip." Gabe introduced the driver. "This is Percy. He's made this run dozens of times. Percy, this is David Gaines. He's the shotgun rider I was telling you about."

"Glad to meet you, Percy."

"Likewise, Mr. Gaines."

Percy was a bowlegged, skinny old gent in his late sixties. He had bright-blue eyes that jumped out from beneath bushy, white eyebrows and a walrus mustache that completely overgrew his mouth. He had a coiled bullwhip in his right hand.

"Percy, were you the driver during the last two holdup attempts?"

"I sure was." Percy pushed his hat back on his head and spit a stream of tobacco juice into the dusty road. "I can't say that either time was much of a holdup attempt. I've been held up before. Been shot at by bandits and chased by Indians a-plenty. I don't think Barta meant any harm. He never put up a fuss about not getting any money. I think he's just bored and lonely, is all."

"You're probably right about that, Percy," Gabe answered. "But there's no sense in taking any chances, especially with our

308

'special' cargo."

"Speaking of that," said David, lowering his voice, "have you loaded the money box yet?"

"That'll be the last thing we load before we leave. It'll be tucked safely underneath my seat." Percy nodded confidently and winked at David.

"Good." David took a cigar from his inside coat pocket, bit off the end, and struck a match to it. "Now, I'd like to see a map of the route, if you have one handy."

"Sure," said Gabe, "I've got one inside the office."

The three men walked into the Wells Fargo station office. David was impressed with the tidiness and orderly fashion with which Gabe conducted business. He had a large map of the Wyoming Territory on his office wall with the various stage routes marked. They walked over to where the map hung, and Gabe indicated the route the stage would take. Fort Laramie was about one hundred miles from Cheyenne. It was a two-day journey with an overnight stop at a home station at about the halfway point.

Gabe pointed out a route that went roughly north from Cheyenne to Chugwater Creek. Then they followed the creek north by northeast to the Laramie River.

From there they followed the Laramie east to the fort. "There are three swing stations between here and the home station on Chugwater Creek. Then three more between Chugwater and the fort."

David turned to Percy. "Percy, can you show me on this map where Barta made his holdup attempts?"

"Right here past Horse Creek." Percy pointed to the spot on the map. "It's about halfway to the overnight stop at the Chug-water Station."

David stepped up to examine the map more closely. "What's this?" He pointed to a geological feature that was marked on the map.

"That's a hill. Not much of a hill, but steep enough that I take the stage around it and not over it."

"So, the stage approaches this hill from the south, then turns to go around the east side of it before heading north again?"

"That's right," Percy replied. "There are actually two hills, one after the other, that I have to snake my way between." He pointed them out on the map. "I go around the east side of this first one, then I turn west to skirt the next. It slows us down a bit. It's probably why Barta chose that spot to wait for us."

"And where, exactly, does Barta wait for you?"

Percy pointed to a spot on the map that was on the north side of the first hill. "He waits for us here. I guess he's trying to surprise us as we come around."

"All right . . . that's good. Here's what I want you to do." David traced on the map with his finger as he explained his plan to Percy and Gabe. "After you cross Horse Creek, I want you to stop the stage on the south side of that hill, just before you continue east. I'll give you further instructions at the time."

Percy nodded. "All right, Mr. Gaines, if that's what you want."

Gabe pulled a watch out of his vest pocket to check the time. "You better get a move on, Percy."

Gabe walked over to the wall safe that was behind his desk. Spinning the knob, he dialed the combination. The handle made a metallic "click" as he pushed down and swung open the door. He pulled out the money box and set it on his desk with a thud. "Be careful with that," he said with a sigh. "There are a lot of soldiers up at the fort depending on that money."

"We'll get it there safe," David promised.

Percy grabbed the handles on each side of

the chest and carried it out to the stage, where he tucked it under his seat. David followed him outside. A moment later, Gabe stepped outside as well. He was holding a Remington ten-gauge coach gun.

"You may need this, but I hope not." He handed the shotgun to David.

David, in turn, handed it to Percy, who had climbed up on the seat and was untying the reins. "You keep this up with you. I'm handier with a revolver than with that scattergun. Besides, I'm gonna ride inside for the first leg and try to catch a nap. This early morning routine is for the birds."

Percy laughed. "Would you like a wakeup call?"

"That depends. If I'm dreaming of blonds, wake me up in an hour. If I'm dreaming of brunettes, wake me up in two hours."

Percy smiled and said, "What if you're dreaming of redheads?"

"If I'm dreaming of redheads, you better let me sleep," David replied. "I'll need my rest."

He climbed inside the stage and pulled the doors shut behind him.

Percy let loose the brake and gave the reins a shake to urge the six-horse team down the road. The creaking of the Concord's leather braces and the swaying motion of the stage soon had David dreaming of redheads.

CHAPTER THIRTY-FIVE

David woke up with a jolt when the stage traversed a small incline into Lodgepole Creek and climbed up the other side. The first swing station was on the north side of the creek, so the stage pulled into the yard.

Percy got down and opened the door to speak to the passengers. "We've got a fifteen-minute stop, folks, while we swap out the horses. You might want to stretch your legs. There's privies in the back of the station, and there's a water pump in the station house if you need to wet your whistle. Could be old Jim's got a pot of coffee brewing inside as well." He proceeded to help the station hand unhitch the horses and hitch up the new team, while the passengers stepped down out of the stage one at a time.

David checked his watch. It was eight-thirty. They had made good time.

He ducked his head as he exited the Concord coach and stepped down onto the running board. He was the last passenger off of the stage. The morning sun was bright, so he shaded his eyes to have a look around.

The swing station wasn't much more than a single room soddie station house and a wooden barn and corral to keep the extra string of horses that the stage would be exchanging. Swing stations were built every twelve to thirteen miles along a stage route. A "home" station was built at the end of a day's journey. At the home station, the passengers could get a hot meal and some shut-eye before continuing on their way.

The other passengers had either made their way back to the privies or had gone into the station house for a cup of coffee, so David went over to talk to Percy, who was busy helping old Jim harness up the new string of horses to the stage. From where he was standing he was able to watch the stage, keeping an eye on the strongbox.

"Well, Percy, we made good time."

Percy finished checking a buckle on the breeching of one of the lead horses, then checked the position of the sun in the sky. "Yep, we did. It's a nice morning, and the horses like to run when the sun is low in the sky. We'll slow down a mite once it warms up."

"How much farther is it to that hill we were looking at on the map?" David wasn't sure how much Jim knew about their situation, so he thought it best to speak in non-specific terms.

"Horse Creek is our next swing station, then I'd say it was about five or six miles past there. So figure another four to five hours."

David turned to the old Negro station hand. "Is that coffee of yours worth drinking, Jim?"

The white-haired gent smiled, revealing two rows of crooked teeth. "Well, I wouldn't have vouched none for it when I set it to boiling this morning, but it should be strong enough now to set a post in."

David smiled back. "That's the way I like it."

He made his way toward the soddie but paused when the door opened and the female passenger stepped outside. She was a young woman in her early twenties, pretty with long, blond hair that hung down in a braid beneath her bonnet.

David removed his hat, "Excuse me, Miss. My name is David Gaines. I apologize for not introducing myself earlier."

She held out her hand. "No apology is necessary, Mr. Gaines. My name is Elizabeth Hall. My husband is Lieutenant Christopher Hall. He's stationed at Fort Laramie, where I'm going to join him."

David took her hand and bowed. "It's a pleasure to meet you, Mrs. Hall."

"The pleasure is mine, Mr. Gaines. I hope you are refreshed after your nap."

David felt the color rise in his cheeks as he flushed. "I'm afraid that was rather rude of me. I'm not much of a morning person."

"Don't be ridiculous, Mr. Gaines. I may have dozed off myself before we arrived here, so we're even."

"Mrs. Hall, I've played worse odds than 'even' many times, and I usually come out ahead."

She was curious. "So you're a gambler, Mr. Gaines?"

"I play a lot of cards, but I rarely gamble. If you'll excuse me, a cup of coffee would go down good right about now."

"If you are planning on drinking that coffee, Mr. Gaines, you are more of a gambler than you realize," she said laughing and walking back to the stage.

Ten minutes later they had resumed their seats onboard as Percy urged the horses forward toward their next stop at the Horse Creek station.

CHAPTER THIRTY-SIX

With only four passengers on a stage that could carry nine inside, there was plenty of elbow room for David and the others to relax and enjoy the journey. Once under way, David introduced himself to the two male passengers.

The younger of the two couldn't have been more than eighteen or nineteen years old. He was about the same size and build as David. He was a private in the Army, stationed at Fort Laramie, and had been granted an emergency leave to visit his dying mother in Cheyenne. He reached across the stage to shake hands with David, who was seated on the opposite seat next to Mrs. Hall. "I'm pleased to meet you, Mr. Gaines. I'm Michael O'Rourke."

"I'm pleased to meet you as well, Private. I'm sorry to hear about the passing of your mother."

"Thank you, sir. I appreciate that." A

lump formed in his throat, and his eyes moistened as he continued. "She was only forty-four years old. She got pneumonia and died before I could get home to say good-bye."

David felt pity for the young man. "You have my heartfelt condolences. I am sure your mother was proud of your decision to join the Army."

The private bit his lower lip and nodded his head.

David turned his attention to the other man seated next to the private. In his late fifties, he was slightly taller than David and was a burly man of about two hundred pounds. He had bushy, black muttonchops flecked with grey. He wore a dark sack coat with light grey trousers and had a black bowler hat perched on top of his head. A pair of wire-rimmed spectacles gave him a studious look. David had the feeling they had met before, but he couldn't place him. The man introduced himself as Gideon Longacre.

"Have we met before, Mr. Longacre? You look familiar."

Longacre shook his head. "I don't believe so, Mr. Gaines."

"What is it you do for a living, if you don't mind me asking?"

"Not at all, Mr. Gaines. I'm a writer . . . a biographer of the famous and infamous." He reached into his jacket pocket and pulled out a small book, which he handed to David. "Here is a copy of my latest book."

David looked at the cover: *Cain Mason, Scourge of the West.* It was published by Beadles and Adams and written by Professor Gideon Longacre. He flipped through the pages, reading sections of the biography. The book was full of accounts of robberies and murders that Professor Longacre attributed to Cain Mason. Well, now he knew where the rumors had been coming from, David thought as he handed the book back to the professor.

"That's fascinating, Professor. Tell me, how do you get your information for your biographies?" David asked.

The professor returned the book to his pocket. "I gather most of the information from accounts written in newspapers across the country. But, for this particular book, I was fortunate enough to be able to interview Mr. Mason as well."

Mrs. Hall recoiled at the thought. "You actually met and spoke with that monster, Professor?"

"Indeed I did, Mrs. Hall." The professor brimmed with self-satisfaction as the passengers on the stage looked at him, waiting for him to tell his story.

"Where was that at, Professor?" David inquired.

"That was in Salina, Kansas, back in '71. I was eating breakfast at a local restaurant when a gentleman ran into the dining room. He was pointing up the street, talking excitedly, and I soon discovered the reason for his agitation. It seemed the sheriff had managed to capture Cain Mason and had incarcerated him in the town jail. I had been contemplating a series of books on outlaws of the western states, so I asked Mr. Mason for an interview. To my surprise and delight, he was more than happy to oblige."

"But weren't you frightened?" asked Mrs. Hall.

"Not at all. In spite of his reputation — and make no mistake about it, the man is a cold-blooded killer — I found him to be an educated man, congenial and well mannered. He was rather willing to talk and held back nothing of his exploits. It was several months later, after my book had gone to the printers, that I learned that Cain Mason had killed a deputy and escaped from jail."

David listened as the professor continued to give Mrs. Hall a history of his interview with Cain Mason. The professor was quick to share some of the outlaw's atrocities that never made it into his book but added, "There are certain things, madam, which could not be put into print, due to their heinous nature."

The professor's story didn't make sense, and David couldn't shake the feeling he had met the man before. "I'm curious, Professor Longacre," David inquired, "I have heard that Cain Mason served time in prison in Philadelphia for killing his wife and brother."

"That is correct."

"I read somewhere that he got into a fight in prison and has a scar above his left eye. Is that true?"

Professor Longacre locked eyes with David for several seconds before answering. "That is all true, Mr. Gaines, except the scar is above his right eye, not his left."

The two men stared across the stage at each other for what seemed like a long minute while no one spoke. The professor broke the silence and asked, "What about you, Mr. Gaines? What is your occupation?"

Mrs. Hall spoke up. "Mr. Gaines plays cards for a living but doesn't consider himself to be a gambler. Isn't that right, Mr. Gaines?"

"How is that possible? Aren't all games of

chance a gamble?" asked Private O'Rourke.

"That's the thing in a nutshell, Private. I don't believe in chance. People talk about chance as though it were a person or a force that could produce an effect. In actuality, chance is nothing more than a way of expressing mathematical probabilities. We toss a coin into the air, and we say that there is a fifty-fifty chance that it will land heads up."

The young man looked confused. "I'm not sure I get your meaning."

David pulled a deck of cards out of his inside coat pocket and spread them out face up on the bench between them. They appeared to be randomly scattered with no particular order to them. "As you can all see, this is an ordinary deck of cards."

He then gathered up the cards and shuffled them, dealing one card face down on the seat. "Now tell me, Private: what are the odds of this card being an ace?"

The young man thought for a moment. "Well, there are four aces in a fifty-two card deck, so that's one in thirteen."

"Correct. Expressed as a percentage we would say that there is roughly an eight percent 'chance' that this card is an ace. Those aren't very good odds." He turned the card over to expose a two of diamonds.

He returned the card to the deck. Shuffling them a second time, he placed the deck face down on the seat.

"Now, we have exactly the same odds that the top card will be an ace — one in thirteen."

They all agreed.

"Private, would you turn over the top card?"

The young man reached over and turned over the top card as directed, revealing the ace of clubs. "How did you do that?" he said, wide eyed.

Mrs. Hall squealed with delight and clapped her hands.

The professor was more skeptical. "That could be luck," he sneered.

"Luck is just another word for chance, Professor. And, I told you, I don't believe in chance." David reached down and turned over the next three cards on the top of the deck, revealing the remaining three aces.

Mrs. Hall and Private O'Rourke both sat motionless in their seats with their jaws hanging low. The professor glared. "So what you are telling us, Mr. Gaines, is that you're not a gambler, you're a cheat."

David glared back with equal intensity. "I never cheat at cards, Professor. I did this only to illustrate a point."

"And what, exactly, is your point?" the professor asked.

"My point is this: what we refer to as 'chance' is nothing more than an accumulation of any number of variables that are in play to affect an outcome. If a player manipulates the cards, as I have done, then that would be cheating. But there are many other variables that can influence the outcome of a game."

"Such as?" asked Mrs. Hall.

"Such as knowledge of the odds, for one thing. For instance, I know that in five-card stud, the odds are one in six hundred and ninety-three that you will draw a full house. I also know there are thirty-six different possibilities for a straight flush."

Private O'Rourke laughed uncomfortably. "Sounds like I'm back in school again. That's too much arithmetic for me."

Mrs. Hall was fascinated. "Please do go on, Mr. Gaines. What are some of the other variables?"

"They are almost too many to mention: What time of day do you choose to play? Are you well rested? Have you eaten? What is the weather like?"

"Would you have us believe that you can control the weather, Mr. Gaines?" asked Professor Longacre.

"Of course not. But if it is hot out, and you choose a seat at the table where you have a breeze from an open window, and your opponent is sweating and uncomfortable, he may be distracted. You can use that to your advantage."

"I see," said Mrs. Hall. "I never viewed poker as anything more than a silly game, but you seem to have made almost a science out of it."

David continued, "One of the most important variables is to know your opponent. What are his betting habits? What are his 'tells'? Learn to read his facial expressions and his body language. The old adage is that you play your opponent, not your cards."

"I imagine you've become an adept reader of people," Mrs. Hall replied.

"Some people are easy to read, Mrs. Hall. Some people are more difficult."

David glanced at the professor, who turned away and stared out of his window in silence with his arms folded across his chest.

The stage rolled on across the gently rolling eastern plains of Wyoming, while the sun rose higher in the sky. A pronghorn antelope appeared about fifty yards in front of the horses and kept pace with the team for a few seconds before darting across their path and disappearing down a small wash.

The passengers passed the morning hours as best they could. Mrs. Hall told endless stories about her husband, the lieutenant, and his brave exploits. It seemed as though the young officer had single-handedly tamed the frontier, subduing hostile Indians, while garnering the love and adoration of his men and undying respect of his superiors. During lulls in the conversation, they sat looking out of their windows at nothing much in particular. David read some from his book while Private O'Rourke dozed.

In this manner, the morning hours slipped by peacefully for the stage and her passengers. Then, sometime before noon, the driver rapped on the side of the coach with his bullwhip and shouted down, "Horse Creek station ahead."

CHAPTER THIRTY-SEVEN

The Horse Creek swing station seemed to be an exact copy of the previous stop, even to the placement of the outhouses. However, this station seemed a bit tidier than the one on Lodgepole Creek, with the aroma of tortillas and beans wafting out from the inside of the station house. There were also pies cooling on the sill of an open window. Horse Creek being the noon stop, the passengers got a full thirty-minute rest and had the option of paying for a bite to eat before continuing on their way.

The station hand looked to be every bit as old as "Old" Jim, but he was a Mexican by the name of Jorge. He had bright eyes that were overhung by bushy white eyebrows. He wore an oversized straw sombrero and a brightly colored wool serape.

The passengers went inside for a bite to eat. Percy followed them into the station house, carrying the money box, which was never out of his sight.

David approached Jorge and asked, "Have you seen any riders around today?"

Jorge had finished unhitching the last pair of horses and was leading them into the barn. He looked at David from underneath his sombrero as though he were deciding how much information to give him, and how much David might pay for it. On the western frontier, where you often went days without seeing anyone and your nearest neighbor might be miles away, information could be as valuable a commodity as silver and gold. David had learned that certain people — bartenders, liverymen, even the town drunk — were often adept at gathering information, and they traded in it like a merchant traded in dry goods.

"Maybe I see someone, *señor.* I am an old man. Sometimes it is hard to say what I see and what I only think that I see."

David smiled and flipped a silver coin into the air that he had already pulled out of his pocket. He knew how the game was played.

Jorge plucked the coin out of the air with unexpected agility and speed. He inspected the coin for a moment before slipping it inside his sleeve. "I see an old *gringo* on a mule pass by on the road." He pointed at the road to the west that the stage had been following.

"When was this?"

"Yesterday afternoon. I see him ride by before, but he never comes into the station. He is just a crazy old gringo, but I think he is harmless. I think maybe his mule is more crazy."

"Gracias, amigo." David turned to the station house for a slice of pie and some coffee.

He had only gotten a few steps when Jorge replied, "I think that the other one is not so harmless."

David turned. "The other what?"

Jorge pointed to the east. "The other rider. I see him this morning. He stays to the low ground. He thinks that Jorge doesn't see him, but Jorge sees."

"Can you tell me anything else about him? Was he young? Was he old? What kind of horse did he ride?"

Jorge shook his head. "It is hard to say. Jorge's eyes not so young anymore."

David reached into his pocket for another coin, but Jorge waved him off.

"I think he was another gringo. Not too old. Riding a paint and leading a second horse."

"What direction was he headed?" asked David.

The old Mexican turned and pointed to the north.

"You have been a lot of help, Jorge. I appreciate it."

"De nada." Jorge started for the barn and then turned to face David again. "There is one other thing that Jorge can tell you. This other man, *señor,* there is something peculiar about the way that he sits on his horse."

"What do you mean by peculiar?"

Jorge looked down at the ground and shook his head. He seemed to be hesitating. David wasn't sure if he was struggling to find the right words in English or if he was uncertain about what he saw. After a moment, he looked up at David again and said, "Jorge cannot be certain, *señor,* but Jorge thinks that the hombre was actually a *mujer.*"

"A woman?" exclaimed David.

"Si, señor."

Now, why would a woman be riding alone out here? He thanked Jorge for the information.

"Vaya con Dios, mi amigo," replied the old man as he turned toward the barn.

David made his way to the station house. He definitely needed a cup of coffee now. This new information was going to require some pondering.

CHAPTER THIRTY-EIGHT

It was almost two o'clock in the afternoon when Percy pulled back hard on the reins and brought the stage to a stop with a sway and a creak of the leather braces. "Here's your stop, Mr. Gaines."

David climbed down from the seat he had taken alongside Percy when they left the Horse Creek station.

The three passengers inside the coach stuck their heads out of the windows. "Why have we stopped?" asked Mrs. Hall. "Is there anything the matter?"

"It's nothing to worry about, Mrs. Hall," David assured her.

"You're not getting off here, are you? There's nothing but sagebrush and prairie dogs," exclaimed Private O'Rourke.

"I'll rejoin the stagecoach momentarily. I assure you, there is no need for alarm."

Percy climbed down from his seat on the coach and motioned to David. The two men walked a few yards in front of the horses.

"What's your plan, Mr. Gaines?"

"Well, Barta seems to be a creature of habit, so if he sticks to his pattern, he should be waiting for you on the north side of this hill. He will be facing east, because that's the direction the stage will be coming from. So I'm going to make my way around the west side of this hill and try to come up behind him. Give me about twenty minutes before you set out again. That should give me enough time to get in place."

Percy thumbed his hat back on his head. He looked troubled. "I sure would hate to see him get hurt. I don't think he means any harm. He's more of a nuisance than a threat."

"Don't worry, Percy. No one is going to get hurt today. I'm here to have a talk with him, that's all."

"All right, Mr. Gaines, I'll catch up with you directly. Good luck."

David made his way around the west side of the hill. The surrounding sedimentary rock had eroded away to leave a granite protrusion that rose one hundred feet above the prairie. The bottom of the hill was littered with rocks and boulders, some of them as tall as he was. Rattlesnakes were abundant in this part of the country, so David kept his eyes peeled as he navigated the perimeter of the hill.

Rounding an especially large boulder, he found himself standing on the rutted path of the stagecoach. There in the road about fifty feet ahead of him was an old man on a mule, facing away from him, peering down the road to where the stagecoach would be coming.

Lloyd Barta sat on his mule in the middle of the road, waiting for the stage to arrive. He had no real plans to rob the stage. He just wanted people to know that he was still a force to be reckoned with. He knew that his niece's husband, who ran the stage line, was a stickler for schedules and being on time and such, so he knew when to be there waiting for them.

He had been a mountain man in his youth and had trapped beaver and fought Indians alongside some of the greats — men like Kit Carson, Jim Bridger, Hugh Glass, and Philo Gaines. He had hunted grizzly bear and buffalo and had survived Rocky Mountain blizzards, prairie fires, and flash floods.

His old, grey mule, Harley, lowered his head and bit the flower off of a prickly pear cactus that was growing in the middle of the road. Lifting his tail, Harley farted and then turned his head to look back at Lloyd as if to say, "Top that, if you can."

Lloyd wrinkled his nose. "Harley, what have you been eating, you flea-bitten bag of bones? You're rotten enough to knock a buzzard off a buffalo corpse. If it's a showdown you want, then you better be up to the challenge."

Shifting his weight to one side, Lloyd lifted his leg and let loose with a fart that reverberated like thunder off of his leather saddle. Grinning with pride, he said, "How do you like them apples?"

Harley pinned his ears back and shook his head violently.

"Whew! That's about as rancid as it gets. I don't think either one of us thought this through all the way. We better relocate upwind a bit."

He kicked his heels into the sides of the mule and clicked his tongue. When Harley had moved ahead a few feet, Lloyd pulled back on the reins and said, "Whoa there, Harley. That should be good enough as long as you behave yourself and don't go provoking me again."

In response, Harley turned his head to look up at Lloyd, lifted his tail, and farted a second time.

"It sounds like that mule of yours might be a bit colicky."

Lloyd froze at the sound of the voice behind him on the road. His hand tightened over the stock of the Henry rifle that rested across the saddle swell in front of him. Without turning around, he said, "I reckon he swallowed too much sand. This old crow bait will eat just about anything."

Lloyd expected a bullet in the back at any moment, but, oddly enough, he found himself more invigorated than frightened at the prospect.

"If you're planning on robbing me, mister, you're barking up the wrong tree. I spent the last of my coin on whiskey more than a week ago. I reckon there's enough left in the bottle to wet your whistle if you're thirsty. Mind if I turn around?"

The voice behind him answered, "That's fine by me, Lloyd. Just promise to keep that Henry out of play. You and I need to have a conversation."

Lloyd was surprised by the use of his name, but he turned Harley around to face the man who had managed to sneak up behind him. The sun had started its descent toward the mountains to the west, and Lloyd had to squint to get him into focus.

Lloyd kept a firm grip on the stock of his rifle but didn't lift it off of the saddle, as he faced the man in front of him. He was a rather short, thin man, dressed in a black frock coat with black trousers and a matching grey, single-breasted vest. On his head, he wore a black bowler hat. The thing that bothered Lloyd the most, however, was the single action Colt the man held in his hand. Lloyd could tell by the comfortable and at-ease way that he held the gun that the stranger was no novice when it came to gunplay.

"You seem to have me at a disadvantage, mister. How do you know my name? And where's your horse? You're not a-foot, are you?"

"I'll answer your questions, but tell me first . . . if I put my gun away, are we going to have a civilized discussion, or am I going to have trouble with you?"

Lloyd lifted his Henry rifle. David tensed and leveled the Colt at Barta. Then Lloyd slid the rifle into the boot that hung on the left side of his saddle. "I reckon I can be civilized enough for conversation . . . if you're not too long winded, that is," Lloyd replied. "Who are you?"

David holstered the Colt. He sat down on a boulder on the side of the road and took a cigar out of his inside coat pocket. Biting off the end and spitting it out, he lit it up and took a long draw. "Can I offer you a cigar?" he asked.

"Never took up the habit," Lloyd replied. "But I'll take some chawin' tobacca if you got any."

David smiled. "Sorry. I never took up *that* habit."

Lloyd remained stoic. "Well, we're off to a good start, aren't we?"

David took another draw on his cigar and exhaled slowly as he considered the old man on the mule. He wore an old, beat-up, open-brimmed slouch hat with an eagle feather sticking out of a beaded Indian headband. He had shoulder length, white hair with a beard to match. He had on a buckskin shirt and trousers, and a pair of leather moccasins on his feet. Ornately decorated botas covered his calves from the tops of his moccasins to below the knee. An equally ornate belt around his waist held a sheath with a Bowie knife.

"My name is David Gaines. I've come here to talk . . ."

Lloyd cut him off in mid-sentence, "I knew a fellow named Gaines once. We spent some time up on the Yellowstone trapping beaver and trading with the Crow. That must have been about — oh, thirty years ago, I reckon. He was a hell of a mountain man, name of Philo Gaines. I heard he went back East and married a gal and had some youngins. Is he your pa?"

David hung his head and chuckled. He looked up again and said, "No. My father owns a saloon in Galena, Illinois. But as I was saying . . ."

"That's too bad." Lloyd interrupted again. "You kind of look like him, only you're scrawnier."

David ignored the remark. "As I was saying, I came here to talk to . . ."

"Come to think of it, it was more like thirty-five years ago. Yep . . . it was at least that long. I remember when . . ."

David drew his Colt and leveled it at Lloyd. "Are you going to let me get a word in? We're kind of working against the clock here."

Lloyd was taken aback by the sudden appearance of the gun in David's hand. "Ain't no need to be rude, young fella. You go ahead and say what you mean to say. I won't say another word."

David holstered his gun. "As I was saying, the stage line sent me out here to have a word or two with you."

Lloyd started to say something, but David held up his hand, and Lloyd relented.

David continued. "This business of trying to hold up the stage has to stop. You have been fortunate so far. No one has gotten hurt. But sooner or later there could be gunplay, and your niece is worried you might be injured."

"Have you talked to Maggie?"

"No, but I've spoken with her husband. He's the one who sent me out here to talk with you. He said she's worried about you, especially the way you up and disappeared."

Lloyd sat for a few moments without replying. He turned his head toward the north. In the distance, he could see a group of about a dozen antelope grazing on the prairie grass. He turned back to David and said, "I remember one winter . . ."

David sighed and shook his head in frustration.

"Now hear me out, son. This here is pertinent."

David shifted his position on the boulder he was sitting on. Taking another draw on his cigar, he waved to Lloyd to continue.

"As I was saying . . . I remember one winter on the Snake. A party of Shoshoni surprised me as I was midway across the river. I didn't even know they were there until I had an arrow in my leg. The arrow came from the side of the river I was making toward, so I turned my horse and spurred him back to the opposite shore.

More Indians came out of the trees on that shore as well. I aimed my rifle at the nearest brave and fired. I don't know if I hit him or not, because at that moment another arrow hit me in the shoulder. I dropped my rifle in the river and almost fell in after it, but I managed to hang on as my horse turned and splashed downriver as fast as he could go. Arrows were flying all around me. I had three of them caught in the folds of my buffalo robe. Just when I thought we were going to be able to outrun them, my horse caught an arrow in his neck. He reared up and fell over backward, dumping me in the icy waters of the Snake.

"Lucky for me, I floated downriver faster than those Shoshoni could follow. They got my packhorse and all my gear, as well as every dad-blasted plew I had trapped that winter, and I was having a good season, too.

"I managed to catch a low hanging branch, so I pulled myself out of the river. My whole body was numb, and I was shaking so bad I thought my bones would all come apart at the joints. The arrow in my leg had almost gone all the way through, so I snapped it in two, pushed it through the rest of the way, and pulled it out the other side."

David winced at the thought. "What about

the arrow in your shoulder?"

"The arrowhead's still in there. Never did get it removed."

"What did you do next?"

"I still had a piece of flint and my Bowie knife, so I was able to get a fire going. I got a fever from the cold, and then my wounds got infected. After a few days, the fever broke, and I got a mite stronger every day after that. It took me near a month, but I tracked down those Shoshoni and got every bit of my stuff back."

"Did you kill the Indians that jumped you?"

"I got every last one of them. But you know what? I never had any hard feelings toward them. They were just being Indians, doing what Indians do. And after I got my strength back and went after them, I was just being me, doing what I needed to do."

Lloyd stopped talking and looked north again. Some of the antelope had wandered down into a wash, and only a few of them could still be seen grazing. Lloyd wasn't looking at them anyway. He was looking down the corridor of time, reliving events and reacquainting himself with people who populated the memories that, for whatever reason, he cherished and held onto, like moss hangs onto a rotting tree stump.

342

There was sadness in the old mountain man's eyes when he turned back to face David and continued with his story.

"You know what, young fella? Even though I was half froze and delirious with fever, that's the most 'alive' I've ever been. Tracking those Shoshoni, I was being 'me.' I ain't been me in years."

As quickly as it had come, the sadness left his eyes, driven away by a staunch look of determination. Lloyd moved Harley a few paces closer to where David sat. With a mobility that was more characteristic of a man half his age, Lloyd pulled his rifle from the saddle boot and brought it to his shoulder, aiming it directly at David. "I'm not goin' back to that rockin' chair, and I ain't sitting in no jail cell either. So, if you want to swap lead with me, you just go ahead and make your play."

David's cigar had burned down to a stub, so he rubbed out the tip on the boulder he sat on. He tossed the stub into the rocks. "I'm afraid you misunderstand my intentions, Lloyd," he said as he stood to his feet, brushing the dust from the back of his pants.

He walked up alongside Harley and, placing his hands on his hips, stared up at Lloyd, who still had the Henry rifle aimed at him. "I didn't come here to take you back with me. I came here to offer you a job."

Lloyd lowered the rifle slowly. He wasn't sure he had heard correctly. Lines of bewilderment creased his brow as he replied, "Come again?"

"You're too good of a man to spend your final years chained to a rocking chair. I'm here to offer you a job with the stage line."

"What kind of a job?"

"Shotgun rider."

"You think you can keep me from robbin' the stage by offerin' me a job ridin' shotgun? Isn't that kinda like putting the fox in charge of the hen house?"

"I'm not offering you the job to keep you from robbing the stage. I'm offering you the job because I need your help. I have reason to believe that, before this day is over, someone is going to try to rob the stage in earnest . . . no offense," he added.

During the next couple of minutes, David laid it out to Lloyd: the payroll for the fort, the rumors of Cain Mason being in the area, the lone rider that Jorge had seen the previous evening.

When Percy brought the wagon around the east side of the hill and turned it along the dusty road back toward the west, he could see two men in the road ahead of him. One was on an old grey mule. The other was standing next to him on the road. The two men were shaking hands.

CHAPTER THIRTY-NINE

The stage pulled into the Bear Creek swing station about three thirty in the afternoon. David had ridden inside the coach, while Barta sat next to Percy on the driver's seat. The two old-timers exchanged stories about their younger days, and Barta embraced his position as a shotgun rider, holding the coach gun across his lap. The old mountain man would put more energy into protecting the stage than he had ever invested in trying to rob it.

Harley had provided a bit of comic relief for the passengers. When David asked Barta what he wanted to do with the mule, Barta said, "Just turn him loose. He'll keep up with us. He knows that I'm the only one that'll put up with his shenanigans."

When the stage took off, it was just as Barta had said. Harley ran right alongside. Occasionally he would veer off the road to examine some bit of sagebrush or prickly pear; then, just as quick, he would be back running with the stage, usually staying so close to the old mountain man that Barta complained about the smell every time Harley belched or passed gas. "He's half mule, half jackrabbit, and half lap dog," Barta told everyone.

The talk inside the stagecoach for the past hour had been all about Cain Mason, and David was convinced that something was in the works. He believed that the stage was going to be held up, maybe tonight, maybe early tomorrow. He didn't think it would happen much past the overnight stop on Chugwater Creek, because the thief, or thieves, would want to wait until the stage was equal distance between the police in Cheyenne and the army at Fort Laramie. That would give them the greatest amount of time before anyone could be notified and begin pursuit.

The stop at Bear Creek was uneventful. The passengers took a few minutes to stretch their legs or visit the outhouse while the horses were swapped out.

David noticed Professor Longacre standing in the shade of the coach. Pulling a cigar out of his coat pocket, he walked over to where the professor had just lit a cigarette.

"Mind if I get a light from you?" David asked.

The professor cupped the lit match in his hands and held it out for David. "What's your business at Fort Laramie?" asked the professor. "If you don't mind me asking."

David rolled the smoke around in his mouth and exhaled slowly. "I don't have any business there," he replied. "I was only along to deliver a message to Mr. Barta." David didn't see any reason to tell anyone about the twenty thousand dollars tucked up under the driver's seat.

"What about you, Professor? Are you thinking of enlisting?" David asked with a grin.

The professor huffed. "Hardly," he replied. "I'm considering writing a book about army life on the frontier. So you could say that I'm on a research trip." He took a draw from his cigarette and knocked the ashes from the tip. They floated down and landed on his knee, so he reached down to brush them away.

"Have any of your research trips ever taken you to Philadelphia?"

The professor's head jerked up. He looked at David and then looked down as he continued brushing the ashes from his knee. He stood up and took a long draw from his cigarette, then shook his head and replied, "No . . . no, I've never been to Philadelphia. Why do you ask?"

David had been playing cards for far too long not to be able to tell when someone was lying. "Oh, no particular reason," he replied. "It's an interesting city. You should check it out sometime when you get a chance."

David started to walk away but turned to ask the professor another question. "Tell me something, Professor. You're the expert on Cain Mason. Do you think he's in the area?"

"That's hard to say, Mr. Gaines, but I hope not. The man is a cold-blooded killer . . . an animal without conscience."

"Thank you, Professor." David turned to walk away.

"I'll tell you one thing more, Mr. Gaines," the professor added. "If Cain Mason does show up, give him whatever he wants. Don't try to stop him. Don't get in his way. If you try being a hero, then you'll die. We might all die."

A small grin curled the corners of David's mouth. "Don't worry, Professor. There are no heroes in my family. They're mostly gamblers and saloon owners."

Percy and Barta were calling the passengers back to the stage to load up for the last leg of the journey for the day. The Chugwater home station was about fifteen miles away. The country near Chugwater would be rougher than what they had traveled through so far. Percy said that it would take all of four more hours to reach the station. If all went well, that would put them at their destination just before sunset.

David took Percy and Barta aside to talk to them after the last of the passengers had taken their seat inside the coach. "If I was a betting man . . . and I am a betting man," he said, "I would wager good money that someone is going to try to rob this stage, either tonight or early tomorrow." Percy and Barta looked at each other. "I can't say for certain," he added, "but I think it will happen when we get near Chugwater."

"Do you think it's Cain Mason?" asked Percy.

David frowned and was silent for a few seconds before answering. "I have my suspicions on who it might be, but I don't want to say anything at the moment."

"Cain Mason can go to hell," exclaimed Barta. "Whoever tries robbing this stage better be ready for trouble." He was turning red and was clearly agitated over the possibility of someone trying to sully his first day on the job.

"I knew you would make a first-rate shotgun rider, Lloyd," said David, slapping the old man on his back. "Just be alert. I could be wrong. After all, I don't win every hand of cards that I play."

"Well, I bet you win a lot more than you lose," replied Barta as he climbed up and took his seat next to Percy.

David took one last look around, carefully scanning the horizon to the north in the direction they would be traveling. He hoped he was wrong, but inside he knew he wasn't. He knew the chances were good that by this time tomorrow they might all be dead.

He placed his foot on the step of the coach and crawled inside. A moment later, Percy gave the reins a shake, and the six-horse team stepped out onto the road to the Chugwater station, with a flatulent grey mule keeping pace.

CHAPTER FORTY

It was just past eight thirty in the evening when the stage pulled into the home station at Chugwater. The setting sun had cast a crimson glow across the low hills to the west. A killdeer darted under the bottom rail of the corral. The aggressive trill of its voice sounded an alarm, announcing to anyone within earshot that the stage had arrived. Then it flew off somewhere behind the barn, having fulfilled its responsibilities as a watchman for the station.

David noted that the station was eerily quiet as Percy brought the team to a halt in front of the single-story, wood-framed building that served as the station house. Overnight home stations were usually larger and in better shape than swing stations. Passengers wanted at least a measure of comfort and security when they were expected to spend the night. There was no sign of anyone in the yard, and there was no light inside the station house. He noted the lack of smoke rising from the chimney. The place looked deserted.

David opened the door to the coach and stepped down. Turning to the remaining passengers, he said, "It might be a good idea for the three of you to remain in the stage for a few minutes until we can have a look around."

Mrs. Hall sat nervously in her seat with her hands folded on her lap. "Is this where we are spending the night, Mr. Gaines? It looks abandoned!" she exclaimed.

David smiled reassuringly. "There's nothing to be alarmed about, Mrs. Hall. We're going to have a quick look around, then you and the other passengers can unload and settle in for the night."

Percy and Barta had climbed down from their perch and were standing next to the horses, cautiously scanning the yard and the premises.

"Something ain't right, Mr. Gaines," Percy acknowledged as David drew near. He pushed his hat further back on his head and idly stroked one side of his mustache. "Ed usually comes out to help unhitch the horses and get 'em squared away for the night, and his wife, Sarah, always comes out to greet the passengers."

"I don't like the looks of this," remarked David. Slipping his Colt out of its holster, he said, "Lloyd, why don't you go have a look in the barn. I'll check out the house. Percy, you stay here and keep an eye on the passengers and the money box."

The two men nodded their agreement. Lloyd, shotgun in hand, crept cautiously toward the barn, while Percy climbed back up onto the driver's seat of the stage.

Dusk was turning into full-blown night. David walked up to the front of the station house. There was a window on either side of the front door, so he walked over to the nearest one and cupped his hand around his eyes to gaze inside. It was too dark to see anything. He stood quietly for a few seconds to hear if he could detect any sounds coming from inside, but the only sounds were the snorting and stomping of one of the horses.

He lifted the latch on the door and pushed it open. The light inside was too dim to reveal many details about the room.

There was a lantern hanging on a hook next to the door, so he took it down and set it on a table inside the entrance. Lifting the globe, he struck a match and touched it to the wick. A flame stretched upward, illuminating more of the inside of the station house. David replaced the globe and adjusted the length of the wick so that the lamp cast a warm glow across the main room.

There was a six-burner, step-top cookstove in the middle of the room. David held his hand out to the sides of the stove. There was only slight heat radiating from it. A mixing bowl sat on a counter with flour and eggs in it ready to be mixed, but there was no sign of anyone.

He checked the other rooms in the building. There were four small sleeping rooms for the passengers and a larger bedroom for Ed and his wife. There were no signs of a struggle, but the couple who ran the stage stop was nowhere in sight.

David walked back out into the yard as Lloyd was coming out of the barn. The old mountain man motioned for David to join him.

Percy climbed down from his seat and joined them in front of the stage. Lloyd said, "The horses are gone."

"All of them?" asked Percy.

"Every stall is empty, the corral, too," answered Lloyd.

"Ed and Sarah aren't here as well," added David. "I can't see any sign of what might have happened to them either. What do you think, Percy? Has this ever happened before?"

"Well, it's policy to turn the horses loose in the event of a pending Indian attack. It makes it more difficult for the thieving bastards to get their hands on 'em. The horses usually make their way back to one of the station stops along the route."

"What about Ed and Sarah? What would they do?"

"They would skedaddle either up line or downline to the next nearest station, depending on which direction they thought the attack was coming from."

"That makes sense," said David, "but I don't see any sign of Indians around here."

Lloyd opened his eyes wide and lowered his voice so it wouldn't carry any farther than the three men gathered there. "I don't think it was Indians. Come take a look at what I found in the barn."

Indicating that they should follow him, he led the two men into the barn. Percy stood just inside the entrance to the barn, where he could keep an eye on the stage in the yard.

A sliver of moon shone down through the loft window. Its beams cast a soft glow on the floor of the barn. There was something nearly invisible on the wall next to the door.

"What's that?" asked David.

"I asked myself the same question," replied Lloyd. He reached into a pocket and pulled out a match. Striking it against a wooden post, the flame shot up, illuminating the wall in front of them. About four feet up from the floor, scrawled in dripping red letters at least a foot high, was the word CAIN.

The three men stared silently at the marks on the wall. Percy broke the silence when he whispered, to no one in particular, "It's the mark of Cain."

David asked Lloyd, "I don't suppose that's red paint?"

"Nope," he answered. "I checked. It's blood."

David turned to Percy. "Any chance we can make it to the next swing station tonight?"

Percy shook his head. "The horses need to rest. They could be ready in another two . . . three hours, but it's too dangerous to try to travel at night. No, we're gonna have to stay here and wait for daylight."

"Besides," added Lloyd, "how do we know Mason hasn't been there as well? He could have hit every station between here and Fort Laramie."

"You make a good point," said David.

"It happens ever' now and then," Lloyd replied.

"All right, let's do this then . . . Percy, you and Lloyd unharness the horses and put them in the barn, and don't forget the strongbox. I'll take the passengers into the station house and see if I can't rustle up some grub for them. After they are asleep, the three of us will take shifts keeping watch. I'll do the first shift, then Lloyd, and then you, Percy."

"What are you going to tell the passengers?" inquired Percy.

"Let's keep this business about Cain Mason to ourselves for now. There's no use scaring the passengers when we aren't sure ourselves what happened here. I'll tell them that for unknown reasons, the station was abandoned, but we are still on schedule, and everything is under control."

The two men agreed that David's plan was the best course of action. While they worked on unharnessing the team and walking them into the barn, David opened the coach door to speak with the other passengers.

"Here's the situation, folks. For some reason or other, the couple that runs the station is not here right now."

"Where did they go?" asked Private

O'Rourke.

"We don't know, Private. There may have been an emergency . . . an illness or an injury of some kind so that they had to leave in a hurry. But we are still on schedule, and everything is fine. So let's get everyone inside and see if we can't find us something to eat. I know I'm famished. I'm sure all of you are as well."

They agreed with nods and various affirmations that they were hungry and could use a meal and some sleep. One by one, they exited the stagecoach and followed single file as David led them into the station house.

Mrs. Hall volunteered to cook up something for everyone to eat, so while Private O'Rourke got a fire going in the stove, she began searching the cupboards and the pantry to see what provisions were available.

David went back outside to see if he could help Percy and Lloyd, but they were already finishing with the last pair of horses.

"What about the strongbox?" David asked Percy.

"I'll carry that inside. There's a door on the other side of the building that goes into Ed and Sarah's room. We usually take the strongbox in that way so the other passengers don't see it. There's a small closet inside Ed and Sarah's room with a padlock on it, and I'm the only one with a key." Percy gave a wink and began to pull the strongbox out of its hiding place beneath his seat. A few minutes later, it was safely locked away inside the closet in the missing couple's room.

Mrs. Hall found some potatoes in a pantry, so she fried them up with onions and bacon. She mixed together some biscuit dough and made some bacon grease gravy to go with them. Everyone ate their fill and then spent the next few hours talking or playing cards.

Even though it was after eleven o'clock, no one seemed eager to go to sleep. They speculated among themselves about the missing couple and where they might have disappeared to. At first, the going theory was that Indians had threatened to attack and had driven the couple to seek greater safety at the next stage stop. But Professor Longacre insisted it was the work of Cain Mason and that they would all shortly be attacked and slaughtered by the outlaw.

David was annoyed by the conversation. He didn't understand why Longacre was so obsessed with Cain Mason and why he so persistently managed to steer every conversation back to his biography of the man.

Mrs. Hall had put on a pot of coffee, so David helped himself to a cup. Then he poured a cup for Barta, who was moving from room to room to do a more thorough examination. He was looking for any clue that might have been overlooked that would help them to understand what had happened to Ed and Sarah.

He finished his search of the station house and walked over to where David was looking out of one of the two windows that were on either side of the front door.

"Did you find anything?" asked David.

"Not a dad-burned thing," Barta responded. "It's too bad it was getting dark out when we rolled in. I'm sure there are tracks out there that will tell us more than we know now. Come daylight I'll have a look around." Barta took the cup of coffee that David handed him. "I don't get it."

"It doesn't seem to make much sense, does it?" said David.

Barta blew across the top of his cup and took a sip of his coffee. David noticed the old mountain man was still clutching the shotgun in his left hand. "If it is this Cain Mason fella and he is after the strongbox, why didn't he rob us out on the road? That's what I would've done."

"I know. I was thinking the same thing."

"I've been listening to this Professor Longacre tell his stories about some of the things that Mason is supposed to have done. If he is the one behind all this, I think I would rather deal with the Indians."

"Don't believe everything you hear . . . or everything you read," replied David, as he tilted his head back and drained the last of the coffee from his cup. "Though I do wish the good professor would stop flapping his gums about Mason," David added. "He's getting people all worked up and scared out of their wits. Mrs. Hall looks like she is going to be ill every time he tells one of his gruesome stories."

"Oh, I reckon he's just trying to sell more books," replied Barta.

David looked around and saw that no one was listening to their conversation. He lowered his voice to a whisper. "Keep this to yourself, Lloyd, but I have every reason to believe that Cain Mason isn't within a thousand miles of this place."

Barta furrowed his brow and cocked his head slightly. "What do you make of all this, then?"

David shook his head and frowned. "I don't know, but there is more going on here than what's apparent. I haven't put all the pieces together yet."

"I'll tell you one thing," answered Barta, "whoever it is gives us honest stage robbers a bad name." He gave David a wink and walked over to help himself to some of the leftover bacon and potatoes.

David refilled his coffee cup and grabbed a couple of biscuits. He resumed his position next to the window and stared out into the darkness.

He got to thinking about some of the preparations they would need to make for their departure in the morning. Calling Percy and Barta, he took them to one of the small bedrooms that were off to the side of the main room of the station house to talk to them privately before everyone settled down for the night.

"Percy, I want to leave as early as we can in the morning. As soon as it's light enough, I want the horses harnessed and ready to go."

"That sounds fine by me," Percy replied. "This place is giving me the spooks."

"Lloyd, I'm going to have you scout ahead of the stage tomorrow. Maybe we can get a heads up on any trouble that might be waiting for us down the trail. Do you think Harley is up for the job?"

"Don't you worry about ol' Harley," said Barta. "That mule is almost as good a tracker as I am."

"Excellent," David replied. "Now, why don't the two of you try to get a few hours of sleep."

Percy asked, "Are you sure you don't want one of us to stand guard for a while? You must be getting plumb tuckered out."

David shook his head. "I'm still working off all of this coffee I've been drinking. If I get tired, Lloyd, I'll wake you up."

Barta nodded his consent, and Percy remarked, "If that's the way you want it. Just don't keep that blond waiting too long. Or was it a redhead?"

David smiled at the old man. "It was a redhead. It was definitely a redhead."

CHAPTER FORTY-ONE

Longacre watched as David, Percy, and the old mountain man made their way to one of the side rooms. When they had gone inside and had closed the door behind them, he stretched and yawned and said, "I believe I'll venture outside and have a smoke before turning in. I sleep better after a smoke."

Mrs. Hall and Private O'Rourke continued their conversation and paid no attention to the professor as he slipped out the front door.

Once outside, he walked down the road until it crossed over Chugwater Creek. There was a rocky outcropping to his left a couple hundred yards from the road. Picking his way carefully across the prairie at night, he made his way to the far side of the rocks. There were two horses picketed and chewing on some sagebrush. It was an easy climb up to the top of the limestone rocks, and it only took a minute to reach the summit.

The figure of a person lay prostrate on the ground, holding a rifle aimed down toward the station house off in the distance. As Longacre reached the top of the ledge, the person rolled over and said, "Howdy, Pa. Did you have any trouble down there?"

Longacre sat on a rock and pulled off one of his boots. Upending it, he emptied it of some sand that had worked its way down inside.

"Nope, there are no problems. Everything is going according to plan." He pulled his boot back on. "How about you, Bess? Did you do everything just as I said?"

Longacre's daughter, Bess, rose to her feet and brushed the sand and grass from her shirt and pants. She was a rather petite girl in her early twenties, but a person would have had to take a close second look to find anything feminine about her. She had short, tangled, brown hair under her slouch hat. She wore men's clothes, and one side of her face puffed out where she had a wad of tobacco tucked under her lip. The least feminine thing about her, though, was the Colt Navy revolver tucked into the belt that was holding up her britches, which were at least two sizes too large for her.

"Yes, Pa, I rode into the station this morning and told them the Sioux were raiding along the stage line to the south and that they had attacked the stage and burned it and killed everyone." Bess spat on the ground and then chuckled. "You should have seen that old couple that runs the station. They couldn't get out of there fast enough. They hitched up a wagon, let the horses out, and tore out of there just like you said they would. Then I killed a jackrabbit and used its blood to write the word CAIN inside the barn.

"You did a fine job, Bess. That should seal the deal. I've got them all so frightened of Cain Mason right now; they won't dare offer up any resistance."

"I still don't understand something, Pa," Bess said as she scratched at some insect bite on the back of her neck. "Why didn't we just rob the stage on the road? Why go through all this bother?"

Longacre shook his head and sighed. "Bess, I've explained this to you already." Bess had never been very bright, and as a young lady, she had no redeeming qualities whatsoever. But she could handle a horse as good as any man, and she could shoot better than most. She had an 1869 .50-caliber Sharps with a long Malcolm scope. It was nothing for her to bring down a buffalo at half a mile.

He summarized for her once again. "This way they won't be looking for us. They will think that I'm dead, and they have no idea you even exist. Instead, they will be searching for an outlaw named Cain Mason. We'll be in the clear with no one the wiser."

"But if we just kill 'em all, doesn't that solve that problem?"

"So far, Bess, we haven't done anything they can hang us for. I want to keep it that way."

"But what if the real Cain Mason finds out we used his name to rob stages? Won't he be mad?"

"Like I told you already, Bess, the real Cain Mason was a man I met in prison back in Philadelphia. No one's heard anything about him since then. For all I know, he died in prison. That's why I picked him, and why I made up all those stories and wrote the book about him."

This was the seventh time they had pulled this routine — robbing stages and pretending to be Cain Mason. It had become a lucrative scam, and they had enough money stashed away to last them a long time. Everything had gone according to plan on each previous occasion, and Longacre had no reason to think that it would be any different this time.

The most difficult part of his plan was in knowing which stage was going to be hauling a big payday. But there was someone . . . a driver, a hostler, a disgruntled employee for the stage line . . . someone who knew. People couldn't keep secrets, not for very long anyway. It was human nature to want to tell others that you had inside information, that you were someone important enough to know what others did not but only if you could share the secret with someone else. Find the person with the secret, add some careful coaxing and manipulation of the conversation, and Longacre could dislodge any bit of information he wanted. He was good at it.

Once he knew which stage to be on, then he would begin to spread rumors that Cain Mason was in the area. On the stage, he would use his time to share horrid and grizzly tales about the outlaw robbing and slaughtering. He would bring out his book and pass it around, letting the other passengers read for themselves the awful deeds perpetrated by the monster. By the time he was through, everyone on the stage would be so frightened of Cain Mason, the boogie man, that it took all the fight out of them.

They practically threw their money at him. But there was still more to do.

"Are you ready, Bess? It's time to go to work."

"I'm ready, Pa. When do you want me to start shooting?"

"Give me about fifteen minutes to get into place, and then you can open up on them. Fire off about six rounds, and then bring the horses down, but stay back behind the barn and out of sight. Once they're gone I'll whistle for you to bring the horses to the front door, and we'll be on our way to San Francisco."

Bess scratched at another insect bite and replied, "OK, Pa, but I still think you ought to let me kill 'em."

"Just do what I tell you. In another hour we'll have that strongbox with the fort's payroll, and we can go to San Francisco like I promised you."

CHAPTER FORTY-TWO

After meeting with Percy and Barta, David returned to his spot by the window and continued with his guard duty. It was close to midnight before things began to quiet down. Everyone was yawning and stretching and looking as exhausted as David felt. Mrs. Hall and Private O'Rourke were preparing to turn in for the night. David didn't see Professor Longacre and assumed that he had already retired to one of the sleeping rooms.

Peering out of the window, something caught his eye. David focused his eyes beyond the area where the stagecoach was parked for the night. There was something moving in the darkness.

With a crash, the glass in the window pane next to him shattered as a bullet barely missed David's head. He dove for cover below the window. "Everybody, get down!" he shouted.

Two more shots crashed through the window. Mrs. Hall let out a scream. She had been standing next to the stove when the second shot ricocheted off of the galvanized stovepipe with a twang. Private O'Rourke pushed her to the floor as Barta blew out the lamp and dove for cover under the plank table. Percy had crawled on his stomach to the other window on the opposite side of the door from where David crouched.

"Is everyone all right?" David shouted.

One of the bullets had hit Private O'Rourke in the shoulder, but he said it was only a scratch and that he was all right. One by one, they said that they were unhurt; all, that is, except for Professor Longacre.

David called into the darkness of the station house, "Professor, are you all right?" There was still no answer. "Has anyone seen the professor?"

From the blackness of the room, David heard Private O'Rourke speak. "I think the professor said he was going outside for a smoke."

"When was that?" asked David.

"That was almost an hour ago," the private answered.

Just then, another bullet crashed through the window above David, and two more buried themselves into the wooden door with a pair of thuds.

During the next few minutes, there were no more shots, but David and the rest of the passengers kept low and under cover.

From somewhere beyond where the stage-coach sat, a muffled voice sounded from out of the darkness. "You, in the station house . . ."

David lifted his head up to the sill of the window and tried to get a look outside. It was too dark to see more than two or three feet beyond the front door. He shouted to the stranger, "What do you want?"

"I think you already know the answer to that."

"Is Longacre all right?" asked David.

"Damn! Was that Professor Longacre? I thought he looked familiar."

David hung his head and sighed. "What do you mean, '*Was* that Professor Longacre?'?"

"Well, he sort of surprised me when he came outside. I don't handle surprises very well. I had to slit his throat. Don't worry. He didn't linger."

There was something strange about the voice. David couldn't figure out what it was.

"Who are you, and what do you want from us?" David shouted.

"You know damn well who I am. I'm Cain Mason, and I want the strongbox."

CHAPTER FORTY-THREE

"Who are you, and what do you want from us?" Longacre heard David Gaines shout from inside the station house.

He figured Gaines would be the one doing the talking. He had been hired by the stage agent to ride shotgun at the last moment, and he seemed to be the one giving orders throughout the journey.

Longacre held a handkerchief over his mouth and spoke in a lower register than normal. He had had a lot of practice over the past year in disguising his voice, and he had no doubt that it would be sufficient to fool everyone inside the station house.

"You know damn well who I am. I'm Cain Mason, and I want the strongbox."

The professor was glad to be rid of the other passengers, particularly Gaines. He had been afraid all day long that the gambler would remember him. They had met before, about three years ago. They had been in the same faro game in Abilene. Of course, his name wasn't Longacre back then, it was Dutch Cooper. It wasn't until he came up with the Cain Mason scam that he changed his name to Longacre, donned a pair of spectacles, and assumed the persona of the bookish professor.

There was no reply from inside for several minutes. Longacre guessed that they were debating with each other what the best course of action would be. He knew that of them all, Mrs. Hall would be the most hysterical. She had recoiled in horror with each new revelation of the murderous nature of Cain Mason. She wouldn't be a problem. Gaines, Percy, and the old guy, Barta, worked for the stage line. They wouldn't like the idea of losing the strongbox and its contents, but their primary concern was for the safety of the passengers. The stage company wouldn't risk the lives of the passengers. Besides, the money in the strongbox wasn't theirs anyway. It was government money. The government would just send more to replace it, so even Private O'Rourke, who some of the money belonged to, wouldn't want to take a chance.

Longacre cleared his throat and called, "What do you say? Do we do this the easy way?"

"We don't want anyone else getting hurt," David called out. "Do you guarantee our safety if we turn over the money?"

Longacre smiled to himself. "To tell you the truth, I'd as soon kill each one of you and fry up your livers for my breakfast, but I'm feeling kinda sorry about Professor Longacre. I liked the guy. I liked what he wrote about me. So I'll tell you what I'll do . . ."

He paused a long moment for dramatic effect. If he hesitated for a minute before continuing, it would build tension inside the station house. It would make them all the more eager to hear what he was offering, and the more eager they were to hear it, the more likely they would be to comply without question. He grinned at his cleverness.

When he thought that he had waited long enough, he continued. "I want you to put the strongbox on the table, just inside the doorway. I'll give you five minutes. Then I want each of you to step outside and start walking north towards the next stage stop. Leave the horses, leave your baggage, and leave your guns inside the building. Just step out with your hands in the air and start walking. If I don't see five people exit the building, or if you don't follow my instructions exactly, I won't hesitate to kill every one of you . . . except the woman. I'll have some fun with her first. Then I'll kill her."

It only took a minute for their reply to come back. "All right, we'll do what you say. But one of your shots hit Private O'Rourke. We thought it was only a flesh wound, but we couldn't stop the bleeding. He's dead. There are only four of us left."

Damn, thought Longacre. No one had ever died before. That could complicate things. Still, the authorities would be looking for Cain Mason, not Professor Longacre, and certainly not Dutch Cooper and his daughter, Bess.

"All right, then the four of you have five minutes. After that, I'm killing every one of you. The clock is ticking."

CHAPTER FORTY-FOUR

It was a few minutes after midnight when Longacre heard Gaines shout from inside the station house, "Don't shoot. We're coming out."

He crouched in a ditch on the opposite side of the road and waited. He had a Spencer rifle Bess had brought for him. Resting the rifle on the top bank of the ditch where he could train it on the stage passengers, he watched as they came out of the station house one by one with their hands in the air.

The partly cloudy night sky diffused what little moonlight there was, playing a symphony of light and shadow across the station yard. At the moment, enough light shone down so that Longacre could count each person as they stepped through the doorway and started walking up the road to the north.

He saw Gaines come out first. It was easy

to make out his slight frame covered with his frock coat and topped off with his bowler hat.

The next to come out was Percy, followed by Mrs. Hall. Bringing up the rear was Barta, the old mountain man. They kept their hands in the air. The only sound was the shuffling of their feet in the gravel as they made their way past the barn and up the road. He watched them as long as the moonlight would allow. Then he waited another five minutes before he crawled out of the ditch and sprinted for the front door.

It was dark inside, so Longacre struck a match and lit the lamp that was still sitting on the table. He kept the wick low so that the lantern would only cast a dim light inside the station house.

He could see the strongbox sitting on the table next to a pile of weapons that included the coach gun, some rifles, and several assorted handguns.

Near the center of the room, next to the stove, he saw the uniformed body of Private O'Rourke lying on the floor, where he had fallen after being hit when Bess had fired into the building.

Longacre turned his attention to the strongbox. Gaines had set the box on the table as instructed, but Longacre had neglected to order him to unlock the box before they left. *No problem,* he thought. Raising his rifle into the air, he brought the butt end of the Spencer down against the lock. It took two more attempts before the lock broke open.

Longacre set the rifle down on the table and reached into the box, which was filled with mail for the fort as well as stacks of new bills and a couple bags of silver dollars. He tossed the packets of mail aside and took out one of the bundles of fresh, green bills and began counting them.

"Don't make a move, Professor, or I'll have to shoot."

Startled by the sound of the other voice in the room with him, Longacre froze in his place. Turning his eyes in the direction of the voice, he was shocked to discover that the body of Private O'Rourke was no longer on the floor next to the stove. He could see a vague shadow of a man with a gun in his hand pointed right at him.

"Reach over slowly, Professor, and turn up the lamp. Let's have a little light in here," the shadowy figure directed, "but don't make any sudden moves."

Longacre did as directed and adjusted the lamp's wick to illuminate the inside of the station house. Standing in front of him holding him at gunpoint was not Private O'Rourke, as he had expected, but David Gaines dressed in the private's uniform.

"Put your hands in the air and step away from the table," David said.

Longacre complied. "That's a slick trick, Gaines. I never saw that coming."

"I got the idea from you," replied Gaines. "I figured if you could pretend to be a professor, I could pretend to be an army private."

"So you do remember the first time we met?"

"It took a while, but it came to me. It was at a faro game in Abilene about three years back. You looked different then. You didn't have the sideburns or the glasses."

David took a step closer and indicated a chair next to the table. "You might as well have a seat. The others will be back shortly. They were going to walk for fifteen minutes, then turn around and come back."

Longacre took the seat that Gaines had indicated. He glanced at his rifle on the table next to the strongbox about three feet from where he sat. He tried to estimate his chances of reaching his Spencer without getting shot, but Gaines still had his gun pointed at him.

"You never did buy into the Cain Mason

story like everyone else," said Longacre. "Why not?"

"It's simple," David answered. "I know the real Cain Mason. I know where he is, I know what he's doing, and I know he hasn't picked up a gun since he got out of prison seven years ago."

That's one thing Longacre never counted on. "I take it Private O'Rourke wasn't really shot."

"Oh, he was shot," replied David, "but it was only a scratch. The private and I are about the same size, so I came up with the idea of telling you he was dead, then switched places with him. It worked out nicely if you ask me."

"What's taking so long, Pa? I was waiting like you said —" Bess Cooper walked through the door at that moment. Her rifle was lowered toward the floor, but, when she saw David Gaines, she raised her rifle and pulled the trigger.

David dove for cover behind the stove. Bess's shot went wide and slammed into the floor next to him.

Longacre sprung out of his chair, grabbed the Spencer off of the table, and dove to the floor.

Bess dropped the Sharps that she carried and ducked back out through the doorway.

Using the doorjamb for cover, she pulled the Colt from her belt and fired into the building.

David peeked around the side of the stove and saw Longacre crawling on his belly, trying to flank him. Their eyes met, and Longacre rose on his knees to bring his Spencer up to fire. David ducked back behind the cover of the stove, at the same time thrusting his Colt out and firing two shots at Longacre. He heard him grunt as one of his shots hit Longacre in the *V* of the neck. The robber clutched at his throat as the blood pumped out between his fingers. He collapsed face down on the floor in an expanding pool of blood.

"Pa!" Bess cried out. She fired three shots in David's direction. "You shot my pa, you son of a bitch."

Ducking back behind the stove, David heard a loud crack, followed by Bess's cry of pain. He stuck his head out from behind the stove just as Bess stumbled through the doorway holding her wrist. Behind her, shoving her along, was Percy.

"Don't shoot, Gaines. It's me, Percy." The stage driver was coiling up his bullwhip. "I thought maybe you could use my help."

CHAPTER FORTY-FIVE

Percy and Barta were hitching up the horses to the stage when the thunder of hooves drew their attention to the northern road. They could see a huge cloud of dust kicked up by a large group of riders.

Percy shouted into the station house, "Gaines . . . you better come out here."

David walked out into the station yard, checking the load in his gun, not knowing what to expect.

It had been a long night. Shortly after the gun battle with Longacre and his daughter had ended, the rest of the passengers returned to the station. Longacre's body was placed in the barn. The plan was to retrieve it on the return trip and take it to the authorities in Cheyenne. Bess would go with them on the stage, albeit under restraint. It was likely that she would have to face charges for other crimes she and her father had committed.

They had all discussed it among themselves and decided to get what sleep they could. They wanted to leave as soon as the sun was up and keep the stage on schedule. The sooner they got to the safety of the fort the better they would be.

"We've got company," Percy said, pointing up the road.

David climbed up on the stage to have a better look. Off in the distance, he could make out a line of riders. A few moments later, he saw a U.S. flag at the head of a column of riders, all dressed in blue.

Within minutes, the riders came to a halt, surrounding the stage and filling the station yard with clouds of dust and heaving, sweaty mounts.

A young officer on a lathered bay dismounted alongside the stage and stepped forward. "Are you the passengers from the stage that left Cheyenne yesterday morning?" Worry lines creased his forehead. He looked as though he hadn't slept all night.

David jumped down from the stage to greet him. "We are, Lieutenant, and we're glad to see you."

At that moment, Mrs. Hall stepped out of the station house. "Chris!" she cried.

The lieutenant turned upon hearing his name. The two ran towards each other, meeting halfway. They kissed, then embraced for a long moment, then kissed again.

The cavalry officer held her at arm's length and looked at her. "I was worried sick about you, Lizzy," he confessed. "Riders came into the fort last night and said Indians had attacked the stage and killed everyone on board."

"We've had a terribly frightening time, but it wasn't Indians." She led him back to where David stood next to the stage. "I'll let Mr. Gaines tell you about it. If it wasn't for him, I think we might all be dead."

The officer held out his hand to David. "I'm Lieutenant Christopher Hall, commanding Second Platoon, Company A out of Fort Laramie. I don't know what happened here, Mr. Gaines, but my wife tells me that I owe you a debt of gratitude."

David shook the lieutenant's hand. "You have a very brave wife, Lieutenant Hall, but I believe she is giving me too much credit. Why don't we step inside the station house and have some coffee, and I'll fill you in."

Lieutenant Hall gave orders to the first sergeant for the men to dismount and tend to their horses.

The two men stepped inside the station house, where David told the story from the beginning.

The lieutenant listened intently until David was through. "And you knew from the beginning that the rumors about Cain Mason were a ruse?" he asked.

"I knew that someone was spreading a lot of fear about him, but I didn't know who or why until after the stage had gotten under way. When I remembered where I had met the man who was calling himself Professor Longacre, I knew that he was a phony and figured he would be involved in an attempt to rob the stage."

"But how could you be sure that it wasn't the real Cain Mason who would attempt to rob the stage? He and Longacre could have been working together. Even up at the fort, we've heard stories of the man. If even half of the stories are true," said the lieutenant, "then Mason is a cold-blooded killer."

David smiled and shook his head. "I knew he wasn't involved, Lieutenant, because I know the real Cain Mason."

Lieutenant Hall's eyes grew wide at the revelation.

"His real name is Shane Mason, and he wasn't always a bad man. The fact is he was a school teacher at one time, back East in Philadelphia. One day school let out early, and Shane got home to find his wife sharing the company of his own brother. That's when something snapped. He picked up a revolver and demonstrated a remarkable natural skill in gunmanship that surprised even him, by killing each of them with a single shot through their cheating hearts. That's when people began calling him 'Cain' Mason. The opportunity for a choice biblical reference, with a bit of irony thrown in, wasn't about to be lost on the virtuous citizens of the city of brotherly love.

"Circumstances being what they were, Shane was spared the gallows and was sentenced to twelve years in prison. He did his time, and, when he was released, he took the first train west and never looked back. He started over with a new name and a new occupation.

"I won't tell you where he's at," David said, "but I will tell you that he's the well-respected editor of a newspaper in California. He's remarried and has two children. He's a deacon in his church, and his wife sings in the choir."

"How do you know all this?" asked Lieutenant Hall.

David shrugged. "For some reason, people are comfortable opening up to me. You'd be surprised what people confess to me. My mother said that I would have made a dandy preacher because I'm a good listener."

The two men walked back outside, where Lieutenant Hall shook hands with Percy and Barta and thanked them for their efforts in keeping his wife, and the fort's payroll, safe.

"You men might as well turn back to Cheyenne today," said Lieutenant Hall. "The stage stops between here and the fort have been abandoned because of the Indian scare. I'll sign a receipt for the payroll, and you can turn it over to me here."

David looked at Percy. "How does that sound to you?" he asked.

Percy scratched his whiskered chin. "We might as well turn back. There won't be any fresh horses to the north if they were all turned loose."

"All right," David agreed. "That's what we'll do."

"I'll send two of my men with you to escort your prisoner back to town. You folks don't need any more trouble than you've already had on account of the army." Lieutenant Hall issued the orders to the first sergeant, who "volunteered" two privates to accompany the stage back to Cheyenne.

Soon, the stage was ready to make the return trip to Cheyenne. David, Percy, and Lloyd shook hands with Lieutenant Hall and said their goodbyes to Mrs. Hall and Private O'Rourke, who would be leaving with the soldiers when they returned to Fort Laramie as soon as the horses had rested.

As the stage pulled out of the station yard, the killdeer landed on the top rail of the corral fence, trilling a farewell to the passengers. When the dust had settled, she took wing and flew out over the prairie in search of grasshoppers for breakfast.

CHAPTER FORTY-SIX

The stage arrived back in Cheyenne some-time after eight o'clock that evening. The sun's rays split open the western sky, spill-ing orange and pink across a canvas of clouds that hung low over the horizon.

Percy pulled the team up in front of the Wells Fargo office and set the brake. Gabe came out of the office as David climbed down from the stage. Gabe was pale and looked concerned as to why the stage was back in town two days early.

"Don't worry," David volunteered before Gabe could ask. "The fort's payroll is delivered, and all the passengers are safe. Well . . . most of them, anyway," he added, remembering that Longacre's body was rolled up in a tarp and tucked away in the rear boot of the stage.

Gabe noticed Barta up on the wagon seat next to Percy. He spoke in hushed tones as David stepped up on the boardwalk. "Did you have any trouble with Lloyd?"

"None whatsoever. As a matter of fact, I'm glad he was with us."

"Okay," Gabe replied slowly, looking even more confused.

"Oh . . ." David added, "He's also on your payroll as the new shotgun rider."

"What?!"

"Do you have anything stronger than coffee in your office? I'll explain all."

The two men went inside while Barta went to find a police officer. They would need to file a report and turn their prisoner over to the authorities. Percy remained outside with the stage guarding Bess until Barta could return with the law.

David related the story to Gabe, not leaving out any of the details of the last thirty-eight hours.

After listening, Gabe expressed his gratitude for the way things had worked out. "Offering Lloyd the job of the shotgun rider was a great idea, Dave. Honestly, I don't know why I didn't think of it myself."

"I'm glad to hear you say that. He and Percy make a good team."

Gabe tilted back his glass and drained the last few drops of whiskey. "Why don't we head on over to Frenchy's? Let me buy you dinner and a couple more drinks. Percy and

Lloyd, too; I'll buy dinner for all of you."

David waved off the offer. "The rest of you can go if you want to. All I want right now is to sleep for about twelve hours. I'm sure your stage is as comfortable as any other stage on the road, but as sleeping accommodations, they leave a lot to be desired."

Gabe agreed to give David a rain check on the dinner and drinks, so David said goodnight and began the walk back to his hotel. His eyelids were as heavy as his feet, which dragged along the boardwalk as he made his way down Sixteenth Street.

Soon after, David was beneath the covers of his bed in his hotel room. As he closed his eyes the only sounds were the distant tinny notes of a saloon piano, the faint sounds of laughter, and the occasional soft thump of a horse's hooves in the road outside. Within minutes, he was asleep with no blonds, brunettes, or redheads to populate his dreams.

Chapter Forty-Seven

It was almost noon before David woke up. After shaving and washing, he dressed and went outside. It was a beautiful day, and the streets teemed with people. Some shopped, some sold various items. Others were engaged in the business of traveling from point A to point B.

David's stomach rumbled. He was ravenous, not having had a real meal since the night before last. There was a new restaurant that had opened up two blocks to the south that he hadn't tried yet, so he crossed the street in that direction.

He had just stepped onto the boardwalk on the opposite side of the street when he heard a voice call out his name. David froze. He had forgotten about Ox.

Turning in that direction, he saw Ox striding towards him, rolling up his sleeves, preparing to give him the thrashing that David knew he could no longer avoid. Even

Ox was too smart to fall for any more delaying tactics.

"There you are, Ox. I was looking for you."

Ox slid to a stop in front of David. "You were?" Ox replied.

"Sure I was. I had to leave town for a while, but I'm back now, and we have some unfinished business to conduct."

Ox looked confused, as he often did. He stood with his mouth open, then reached into a pocket in his coveralls and pulled out a piece of paper and handed it to David.

"I got the license all no-to-rized, like you said. The man at the courthouse thought it was a funny license. He laughed when he read it. I don't know why he laughed, Davey, but he put his stamp on it. See here?" Ox pointed to the notary stamp that embossed the bottom of the "license."

David made a show of examining the document. "I see that, Ox. I have to say, you did an outstanding job. This is a real first-rate legal document that you have here." He folded up the piece of paper and handed it back to Ox.

"All right then, Ox, are you ready?"

People began to take note of the two men. A few of them slowed as they passed and then stood off at a distance to see what was about to happen. It was obvious that some kind of confrontation was about to take place. It was equally obvious that the big man could easily kill the smaller man with a single blow.

Ox grinned and formed his hands into fists. "I'm ready, Davey."

"Okay, Ox. There's still one additional thing that we need to decide first, then we can have our duel."

Ox appeared heartbroken. Dropping his fists, he exclaimed, "What now, Davey? I did all the pro-to-col. I got the license, and I got the no-to-rize. What's left to decide?"

"You have been very patient, Ox. I couldn't have asked for a more patient opponent than you have been. And I promise that we are going to have our duel right now, right here. But there is one more piece of protocol that we need to follow, and it is the most important protocol of them all."

Ox looked at David, and then he looked around at the people who had gathered to witness their duel. There were close to a couple dozen bystanders who had stopped to watch what the big man and the little man were up to.

"Ox wants to follow all the pro-to-col, Davey. You know that."

"That's excellent, Ox," David replied. He

turned to the crowd and announced, "I want everyone here to bear witness that Ox is a fair opponent and a good sport and that he would never break protocol."

The onlookers, who sensed that they were now a part of whatever theatrics were about to take place, began to applaud and cheer for Ox, who smiled broadly.

"The last piece of protocol, Ox, is this . . . you challenged me to the duel. That makes me the challenged party, and, as such, I choose the weapons for our duel."

Ox looked confused. "You mean we're not going to pound on one another?"

"Oh, that would hardly be fair, Ox. You're three times my size. You could put me in the hospital if you didn't kill me outright."

Ox agreed that that wouldn't be fair, and he added that Davey was his friend, and he didn't want to put him in the hospital, so both men thought about it for a moment.

David said, "I know! We could use guns."

Ox looked frightened at the mention of guns. He shook his head back and forth. "Ox doesn't like guns, Davey. They hurt Ox's ears."

"You're right, Ox. That's not a good idea. Besides, that would give me the advantage. We need to think of something that would be fair to the both of us."

Again, the two of them resumed their deliberations while they pondered their dilemma.

Looking up, David snapped his fingers. "I've got just the thing. How are you at throwing things, like rocks and such?"

"Oh, you bet, Davey. Ox is the best rock chucker there is," he boasted, sticking out his chest and smiling broadly.

"I don't know about that, Ox. I'm a better than average rock chucker myself. You wait right here a minute."

Turning to the crowd, David called forward two boys who were eager to volunteer their services. Pressing a coin into the hand of each boy, he bent down and whispered in their ears. A moment later, the two boys took off down the street and around the corner. Soon, both boys reappeared, each of them carrying a bucket. Then they took off in opposite directions down the middle of the street. Periodically, each boy would stop, bend down, pick something up, and place it in his bucket.

When they had filled their buckets, the two boys ran back to where the combatants waited and turned them over to David, who handed one of the buckets to Ox.

"This is what we'll do, Ox . . . we'll take our buckets and go out into the street and . . ."

Ox didn't need any more instructions or delays. Before David could finish, Ox reached into his bucket and pulled out a fresh horse turd and flung it at David, hitting him in the shoulder. Ox laughed. He slapped his hand on his knee and pointed at David. "I got you, Davey. I got you good."

David had been caught off guard with Ox's delivery. His eyes were wide as he said, "So that's the way you want to do it, huh?" He reached into his bucket for a handful of the horse excrement.

Ox turned and ran down the boardwalk, giggling like a school kid. He ducked behind a post that was far too thin to offer any protection for his size. David's aim was off, and Ox easily ducked the horse apple as it flew past his face.

David didn't stay put. Figuring a moving target would be harder to hit, he turned and ran back toward his hotel across Sixteenth Street. Another horse apple whooshed over his head as he took refuge behind a freight wagon.

The bystanders on both sides of the street laughed and shouted words of encouragement; some were for David, but most seemed to be cheering for Ox.

David peered over the edge of the wagon

that was sheltering him from the barrage of flying fecal matter. Ox had set his bucket on the boardwalk behind him so that he could fill his hands with more of the aromatic projectiles. When Ox had emptied his hands and turned around and bent over to replenish his supply, David stood up and let one fly that landed squarely on Ox's backside.

The crowd erupted in laughter.

The two boys who had gathered up the weaponry positioned themselves on either side of Sixteenth Street — one on David's side and one on Ox's side. They decided that this looked like too much fun not to take part themselves, so they began lobbing horse turds at each other.

One of the bystanders, who had been lending his encouragement to Ox, got his hat knocked off by someone's poor aim, so he picked up the spent projectile and returned fire.

By this time, both Ox and David were laughing so hard that they couldn't aim with any kind of accuracy. Their shots were wild, striking others in the crowd, smashing into the fronts of the buildings, and forcing others to run for cover.

Soon, opposing armies had formed up on either side of the street, with horse apples flying through the air like lead at the battle of Chickamauga.

The battle, though fierce, burned itself out in less than ten minutes. David called a cease-fire and declared Ox the winner of the duel. Brushing themselves off, David and Ox met in the middle of the street and shook hands.

"See," said Ox, "I told you I was a good chucker."

"You did indeed tell me that, Ox. And if I'm ever in need of a first-rate chucker, you're the first man I'll call on."

Ox shook hands with several of the bystanders, who slapped him on the back and congratulated him on his victory.

"Mr. Gaines."

David turned around. The manager of the Rollins House was walking toward him with a piece of paper in his hands.

"Mr. Gaines," he repeated. "You left without checking your messages. This telegram came for you this morning."

Smiling, David took the telegram and read it. Seconds later, the smile left his face. His eyes narrowed, and his jaw tightened. He said to the hotel manager, "Can you arrange a train ticket for me? I'll be checking out. I want to leave as soon as possible."

"I'll be happy to do that for you, Mr. Gaines. Where will you be traveling to?"

David shoved the telegram into his pocket. "Mustang Flats, Texas."

■ ■ ■ ■

Part Four
The Sons of
Philo Gaines

■ ■ ■ ■

"I remember seeing the three of them standing there in the middle of Main Street — the school teacher in the middle with the taller one on his right and the gambler on his left. I knew what had been happening in town, but, like everyone else, I looked the other way — too afraid to stick my neck out. Then the Gaines boys came to town, and I knew that Mustang Flats was going to change forever."

— John Lathrop,
Manager of Tolliver's Mercantile,
Mustang Flats, Texas

CHAPTER FORTY-EIGHT

Matt and Luke escorted Katie back to her ranch. She was planning to sleep at the hotel but spend the rest of the time taking care of Tom while he recovered from his injuries.

As the three of them rode into the yard, Katie saw her foreman, Ben, coming out of the barn, so she called to him. She explained that Tom was no longer a prisoner and that she would be staying in town until Tom was able to return to the ranch.

"You and the rest of the men can handle ranch details until Tom and I return."

"Yes, ma'am," he replied. "Don't you worry none. We'll take good care of the place."

"Please hitch up the carriage and bring it around to the front door for me," said Katie.

"I'll do that right away," replied Ben. He started for the barn, then turned and said, "Miss McCutchen, if I'm not out of line to say so, me and the boys never thought that

Tom was guilty. We saw the way that Tolliver and his men were spreading lies about him, but —" He stopped in mid-sentence, realizing that he had probably said too much.

Katie felt his discomfort and finished his sentence for him. ". . . but because of my relationship with Amos, you all kept your mouths shut. I know that I put everyone in a difficult position. I behaved like a silly schoolgirl."

"No, ma'am," Ben protested. "I would never say that."

"You don't have to, Ben. I'm saying it because it's true. But the scales have fallen from my eyes, and I see Amos Tolliver for what he is. If he, or any of his men, set a foot on this ranch, you run them off. Do you understand?"

"Yes, ma'am," replied Ben, grinning. "That will be a real pleasure."

He started for the barn but turned again and said, "We want you to know that if there is any trouble, you can count on us."

"I appreciate that, Ben. I really do. Let the rest of the men know that, too, will you?"

Ben smiled and nodded, then went into the barn to hitch up the carriage.

Matt, Luke, and Katie walked inside, and

the two men waited downstairs while Katie went up to her room to pack some of her clothes for her stay in town. After about ten minutes, she came back downstairs with a huge valise in each hand. Luke and Matt looked at each other in bemusement.

"I spent the last month crossing the desert," said Luke, "and I didn't have half that much stuff with me," he teased.

Matt looked at the bags and shook his head. "I see that you have every possible fashion contingency covered."

Katie reached the bottom of the stairs and handed each of them one of the bags. "A woman needs her things," is all she said. "Now if you will be so kind as to place these in the carriage, we can be on our way."

They carried the bags outside to where Ben had the carriage waiting. Placing the bags inside, Luke tied his roan and Matt's chestnut to the back of the carriage while Matt helped Katie to her seat. Then the two men climbed inside, one on either side of Katie. Luke took the reins and gave them a quick flick that set the two-horse team in motion.

An hour later they were back in Mustang Flats.

Amos Tolliver was about as mad as Red had

ever seen him. When he found out that Luke was actually Matt Gaines's brother, he commenced to cussing and throwing things around his office. He made such a racket that he scared three customers clean out of the bank. Katie had just been in to see Amos. She knew that Amos was behind Tom's beating and that he was somehow involved in the burning of the schoolhouse. Katie had a temper, but he had never seen her flashing lightning and spitting fire.

Red stood outside the closed door of Amos's office. After a few minutes, objects ceased crashing against the walls, so he opened the door a few inches and peered inside. Amos was sitting motionless behind his desk. Paper was strewn all over the office. Two of the chairs that occupied the room were on their side, and a third was broken into pieces.

Amos saw Red peeking through the cracked door and motioned him inside.

Red walked tentatively into the room. Picking up one of the upset chairs, he set it upright, took a seat, and waited for Amos to speak.

The two men sat in silence for several minutes before Tolliver turned to Red and said, "We can still salvage this situation. This is what we're going to do. The town finds itself without a marshal, so I'm going to call the town council together and have you appointed in Guthrie's place."

Red fidgeted in his seat and said, "I don't know anything about being a marshal."

"The only thing you need to know is that you work for me," snapped Tolliver.

"Okay, boss," Red was quick to respond. As he considered the notion, Guthrie hadn't known anything about the job either. All he had to do was follow Tolliver's orders, and he had been doing that for years.

"It probably won't be until tomorrow," said Tolliver, "but, as soon as it's official, I want you to arrest Tom McCutchen again. If anyone says anything, tell him we have new evidence; tell him we have an eyewitness that saw him shoot Curly."

"Who are you going to get for an eyewitness?" asked Red.

Tolliver waved his hand through the air. "Don't worry about that. I'll find someone who wants to make some easy money. I think that I can get Pony to go along with it. He can say that he didn't want to get involved at first because he didn't think anyone would believe a Mexican. He can say that he had a change of heart when he heard that Tom had been set free for lack of evidence. Whatever happens, I don't want

Tom leaving that jail alive."

"What about Katie?" Red inquired.

Tolliver let go with a heavy sigh. He reached into his inside coat pocket and pulled out a small velvet covered box. Flipping the box open he revealed an exquisite diamond ring, accented with rubies and emeralds.

"It's ironic," he said with a chuckle. "Luke Gaines carried this all the way from Las Cruces so I could propose to Katie. Now, because of him, that won't be happening. Oh, well," he sighed a second time, "she was a means to an end. It's a shame I wasted so much time and effort into winning her over. It would have been a lot easier if she would have agreed to be my wife, but now we'll do things the hard way."

He snapped the lid shut on the jewelry box and tossed it into a desk drawer. "Neither Tom nor Katie have any heirs, so if something happens to the both of them, then the county will sell the ranch at auction. It's not how I prefer it, but it's the only choice that they are leaving me."

Red listened as Tolliver laid out his plans. He felt sick. He had done a lot of things for Tolliver. He had robbed and killed people — men and women. He had intimidated ranchers and farmers and driven them off of their land when they opposed Tolliver. But he didn't want to kill Katie. It tied his insides up in knots.

Tolliver must have sensed Red's uneasiness. "Make it look like an accident if it helps you sleep better. Remember, you'll be the marshal; you'll have the full authority of the law behind you."

Red nodded.

"And as far as the two Gaines brothers, you can do whatever you want to them. That is if you think that you can handle Luke Gaines," Tolliver said, taunting Red.

Red looked up at the sound of the taunt and stared Tolliver in the eyes. "That dirty son of a bitch sucker-punched me. Just give me a chance at him."

"All right then," said Tolliver, leaning back in his chair. "Tomorrow, this all ends."

CHAPTER FORTY-NINE

The next morning, Matt and Luke left their hotel rooms and made their way to the dining area for breakfast. While they were drinking coffee and waiting for their food, the hotel clerk walked in carrying an envelope.

"This telegram came for you last night, Mr. Jensen." He handed the envelope to Luke, who opened it and read it. A broad smile broke out on his face.

"What is it? Who's it from?" asked Matt.

Luke handed the telegram to Matt. "It's from David. He'll be here on the evening train."

"Boy, it sure will be good to see him again," said Matt. "When was the last time that the three of us were in the same place at the same time?"

Luke sipped his coffee before answering. Setting his cup back down on the table, he said, "That would have been at Linus's funeral."

Both men were reverently silent for a moment. Then Luke lifted his coffee cup to Matt and said, "To Linus."

"To Linus," said Matt, raising his cup to clink it against Luke's.

They finished their breakfast and then decided to check on Tom.

The crisp morning air invigorated the two brothers as they walked along the wooden boardwalk that lined the main street of town. But it wasn't just the cool air that energized them. It had been several years since they had seen each other, and it had been even longer since either of them had been home or had seen their mother or father. There had been the occasional letter, so they had been able to stay in touch to some degree. But to finally have an opportunity to sit down together, to joke and laugh and reminisce, it was almost medicinal to the brothers. Neither Matt nor Luke had realized how much they had missed each other, and both looked forward to David's arrival later that evening.

They arrived at the jail to find Katie serving Tom his breakfast. Tom was in much better shape and could walk around a little before he had to sit down and rest.

The four of them were back in the holding area of the jail when they heard the front door open and close. Matt and Luke went to investigate who had entered the marshal's office and were shocked to see Pony standing by the front door.

On Matt's previous encounters with the Mexican, he had either been on horseback or in a wagon. This was the first time that Matt had seen Pony standing on his feet and was surprised to see how tall he was. At least six feet tall, he was a well-built man with broad shoulders that tapered down to a pair of narrow hips. He had black hair and a square jaw with hard, black eyes. He was clean shaven except for a thick mustache. The scar on the right side of his neck was a shade lighter than the rest of his complexion and ran from under his ear to his chin.

"Buenos dias, amigos," he said.

"What are you doing here?" asked Matt.

Luke saw his brother tense up as he addressed the tall Mexican. "Who is this guy, Matt?" Luke asked. He kept his arms loose at his sides with his hand close to his gun.

"This is one of Tolliver's hired guns," said Matt. "They call him Pony."

"*Si,* schoolteacher, you remember Pony. We old *amigos,* no?" His words were heavily accented as he spoke. "Who is the tall one?" he said, looking at Luke.

"This is my brother Luke," said Matt, "and you and I are not old friends, so state your business or leave."

By this time, both Tom and Katie had appeared. They stood together with Matt and Luke, who were on one side of the office, facing Pony, who still stood next to the door.

"Are there any more peoples here?" said Pony.

"Just us," said Matt, who was growing increasingly worried by Pony's presence.

"Listen, friend," said Luke, taking a step forward and clenching his fists, "if you have something to say to us, then say it. We're minding our own business here, taking care of our friend who was badly beaten by two men hired by your boss. Your presence here is not welcomed."

Pony clenched his teeth and took a step closer to Luke. His dark eyes squinted as he looked from person to person in the room. Then he tilted his head back and started laughing. "Man, if you aren't the spitting image of Philo when he was younger." The words were spoken in excellent English, without a trace of an accent.

Luke and Matt looked at each other when Pony mentioned their father's name. They looked back at Pony, who was still laughing at his joke, and waited for an explanation.

"I apologize for the subterfuge, gentlemen. My name is Cisco Perez. I'm the deputy U.S. marshal for the western district of Texas." He stepped forward and shook hands with Matt, who was in shock.

Matt looked at the others gathered there in the town marshal's office, then said what they were all thinking. "I'm sorry. I'm confused. You're telling us that you're a U.S. marshal?"

"That's right," said Pony. "I have been since after the war. Before that, I was a Texas Ranger, until we got conscripted to fight for the Confederacy. Being a Ranger is where I know your father from."

"Wait a minute," said Luke, snapping his fingers and pointing at Pony, "Dad talked about a young Mexican kid named Cisco that the Rangers kind of adopted. He said this kid stole most of their horses one night while they were sleeping and got halfway to Mexico before they caught up with him."

Pony laughed. "Yeah, some of the Rangers wanted to hang me, but your dad said that anyone who could steal horses right out from under their noses was someone who had potential and that he needed to be mentored and not hung. I was twelve years old at the time. The Rangers made me their mascot. They took care of me and educated me. When I turned sixteen, I joined up and became a Ranger myself."

"So, Philo Gaines is your father?" Tom spoke up and directed his question at Matt. "I thought you said that you were no relation?"

Matt looked rather sheepish as he replied, "I apologize for that, Tom. My brothers and I have found life less difficult if we're not the sons of Philo Gaines. It's not easy walking in that shadow. It takes off a lot of the pressure if folks don't know that he's our father."

"So why are you working for Amos?" Katie asked Pony.

"I've been trying to build a case against him. I broke my cover so I could talk to all of you. I have a feeling that you're about ready to make some kind of move against him. I want to know what your beef is with him."

Matt proceeded to lay out the entire story to Pony, including his suspicion that Tolliver's real name was Morgan Burnett. Then he showed him the telegrams and explained their significance.

Pony listened intently while Matt finished talking. Then he said, "That helps fill in a lot of the gaps that I have in the information that I've been able to collect in my investigation."

"Why are you investigating Tolliver?" asked Luke.

"We're trying to connect him with a string of bank robberies up north. The information that you gave me about this Major Burnett dovetails nicely with the facts that I've collected, but it doesn't constitute hard evidence. It's not enough to hold up in the district court. I do, however, have enough evidence to arrest Red for Curly's murder and Tolliver for conspiracy to commit murder because he ordered Red to do the killing."

"We figured that Tolliver was responsible for Curly's death but didn't have any proof," said Matt. "How did you figure it out?"

"I have a witness," said Pony.

They exchanged glances with each other.

"Who's your witness?" asked Matt.

"Marshal Guthrie," replied Pony. "I caught him trying to skip out of town. He's got quite a bit of dirt on Tolliver, including how he paid him to arrest Tom for Curly's murder even though it was Red who killed him. The sheriff over in Taylor County is holding him in custody for me. He's agreed to testify against Tolliver in exchange for a reduced sentence."

Luke stood quietly, listening to what Pony had to say. When he had finished, Luke slowly shook his head and said, "It sounds like we have a bit of a conflict of interest, Marshal. You're talking like you want to arrest Tolliver. That's not our plan. He killed our brother-in-law, turned our sister into a widow, and left our niece without a father. He needs to pay for that."

"I expected that you'd feel that way," said Pony, "so here's my proposal. I can arrest Tolliver, but I don't think that he's gonna surrender without a fight. And even if I do manage to take him into custody, he has a dozen guns riding for him. I wouldn't get far against all of them by myself. I'm gonna need some help."

"What's your plan?" asked Luke.

"I was going to wire the district court in San Antonio to send more marshals out here. But if the sons of Philo Gaines want to throw in, we can join forces and take down Tolliver and his men together."

Matt and Luke looked at each other, but neither one spoke.

Pony looked anxiously from one to the other. "I know that you want your revenge. I would feel the same way if I were in your shoes. But I promise you, Tolliver will be facing a number of charges. If I can take him into custody and to San Antonio, he'll wind up spending the rest of his life behind bars. That's got to give you some comfort."

Matt glanced at Luke. He knew his brother. Luke had a distrust of most lawmen. Luke was suspicious of them and branded them as power-hungry hypocrites who considered themselves above the laws that they forced other people to obey. About the only group of people that Luke despised more than hypocritical lawmen were crooked lawyers.

Matt did not understand why Luke felt this way. Their father had been a Texas Ranger, and a darn good one. He was nothing like the caricature that Luke had of lawmen in general.

Matt turned to Pony and said, "The thought of Tolliver spending the rest of his life behind bars works for me. We'll work together with you, Marshal." Glancing back toward Luke, Matt said, "Won't we, Luke?"

Luke rolled his eyes and sighed in disgust. He aimed his next remarks at Pony. "I doubt that you will be able to arrest anyone without a fight on your hands. If anyone shoots at me, I'm not going to ask your permission to shoot back."

Pony nodded as Luke spoke. "I fully

expect that there will be trouble. I also expect that you will defend yourselves if fired upon. I'm only saying that I've put in a lot of time on this case. I'd like to have something to show for it, and I would prefer a conviction over a corpse."

Matt could see that Luke wasn't happy about the arrangement, but he reluctantly agreed. "I do have one condition," Luke said.

"What's that?" asked Pony.

"Our brother, David, is arriving on the evening train," said Luke. "I'd like you to wait until he arrives before you arrest Tolliver. Our family has been looking forward to getting our hands on the man that killed our sister's husband for a long time. I don't want David deprived of the opportunity to be in on this."

"That goes for me, too," said Matt.

"I've waited this long," said Pony. "I can wait a few more hours."

Pony, Matt, and Luke agreed to meet at the train depot later that evening. Then they would ride together to arrest Tolliver and Red.

"That reminds me," said Pony, "Tolliver called an emergency meeting of the town council this morning. His plan is to appoint Red town marshal to replace Guthrie. As soon as it's official, Red is going to come down here and arrest Tom for Curly's murder all over again."

"What!?" Tom cried out.

"How can he do that?" asked Katie. "Tom has a letter from Guthrie saying he is free."

"He's going to claim that they have new evidence," said Pony, "that there's an eyewitness who saw you shoot Curly."

"What eyewitness?" Matt wanted to know.

Pony laughed and said, "Me." He reached into his pocket and pulled out a handful of money. "Tolliver paid me two hundred dollars to say that I saw Tom kill Curly."

Luke chuckled and grinned. "He sure has developed a bad habit of hiring the wrong people to do his dirty work, hasn't he?"

That generated more laughter.

"Seriously, though," said Pony, "if we're going to wait until David arrives before we make our arrests, then Tom, you should stay out of sight of Red. I don't think that Tolliver will be content to have you arrested. I think that he plans to have you killed."

Katie spoke. "But Tom is still hurt too bad to be moved. How is he going to avoid Red?"

There was silence for a moment while everyone tried to think of a solution.

"I think I have a plan," said Pony. "Guthrie's old shack is on the south side of town. It's only about a half mile from here. Tom, if you can make it that far, I doubt that they will think to look for you there."

"I can make it," said Tom. "Don't worry about me."

"Do you have a gun?" asked Pony.

"I'm sure I can get one. Guthrie left some here in the jail when he took off."

"We'll see that he gets there safely," said Matt, "then we'll see you at the train station tonight."

"Bueno," said Pony, reverting back to his heavy accent. *"Vaya con Dios."* He winked as he opened the door and stepped out into the morning sun.

CHAPTER FIFTY

The six o'clock train was thirteen minutes late as it rolled into the station in Mustang Flats. The locomotive's three-chimed whistle gave one long blast as it approached the platform and set the air brakes.

Matt, Luke, and Pony watched from inside the station house out of sight as much as possible from Tolliver and his men as they waited to greet a new arrival.

David Gaines stepped onto the platform. He was dressed in black, as was usual for him, including a frock coat and bowler hat. He carried his valise in his left hand. His right hand hung easy but ready at his side, and, under his frock coat, his Colt revolver rested in a holster buckled around his waist and hanging low.

Luke stepped into the doorway of the station house and gave a quick, low whistle.

David saw Luke duck back into the building, so he followed him inside.

The three brothers greeted each other with an embrace and a slap on the back.

Luke pushed his hat back on his head and grinned. "What took you so long to get here, you old card swindler? We're about ready to start this dance."

David shook his finger in Luke's face. "I haven't had a decent meal or a decent card game in almost a day and a half, son, so don't rile me."

Matt and Luke laughed at their brother's remark. If David had to choose, he would often forgo meals for a game of poker or faro.

David had noticed Pony leaning against the ticket counter watching the reunion. He looked at Matt and tilted his head in Pony's direction.

Matt took David by the arm and led him over to Pony. "David, I want you to meet Deputy U.S. Marshal Cisco Perez." Matt turned to Pony, "This is our brother David."

The two men shook hands. David's eyes widened. "Not *the* Cisco Perez? The one that Dad talked about?"

Luke nodded. "The one and only."

"It's a real pleasure to meet you, Deputy Perez." David chuckled. "If only half of the stories that our father told us about you are true, then this is an honor."

"Please, call me Pony."

"All right," David replied, nodding.

"When we finish this business, I'm gonna sit you boys down and tell you the real, unvarnished truth about those stories Philo told you. I'm sure he left out the more important parts, like how he saved my life on more than one occasion."

David grinned. "I look forward to that."

When David turned back to look at Matt, the grin left his face, and his eyes narrowed and became hard. "Is he here? Is it Burnett?"

"It's him," said Matt. "He goes by the name of Amos Tolliver. He owns a large ranch north of town as well as half of the businesses in Mustang Flats. But it's him."

David turned back to face Pony. "How did you get involved in this?"

"Tolliver doesn't know that I'm a lawman. He hired me to work on his ranch. I've been gathering information on him to connect him with some bank robberies up north."

Pony had been chewing on a wooden matchstick. He used his tongue to move it from one side of his mouth to the other. "Your brother Matt became suspicious and started asking questions. Tolliver, or Burnett if you prefer, doesn't like people poking around in his business, so things have gotten sticky around here."

Pony proceeded to tell David about Tolliver's attempts to kill Matt. "That's when I decided to let your brothers know who I was. I've got enough on him now to arrest him several times over, and his foreman, Red, too."

David looked troubled, so Matt added, "We agreed to work with Marshal Perez in the apprehension of Tolliver and his men, but if they don't want to leave us a choice . . ."

David nodded his head. He understood. The three brothers had talked at length about what they would do if they ever found Burnett. They didn't care about his career as a bank robber, or his other unethical or illegal acquisitions. What they cared about was that he had killed a member of their family, and now he had tried to kill another. This was family business, and they would handle it as a family. If there wasn't anything left over for Perez when the smoke settled, then so be it.

David looked from man to man. Then he set his gaze on Pony. "How do you want to do this?"

"Our goal is to arrest Tolliver and Red. The rest of his men are no good, for sure, but I don't have anything that will stick to them."

A horse passed by on the street, so Pony moved to the window to have a look. It was no one in particular, so he continued. "Red has deputized a dozen of Tolliver's men. They've been searching for Tom all day, but Katie is keeping him out of sight."

Pony tossed his chewed matchstick to the floor. "Except Tom is not the only one he's after. He also wants to arrest your brothers. And when I say 'arrest' I mean 'kill.' He claims they helped Tom break out of jail."

Luke had been listening without saying anything for the past few minutes, but spoke now. "Tolliver's down at the bank. If you can get to him first, maybe we won't have too much trouble with his men. His men are only loyal to one thing — a payday. If they see that dry up, it will take a lot of the fight out of them."

"That's a good idea," said Pony, "but Red will be different. He's been with Tolliver from the beginning. Their fates are intertwined."

Luke looked at Pony. His eyes were the deep blue of cornflowers. "You leave Red to David and me. You and Matt take care of Tolliver."

"All right," said Pony. "There's still one

detail first, though, and I'm afraid you're not going to be happy about it, Luke."

"What's that?"

"I'll have to deputize each of you."

Matt and David both started laughing, while Luke stood with his mouth hanging open.

"What the hell . . ." Luke took a step backwards, as if Pony was infected with smallpox. "You have got to be joking."

David was almost doubled over with laughter.

"I'm not joking at all." Pony handed a badge to Matt, who pinned it to his coat. "It's for your protection. This has to be done legally."

David's laughter slowed to a chuckle, and he took a badge from Pony's hand. He pinned it to the lapel of his frock coat. They stood there, watching Luke, waiting for him to take the remaining badge.

Luke sighed and snatched the badge out of Pony's hand. He glared at his brothers, who were still snickering. "If either one of you ever speaks about this, I'll beat the tar out of you."

Pony grinned triumphantly when all three of the Gaines brothers had their badges pinned on. "Consider yourselves deputized."

David looked at the badge on his lapel

and then at his two brothers. He felt pride well up inside of him. It was something that he never felt when he was alone, only when he was with his brothers. "I wonder what Dad would say if he saw us right now."

Luke drew his Colt and checked the load. Satisfied, he gave the gun a twirl and slid it effortlessly back into its holster. "He'd say, 'Let's go get this son of a bitch.' "

Pony and David checked their weapons also.

Pony noticed that Matt was unarmed. "You need a weapon."

Matt shook his head. "I don't care for guns."

Pony shrugged. "All right, if that's the way you want it. But if there's any shooting, stay behind me."

David stored his valise behind the ticket counter, then, one by one, they left the depot. Once outside they separated into two groups. The train station was on the west side of town. The bank, where Tolliver was, was located on the north side of Main Street, but on the east side of town, with the jail about halfway between on the south side of Main Street.

David and Luke were going to work their way toward the jail in search of Red. Pony and Matt were going to maneuver themselves one block north and then work their way east toward the bank, but on a road that paralleled Main Street so that they could approach the bank from the rear. They didn't want to take a chance that Tolliver would see them coming.

CHAPTER FIFTY-ONE

Luke and David left the train station and crossed Main Street unseen by anyone. It was half past six in the evening. The sun was still visible, but hanging low in the sky. They had the advantage of approaching the jail from the west, and the sun would be in the eyes of anyone facing them.

They crossed the street at a fast walk and ducked between two buildings.

Luke had begun to move out from the cover of the building when David grabbed his arm to hold him back. Luke looked at David. "What's wrong?"

"Nothing's wrong. I was just wondering something."

Luke was eager to get at it. He didn't much care to be held back once he started a task. "Well, I hope it's something important."

"The thing is that I just arrived in town. I don't know all the players. How do I know who the bad guys are?"

Luke stared at his brother like he had three eyes and green skin. Sometimes he didn't know whether to take David seriously or not. "How about you do this . . . if someone is shooting at me then you shoot at them. Does that help clear it up for you?"

David rubbed his chin as though deep in thought. "That sounds like a good plan." He slapped Luke on the back and said, "What are you waiting for? Let's go."

They had stepped out onto the boardwalk along the south side of Main Street and moved east toward the jail. As they approached an intersection, a man on horseback stepped out in front of them. It was one of Red's deputies.

The deputy saw the two men and recognized one of them as Luke Gaines. Drawing his gun, he shouted, "He's here . . . Luke Gaines is here!" He aimed his gun at Luke, but David waved his arms and shouted, spooking the man's horse enough so that when he fired, his shot went wide.

Before the man could fire a second time, Luke reached up and grabbed him by his belt and dragged him off of his horse. The deputy tried to grab the saddlehorn, but he wound up losing his grip on his gun instead.

David drew his gun and leveled it at the

man, who was sprawled in the dust of the street. The deputy found himself unexpectedly on his backside with his gun lying in the road several yards out of reach, so he wisely remained motionless at the feet of Luke Gaines and the man who pointed a gun at his head.

Luke's six feet, four inches towered over the prostrate man. "Where's Red?"

The deputy looked down the barrel of David's Colt and then looked at Luke. "He must have heard my shot. You'll see him soon enough."

"I suppose you're right." Luke nodded at David, who raised his hand and brought the barrel of his revolver down on the side of the deputy's head.

David grinned. "Is that one of the bad guys you were telling me about? Hell, I don't know why you dragged me down here. You and Matt could have handled this yourselves."

Luke picked up the deputy's gun and tossed it under the boardwalk. "We didn't need your help; we just missed your witty banter."

The deputy had been right. His shot had drawn attention. There were several people on the street that heard it and were looking in their direction. They saw the two men, with their guns drawn, slowly making their way up the street, pausing at every window and doorway to glance inside.

Bystanders began whispering to one another and pointing, then ducked into buildings to get off the street.

David and Luke were still a couple of blocks from the jail when four men stepped out of a saloon on the opposite side of the street. Luke recognized each of them as part of Tolliver's crew.

One of the four men was a tall, thin man called Jed. He had been one of the men who had been with Tolliver when he arrived in Mustang Flats.

As Jed stepped out of the saloon, he glanced across the street and saw Luke and another man on the boardwalk making for the jail. "It's Luke Gaines," he told his companions. All four men drew their weapons and started firing at Luke and David.

Luke dove behind a water trough as bullets slammed into the building behind him. Bullets buried themselves into the wooden walls and crashed through a window, sending shards of glass flying. Peering around the side of the water tank, he aimed his Colt at the nearest man and fired. Jed fell backward, dropping his gun, and remained motionless.

When David heard the first shot and saw Luke dive behind the water trough, he turned in the direction of the four men and fired his gun. Then he backed up, pushing his way through a doorway and into the building behind him. He bent below the window and dropped his head as glass from the shattered window pane rained on top of him.

Chancing a glance out of the window, he saw that Luke was unharmed but pinned down, unable to move in either direction. He took aim at one of the three remaining men across the street and put a bullet in his chest.

The two men left standing must have taken stock of their dwindling numbers and decided to take shelter back in the saloon. As they retreated behind the saloon doors, David fired rapidly in their direction, giving Luke time to retreat from the water trough and dash into the building with David.

The two brothers sat on the floor on either side of the window and reloaded their weapons. Several more shots were fired through the window, hitting the opposite wall with solid thuds that splintered the wood and sent wood chips flying.

David picked up his hat, which had fallen from his head during the fight. He turned it around in his hands, examining it for bullet holes. Finding none, he returned it to his head. "Now this was worth the train ride."

"I'm glad you're not disappointed." Luke gave his brother a wink. "At the count of three: One . . . two . . . three." Both men pushed their guns through the window and fired several shots each in the direction of the saloon.

More bullets whipped past them as they threw themselves flat against the floor.

The new town marshal, Red Decker, and several of his deputies had been in the saloon when the first shot rang out. He sent Jed and three other men to investigate. Within seconds, gunfire was ringing in the street in front of the saloon.

Red and his remaining deputies were charging for the door at the front of the saloon when two of his men burst back in, their guns still smoking. One of the men had a bloody gash in his arm. He spoke excitedly as he grabbed a towel off of the bar and pressed it against his wound. "Jed and Andy are down. They killed them."

"Who did? Who killed them?" asked Red.

"Luke Gaines and some other guy. They were across the street when we went outside and opened fire on us. They're across the street, in that old warehouse."

Red crossed hurriedly to the front of the building and looked out one of the windows facing the street. A bullet shattered the window next to him and broke a bottle of whiskey sitting on the bar. The only oc-cupants of the saloon at the time, other than the bartender, were Red and his men.

The bartender took cover behind the solid mahogany bar, and Red ordered his men to take a position up front and return fire.

For several minutes, bullets flew in both directions without much damage other than some broken glass and splintered wood.

During a lull in the shooting, Red stood next to one of the busted windows and shouted across the street, "Gaines, you know this isn't going to end well for you. Surrender now while you have a chance. You have my word that you'll get a fair trial."

He got an instant reply shouted back. "That's funny, Red. I was about to say the same thing to you. If you surrender, you live; well, at least until the court hangs you. But if you don't surrender, you'll be dead before the sun sets."

Red laughed. "What are you talking about? Why should I surrender to you?"

"Not to me, to the U.S. marshals. I've been deputized to arrest you for Curly's murder."

Red laughed again, only this time it was a nervous laugh. He glanced around the saloon at his men, who were staring at him. They had worked with Curly and had all liked him.

"What are you talking about? Tom McCutchen killed Curly. Everyone knows that. We have an eyewitness. Pony saw it. He's willing to testify that he saw Tom shoot Curly."

"Where's Pony now, Red?" Luke's question flew across Main Street and into the saloon like a slug from a .44 and hit Red like a slap in the face from a pretty girl. He had no idea where Pony was. He hadn't seen him all day, and it had bothered Red that he didn't know his man's whereabouts.

Luke continued. "I'll tell you where he is. He's on his way to arrest Tolliver, because Pony is a U.S. marshal. Who do you think deputized me?"

Pony, a U.S. marshal? That can't be, thought Red. He knows too much about Tolliver's operation. This could be bad if it's true.

He shouted back across Main Street, "You're bluffing, Gaines. Pony's worked for Tolliver for over a month. He's no lawman."

Red heard Luke laugh, then he shouted

back, "You don't even know the name of the guy who's been working for you, do you? It's not Pony, it's Cisco Perez. Ever heard of him? He's learned a lot about you and your boss — enough to put you both behind bars for a long time."

Several of Red's men murmured among themselves when they heard the name Cisco Perez. Everyone in Texas had heard of him.

"What's he talking about, Red?" one of the deputies asked. He was a big German that they called Dutch. He had been one of the men in Tolliver's original outfit. Dutch had taken a special interest in Curly, who had been like a younger brother to him. "You told us that Tom McCutchen killed Curly. Did you do it? Did you kill him?"

Red looked at Dutch, then at each of the other men in the room. Every one of them was staring at him, expecting an answer. Drops of sweat had formed on his brow and were running down the sides of his face. He wanted to say something, knew that he should say something, but his mouth wouldn't form any words. His silence was as convicting as any words that he could have spoken.

Dutch's eyes turned hard as they bore into Red. "You son of a . . ."

Dutch's gun was already out. He raised

his hand and brought the gun to bear on Red, who was caught by surprise. Two more of Tolliver's men had their weapons aimed at Red. One of them walked over and relieved Red of his gun.

"What are you going to do, Dutch? Are you going to shoot me? Curly's big mouth was gonna get us all in trouble."

"How could you do it, Red?" Dutch spoke through gritted teeth. "How could you kill Curly? He was one of us. He was with us from the beginning." He aimed his revolver between Red's eyes and thumbed back the hammer.

Red saw the cylinder on Dutch's gun advance. He heard the metallic click of the hammer as it locked into firing position. He could feel the beating of his own heart in his chest and felt the trickle of a drop of sweat as it ran down the side of his face and into his beard.

After a few tense moments, Dutch released the hammer and holstered his gun. He walked over to Red and stood within inches of him. "No, I'm not going to shoot you. I'm going to let Gaines do that, and I'm going to enjoy it."

Dutch drew back his powerful right arm and smashed his fist forward into Red's nose.

Red's head snapped back, knocking him to the floor. Blood ran from his nose and mingled in his mustache and beard.

"Keep an eye on him," said Dutch to one of the other deputies, who stood over Red and kept his gun aimed at him.

Dutch walked over to the window and shouted across the street, "Gaines, this is Dutch Krueger. Me and some of the other boys . . . we didn't know that Red had killed Curly. We don't want any trouble with the marshals."

From across the street, Luke called back, "How many of you are there?"

"There are five of us besides Red. One of us is injured."

"We're not interested in you or any of the other men with you. Just send out Red, and the rest of you can ride away, as long as you leave town and never come back."

"All right, Gaines, you've got a deal."

"Good to hear, Dutch. Come out one at a time. Throw your guns into the street and step off to the side with your hands in the air."

Luke and David Gaines watched as, one by one, the deputies walked through the saloon door and out onto the boardwalk. They tossed their guns into the street and then spread out along the front of the saloon. Each man kept his hands high.

Red came hurling out head first, landing in a heap in the street, as though a great force had propelled him headlong. That great force turned out to be Dutch, who was the last man to exit the saloon.

After tossing his revolver into the road like the rest of the men, Dutch stood in the doorway, his massive shoulders nearly touching each side of the door frame.

"There's your man, Gaines. Do whatever you like with him. I've got no use for a murdering traitor who turns on his own men."

Luke and David stepped out of their concealment in the warehouse, their guns in hand. After looking at Red and seeing the blood on his face, it was plain that Dutch was sincere.

Luke holstered his gun. "Dutch, you did the smart thing. This isn't your fight anymore. You and your men can ride out. But, like I said, leave town and don't come back."

"Our horses are tied up in front of the jail down the street."

Luke turned to David, who still had his gun drawn. "Go with them and see that they get on their horses and ride out."

David looked at the men who were lined up in front of the saloon. He waved his gun in the direction of the jail. "Start walking, boys, and keep in mind that I buy my bullets in bulk, so I have plenty of them left."

The men each stepped off of the boardwalk and into the street. They began walking with David following behind.

Luke stepped into the street and stood over Red, who was lying on his right side, doubled over and moaning in pain. There was blood on his face from his nose, as well as from several cuts on his cheekbones and above his left eye. It looked like Dutch had worked him over before tossing him into the street.

Luke stood with his hands on his hips. "Get up, Red, and start walking. You know the way to the jail."

With effort, Red turned his head to look at Luke, but he remained on the ground. "If you were any kind of a man, you would settle up with me one on one, man to man."

Luke unbuckled his gun belt and laid it on the ground to the side. "If you still feel up to it, let's go."

Red grinned. "Are you sure that you're up to it? I'm not going to give you a chance to blindside me this time."

Luke curled his hands into fists and planted his feet in a fighter's stance. "There's only one way to find out."

When Red rolled over, Luke noticed the gun in his hand. He had landed on it when Dutch tossed him to the ground, and he had kept it hidden underneath him while he waited for his chance.

As Red swung the revolver around, Luke kicked out with his leg. His foot made contact with Red's wrist. There was a cracking sound as Red cried out. The gun went flying, landing several yards further down the road.

Luke bent down and grabbed Red by the collar with his left hand, pounding him repeatedly with his right. After several blows, Luke released his grip, and the man fell backward to the ground, unconscious.

Luke took a few seconds to catch his breath. He reached for his gun belt, buckling it into place. Bending down, he grabbed ahold of Red's feet and began dragging him down the middle of Main Street toward the jail.

CHAPTER FIFTY-TWO

While Luke and David were going after Red, Pony and Matt were making their way to the bank to arrest Tolliver. They could hear the shooting taking place one block south of them.

Pony looked concerned. "I hope your brothers are all right."

"Don't worry about them. They've both been in scraps before and can take care of themselves."

They made their way to the back of the bank, where there was a door opening into an alley. Pony tried the latch, but it was locked. "We're going to have to go through the front of the bank. Tolliver is likely to have one or two men with him, so keep a sharp eye out."

They worked their way cautiously around the east side of the bank. As they approached Main Street, they stopped. Pony peered around the corner of the bank and saw two of Tolliver's men standing in the street. Both men were facing away, looking west into the sun and toward the sounds of gunfire.

Stepping around the corner of the building, Pony stood in the street behind the two men. He had his gun drawn, and he said, "You two boys hold it right there."

The two men froze and then turned their heads toward Pony. One of the men said, "What the hell are you doing, Pony? Where have you been all day? The boss has been asking for you."

"My name is Cisco Perez. I'm a deputy U.S. marshal. I'm here to arrest Tolliver, and I don't want you boys getting in the way."

The two men looked at each other and then back at Pony. Their eyes mirrored the same confusion. "So you're not one of us?"

"Don't take it personal. I'm not here for you boys. I'm here for Tolliver. Drop your gun belts and back away."

Pony had recognized the two men. The younger one was Henry, while the older one — the one talking — was Al. They were brothers from Arkansas who had joined up with Tolliver's crew less than a year ago and found his heavy-handed tactics to their liking.

Al turned to face Pony, who was about twenty feet away. "Cisco Perez, huh? I've heard of you. You're supposed to be some kind of a big-shot lawman."

Pony saw the same look in Al's eyes that he had seen many times before. Al was sizing him up, calculating the odds on whether he could take him.

"Don't do it, Al."

What happened next was only a matter of a few seconds. Al drew his gun, but before he could bring it into play, Pony fired, sending a bullet deep into Al's chest.

Henry drew his gun at the same time that Al had drawn his, but he was luckier than his brother and was able to get a shot off. His bullet smashed into Pony's right arm.

Pony dropped his gun and spun around.

Henry attempted a frantic retreat after shooting Pony. Stumbling backward, he tripped over the edge of the boardwalk and landed on his backside. He scrambled to his feet and ran into the bank.

Matt ran over to Pony, who had picked up his gun and was holding it in his left hand. Blood was flowing down his injured arm, which hung limp at his side.

"I think the bullet broke my arm," Pony said, wincing.

Matt examined the wounded arm. "You're

bleeding badly. Let's get off the street." He hurried him into the mercantile store across the street from the bank.

John and Violet, the old couple that ran the store, had ducked behind the counter when they heard gunfire across the street. When Matt came in with the injured marshal, they emerged.

Violet got some bandages off the shelves to work on dressing Pony's wound and make a sling for his arm. "This will stop the bleeding for now, but you should have the doctor take a look at that."

At that moment, Luke and David burst through the front door. "What happened?" David asked.

Matt filled them in and then asked, "We heard a lot of shooting from your direction. Did you find Red?"

David and Luke grinned at each other. "He's a little worse for wear, but he's presently enjoying a nice nap in the jail," said David.

"In the same cell that Tom had occupied," Luke added.

John disappeared momentarily and then reappeared with a ten-gauge shotgun. "Tolliver might own this store," he fumed, "but I can't tolerate that man's lawlessness any longer."

Matt put his hand on the old man's shoulder. "Hold on a minute, John. This is our fight, not yours. Keep that gun handy to protect yourself and your wife, but leave Tolliver to us."

The old man shook his head and tried to pull away. "You don't understand. He has that woman with him."

"What woman?"

"Katie McCutchen."

Matt spun him around. "Katie is in the bank with Tolliver?"

"Yes. Katie is with him. Two of his men dragged her in there not a half an hour ago." He hung his head as he continued. "It was plain that they were forcing her. I should have done something, but I was too frightened."

"There was nothing that you could have done against them," Luke assured him.

A voice called from the street. "School-teacher, come on out. You and I need to talk."

It was Amos Tolliver.

Matt took a look out of the window and saw Tolliver standing in the middle of the street. He wore a gun belt with two guns and stood smoking a cigar. Two other men had taken positions a few feet from him on either side.

Matt opened the door and stepped out onto the boardwalk, David, Luke, and Pony right behind him. Each of them had his gun drawn. "Unless you want to confess and turn yourself in, I'm not sure that we have much to talk about," answered Matt.

It didn't seem to faze Tolliver that three guns were pointed in his direction. He continued to puff on his cigar. "Why don't you gentlemen holster those weapons? All this brandishing of firearms is counterproductive to a civilized conversation."

"As I said, I don't think that we have anything to talk about. Pony is a U.S. marshal, and he's here to arrest you, Tolliver; or maybe I should call you Major Morgan Burnett."

"Yes, I know about Pony. Henry told me. I'll take care of him later," said Tolliver with a wave of his hand.

Matt had never seen anyone as cocky and self-assured. Even outnumbered, he still seemed convinced that he was going to come out on top.

"Do you deny that you are Morgan Burnett?"

Tolliver pursed his lips and shook his head slowly. "There's hardly a point anymore in denying that. I had a feeling that you had figured it out. You're one meddlesome bastard, you know that, Gaines? Tell me, why does it matter to you?"

"Do you remember a private by the name of Linus Walker?"

Tolliver hung his head while he contemplated the question. After a few seconds, he looked up and said, "It seems like I do recall a private who served under me. His last name was Walker. As I recall, he got himself shot in the back while attempting to run away from the enemy. Was he a friend of yours?"

Luke's jaw muscles tightened. He took a step forward. "You're a damned liar."

Matt held out his arm to block Luke. "He was our sister's husband, and you shot him."

Tolliver snickered. "That's quite an accusation. How do you know who shot him?"

"I know because he didn't die right away. He lived long enough to say you shot him in the back like a coward."

"Well, that is unfortunate. I imagine that my aim must have been off that day. But I assure you, my marksmanship has only improved through the years."

Pony raised his gun and leveled it at Tolliver. "I've had enough of this. Tolliver, I'm placing you under arrest. Drop your gun belt, and put your hands in the air."

Tolliver smiled and replied, "I think not."

As if on cue, the sound of muffled cries came from inside the bank. Everyone's attention was drawn to the front door as Katie McCutchen emerged, followed by Henry, the brother of the man that Pony had shot, and whose body still lay in the street.

Henry had one arm wrapped around Katie's neck. His other hand held a knife. The sun glinted off the blade as he held it to her throat.

Matt saw the look of horror in Katie's eyes as the edge of the knife pressed into her neck. Any movement on her part would draw blood. "Katie, are you okay?" he called across the street.

In tears, Katie replied, "I'm all right, but they killed Tom."

"Tom was a fugitive," Tolliver shot back.

Matt felt a wave of nausea overtake him at the news of Tom's death.

Tolliver grinned, and Matt understood why the man was so confident. As long as he had Katie, he did have the upper hand.

Tolliver's cigar had burned down to a stub, so, after taking one last puff, he tossed it to the side. "I want all of you to toss your guns into the street."

The men on the boardwalk hesitated for a second before tossing their guns into the dirt.

"Schoolteacher, you have been a thorn in my side ever since you arrived in town." He looked down each direction of Main Street, which was eerily devoid of any pedestrian traffic.

Most of the people in town didn't like him, and that was fine with Tolliver; as long as they feared him. As soon as he dealt with the Gaines brothers, he could go back to the way things were before the schoolteacher arrived. No . . . actually, things would be better, because he wouldn't have to pretend anymore.

Lifting both hands in a sweeping gesture, Tolliver said, "I had a good thing here before you arrived and stuck your nose in my business. You should have stayed where you belonged. But since you are so dead set on being a real Texan, then we are going to settle our business the way of Texans."

Walking over to where Pony had tossed his gun, Tolliver picked it up and threw it at Matt's feet. "Get a gun belt and put it on."

Matt looked at the gun lying at his feet. "I really don't care . . ."

"I know, I know," Tolliver interrupted. "You don't care for guns. That's all right. I'm not going to force you . . ."

Without turning around, Tolliver shouted over his shoulder, "Henry . . ."

With a jerk, Henry pulled Katie's head backward, thrusting her neck forward as he leveled his blade for the cut.

"All right!" Matt shouted.

Luke removed his gun belt and handed it to Matt.

Threading the tapered end of the leather belt through the buckle, Matt pulled it tight and fastened it in place. Then he tied the leather thong around his thigh. Bending down, he picked up the gun that Tolliver had tossed at his feet and thrust it into the holster.

Pony stepped in front of Matt and stood to face Tolliver. His right arm was in a sling, but he kept his left arm in the air and pleaded, "Tolliver, don't do this. It's murder. Face me instead. I'm instructing these men right now that if you kill me, they are to let you go. I haven't filed a report yet. No one will come after you."

"No," said Matt. "We're going to do it his way."

Tolliver and Matt moved into the center of the street and stood facing each other about twenty feet apart. Tolliver's two men each stood to the side, pretending that they were only spectators, but Tolliver had given them their orders; after he killed Matt, they were to finish off Pony and the other two

Gaines brothers. This ended now with no one left to get in his way.

Tolliver deliberately positioned himself with the setting sun behind him so that Gaines would have to contend with the glare. He removed his jacket and hung it over a rail. "I want you to know that when I kill you, schoolteacher, I'm going to force Katie to sign her ranch over to me."

Tolliver looked for any signs of fear in the eyes of Matt Gaines, but there wasn't any. Instead, there was a calm self-assurance in the school teacher as he said, "As long as we're being honest with each other, there's something that I should tell you as well. I want you to think carefully about what you have heard me say. I have said on a number of occasions that I don't care for guns. But have I ever said that I don't know how to shoot one?"

Amos laughed, although it was not totally convincing. Matt had planted a seed of doubt. "You're bluffing, schoolteacher. Where would someone like you learn to shoot?"

"Bluffing is my brother David's strength, not mine. When you grow up with Philo Gaines for a father, you learn a thing or two about guns. My brothers and I could all shoot as soon as we were old enough to hold a gun."

At the mention of Philo's name, Tolliver's eyes widened. A rising panic seized him as he realized who he was facing. Matt Gaines the schoolteacher was one thing, but Matt Gaines the son of Philo Gaines was a different matter.

But it was too late.

Tolliver reached for his guns. As his hands touched the grips on his two Colts, he felt a pressure against his chest as though someone had shoved him. Something had stung his arm as well. He thought that he heard gunfire, but his guns were still in his holsters. Why hadn't he fired his guns?

He heard two other shots and saw his men lying in the street. Get up, you fools! What were they doing? And why hadn't he fired his guns yet?

He reached for his Colts again, but his right arm wouldn't move. He could feel the sweat running down the inside of his shirtfront. It felt warm and sticky. Looking down, he saw a crimson stain growing in the middle of his chest.

He realized that he was on his knees in the road. He saw the schoolteacher standing with his gun in his hand. Smoke was trailing from the end of the barrel. He wanted to fire back. Why hadn't he fired back?

He reached one more time with his good arm for his gun and managed to draw it out of the holster, but he couldn't raise the gun to take aim.

Tolliver fell backward into the street and lay there listening. It had gotten quiet, he thought; and it had gotten dark. How did it get dark so fast? I can't see the schoolteacher. Maybe he can't see me.

■ ■ ■ ■

Tom McCutchen was buried two days later on a Tuesday afternoon. It was a cool day, but a sunny one, as they lowered his coffin into the ground beneath a live oak tree in the family plot on the McCutchen ranch next to his mother and father.

A great many of the town's people came to pay their final respects. Most of them were there to appease their guilt over having believed in Tom's culpability in the death of Curly.

The funeral procession marched the small distance between the burial plot and the ranch house. The women had brought with them a pot of stew or a pie or other baked item as a token of their condolences and a small gesture of comfort to the grieving Katie McCutchen.

At about the same time, in the town cemetery south of Mustang Flats, Amos Tolliver and five of his men were being put to rest as well. There were no mourners to send them on their way. There was no meal afterward for the grieving family and friends, because no one mourned their passing . . . unless you counted the yellow dog that stretched out across the fresh mound

461

of dirt under which Amos Tolliver rested.

The few men that had worked for Tolliver who were actually ranch hands and not gunmen decided to stay on and take care of his ranch until the courts could decide the disposition of his properties. The ranch would probably be sold at auction, and Katie McCutchen was planning to be one of the bidders. The irony of the McCutchens acquiring the Tolliver ranch was not lost on her.

Matt and Katie sat side by side in a wicker love seat on the veranda of her home. Most of the mourners had left, and the few remaining were preparing to do so.

They were joined by Pony and David. Luke was off to the side, talking to a group of the town's men.

Matt looked at Pony, who by this time had seen the doctor and had his arm in a proper sling. "How's the arm doing?"

"It could be worse." Pony took a seat in one of the wicker chairs. "The doc said that the bullet chipped the bone but didn't break it. It will be a while before I can handle a gun with my right hand, but it should heal up fine. And, speaking of handling a gun . . . Matt, you surprised the hell out of me. I had no idea that you could shoot like that."

David laughed. "You should have seen the

look in your eyes when Tolliver called him out. I could barely keep a straight face. Everyone assumes that, because Matt doesn't like guns, he doesn't know how to handle them. The fact is my big brother here is faster than anyone I know."

Pony sat in his chair, shaking his head back and forth. "Tell me then, if Matt is the fastest of the three of you, who is the next fastest?"

"That would be me," Luke said as he stepped up on the veranda and took a seat.

David had himself another good laugh over that. "That's what you've been saying since you were thirteen. One of these days we're going to have to settle the matter once and for all."

Luke reclined in his chair with his fingers interlaced behind his head. "Bring it on, brother. Bring it on."

Pony got to his feet. "I'd like to stay around and watch that, but I have to collect my prisoner and hit the road."

"Are you taking Red to San Antonio?" Matt asked.

"Yes, after a short stop in Taylor County to pick up Guthrie. I don't need him to testify against Tolliver anymore, but he still has information about Tolliver's business, and details touching on Red's involvement.

There may be further avenues of investigation to pursue, but I'll leave that up to the court to decide."

"What about Henry?" asked Katie. She wore a scarf around her neck to hide the mark left by the outlaw's blade as he pressed it to her throat. It was more of a wound to her vanity than it was an injury to her person and would disappear in a week's time.

Pony frowned and replied, "I'm afraid he got away. It didn't take long for him to disappear once Matt dropped Tolliver and his men."

Pony shook hands with everyone and said goodbye. Then he collected his horse and rode away towards town.

David had stepped off the porch to smoke a cigar. He was staring off to the west as though he were looking for something, or maybe listening to something in the wind.

Matt had seen that look in his brother's eyes before. It told of a restlessness that kept David on the move, never settling in one place for long.

"What about you, David? Are you going to stick around for a while, or are you returning to Cheyenne?" Matt asked.

David turned to look at his big brother and then turned back toward the waning sun. He waited a moment before speaking, and, when he did find his words, he spoke them without turning back to look at the people on the veranda. "Neither. I'll take the next train that leaves town, and I'll be going further west."

He knocked the ash from his cigar and turned back to face Matt and Luke. "If you need to reach me, I'll be at the International Hotel in Virginia City, Nevada."

Luke had been sipping a cup of coffee. He put the cup on a nearby table and grinned at David. "You're intending to relieve those miners of their hard-earned wages, aren't you?"

David smiled back. "I'm going to do my level best."

Katie had been silent, listening to the brothers' talk. She turned to Luke and said, "What about you? What are your plans?"

They were surprised to see Luke fidget in his chair. His ears turned red as he looked first at Matt, then at David. Finally, he heaved a sigh and said, "Well, you were going to find out eventually. The town council approached me and offered me the job of town marshal."

Matt, Katie, and David stared wide eyed at each other in disbelief. David let loose with a resounding laugh that doubled him over. "I have got to send a telegram back home to let Dad know about this."

Luke sprang to his feet. "If you do, I'll knock you from here to Sunday."

He jumped off the porch in hot pursuit of David, who tried to outrun the much taller Luke, but was laughing so hard that Luke easily overtook him. Soon, the two brothers were wrestling in the grass like they were kids.

Katie adjusted her position and turned to look at Matt. "It was a wonderful idea that Luke had, to hold school in that old warehouse on Main Street until the new school is built."

Matt nodded. "Luke's a good man. He'll be good for this town."

"You'll be staying, too, won't you, Matt?"

Matt smiled down at her. "Well, I am obligated to fulfill the terms of my contract."

Katie smiled and looked down as a rosy blush crept into her cheeks. After a moment, she looked back up and locked eyes with Matt. "I hope that before the school year is over, you'll find other reasons to stay in Mustang Flats."

Matt thought about all that had transpired since he had been in Texas. Then he thought about his life back in Princeton. It seemed far away and long ago, yet it had only been a few short weeks. Texas may not have wanted him, but he had fought to make a place for himself here. He had let go of his past and was pressing on to what lies ahead.

He took Katie by the hand and said, "I don't know what the future holds for me, Katie, but I'm a Texan now. Where else would I go?"

Chapter Fifty-Three

January 1874, Austin, Texas

The carriage clattered over the stone pavement on Brazos Street and came to a stop at the hotel where fifty-seven-year-old Philo Gaines would be staying while in Austin.

As a second term United States senator from Tennessee, Philo had made a number of trips to different states in the service of the government, but this trip was one of the strangest.

Last November's gubernatorial election in Texas had seen the incumbent governor, Edmond J. Davis, soundly trounced by his opponent, Richard Coke, by more than a two-to-one margin. However, Davis refused to leave office and barricaded himself in the capital building, refusing to leave or to let the new administration enter.

It was a situation that President Grant wanted resolved right away and without a fuss. So, he asked Senator Gaines to travel to Austin and talk to Davis, who was a personal friend of Philo's.

It was a cool day in the mid-fifties when Philo stepped out of the carriage. The clouds hung low in the grey sky. A light rain had been falling off and on throughout the morning. The carriage driver handed him his travel bag, and Philo walked through the double doors of the hotel and entered the lobby.

The hotel clerk looked up from his newspaper when Philo approached the counter and asked for a room.

"Certainly, we have a room for you, sir. If you wouldn't mind signing our guest register, I'll get your room key for you."

The desk clerk turned to retrieve a key from the pegboard behind the desk while Philo signed the register.

The clerk handed Philo his room key. "It's number 213, up the stairs and to your left. How long will you be staying with us?"

Philo's deep-blue eyes showed the strain of a long trip as he replied, "I should be checking out by the end of the week."

He had turned to climb the stairs when the clerk looked at his signature in the hotel register.

"Philo Gaines, huh?"

Philo stopped and turned to face the clerk.

"That's right."

"That name sounds familiar," the clerk said as he searched his memory. "Oh, I remember now," he said, snapping his fingers. "Are you any relation to those Gaines brothers in Mustang Flats? Boy, they sure cleaned up that town, I'll tell you . . ."

ABOUT THE AUTHOR

Michael R. Ritt tells people that he is a writer trapped in the body of a consumer safety inspector for the United States Department of Agriculture. An early passion for books turned into a passion for writing while he was in high school, and since then he has been writing everything — short stories, poems, essays, shopping lists, you name it. He currently lives in a small cabin in the mountains of western Montana with his wife, Tami, their Australian Shepherd, Lucky, and their nameless cat. He enjoys studying history, theology, and natural science. He is a member of the Western Writers of America, Western Fictioneers, and American Christian Fiction Writers. *The Sons of Philo Gaines* is his first novel.